The Monstrous Murders

An Alewives of Colmar mystery

Elizabeth R. Andersen

HAEDDRE PRESS

Copyright © 2025 by Elizabeth R. Andersen

All rights reserved.

No portion of this book may be reproduced in any form without written permission from the publisher or author, except as permitted by U.S. copyright law. No generative artificial intelligence (AI) was used in the writing of this work. NONE. The author expressly prohibits any entity from using this publication for purposes of training AI technologies to generate text, including without limitation, technologies that are capable of generating works in the same style or genre as this publication. The author reserves all rights to license uses of this work for generative AI training and development of machine learning language models.

This is a work of fiction based on historical facts that the author researched to the best of their ability. Any omissions or misrepresentations are unintentional. Resemblance of fictional characters in the book to living individuals is coincidence.

Contents

Dedication — 1

Alsace, 1355 — 3

1. A fine morning for mushrooms — 5
2. Beginnings — 11
3. Tryst — 17
4. The knavish and the vexatious — 27
5. A necessary journey — 39
6. The potter's sons — 45
7. A snarl in the dark — 53
8. The houseguest — 61
9. Arne's tale — 71
10. Lonel's tale — 81
11. A grudging confession — 89
12. Enough is enough — 97
13. The posse, the priest, and the nobleman — 105
14. The flames of rivalry — 111

15.	And then there were two	119
16.	For want of a helmet	133
17.	Clues	143
18.	Monstrous accusations	155
19.	Sheriff Werner's suspect	163
20.	A cask full of Kornelius	171
21.	The street sweeper's secret	179
22.	Accusations	187
23.	Strange brew	195
24.	Mummery	205
25.	Les Tanneurs on trial	213
26.	The verdict	225
27.	Just a glance	229
28.	A plea falls on deaf ears	235
29.	Eleven Leporteurs and one vital clue	243
30.	A fortunate homecoming	251
31.	The love token	257
32.	Suspect suspects	269
33.	A confession	277
34.	Labor pains	287
35.	The pieces fall into place	293
36.	All's well that ends	317

37. Prior engagements	325
38. Author's Note	339
39. Acknowledgements	343
About Elizabeth R. Andersen	347
Also by Elizabeth R. Andersen	349

To Louis W. (the Third), who makes a mighty fine homebrew

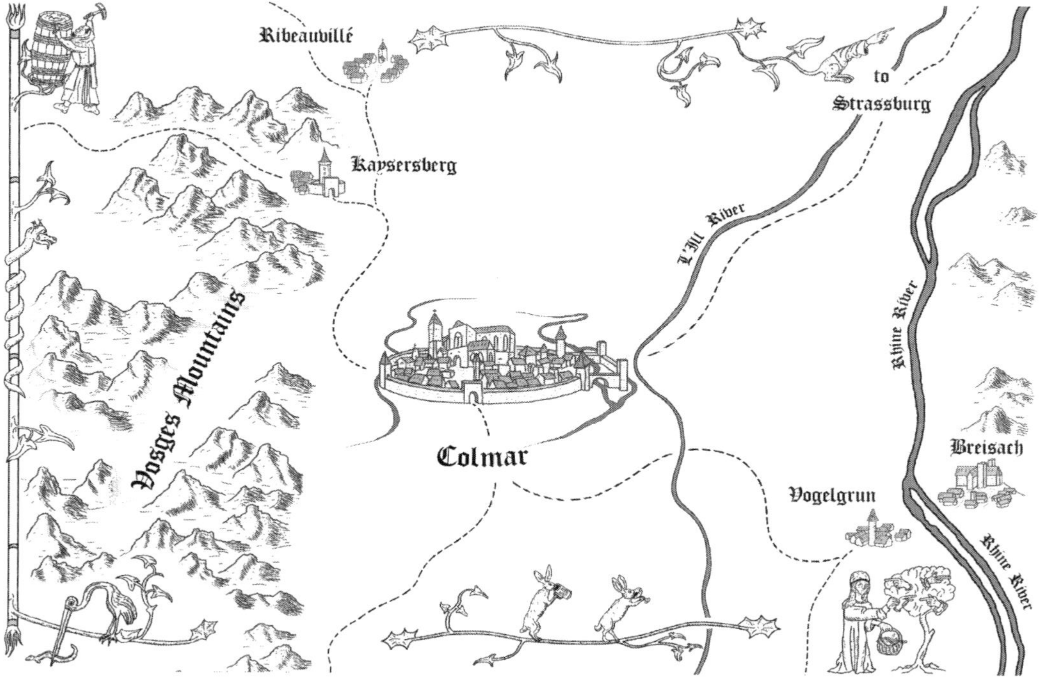
Ribeauvillé
to
Strassburg
Kaysersberg
L'Ill River
Vosges Mountains
Colmar
Rhine River
Breisach
Vogelgrun
Rhine River

A fine morning for mushrooms

In which Frau Appel Schneider shakes off the chains of respectability

THE MORNING DAWNED SPLENDIDLY, as it often did after a heavy storm. Between the Vosges mountains and the Black Forest, the fertile Florival Valley was a green jewel, slashed through the center by the broad, slow-moving waters of the Rhine. On either side of the river, fields of young barley glistened with dew in the new sunlight, and the forested hills rang with birdsong. It was a perfect morning to hunt for mushrooms. At least, that is what Frau Appel Schneider planned to tell anyone who questioned her.

Sliding carefully from the bed she shared with her friend, Efi Kleven, she crept down the rickety wooden staircase which clung to the exterior wall of her house, taking care to hop over the last step, which squeaked. When she reached the bottom, she darted around the corner and re-entered the house through her front door. *Someday,* she thought, *when I have enough money, I shall pay a carpenter to put the stairs inside.* It was a colossal nuisance to dirty her feet in the dust when she needed to move from her bed chamber to her hearth. Nudging her ginger cat from his slumber in her favorite gathering basket, Appel swung a cloak of dark-blue homespun over her shoulders and stepped into the street. "God's bones, I'm late," she groaned.

The street was already beginning to bustle, and the nearby square slowly filled with tanners' wives heading to market, leatherwork apprentices staggering to their masters' workshops, children driving flocks of sheep to the fields to graze and herding raucous gaggles of geese to the pens where they would await their fates at the slaughterhouse.

Appel straightened her shoulders and walked through the square at an unhurried pace. A few of her neighbors called out greetings, and she responded with a graceful dip of her head or a demure wave of her hand. She had nearly made it through the crowded square, and to the main thoroughfare that wound its way through the city of Colmar to the gate, when a young woman called her name.

"Appel! Frau Appel!"

"Ah, Rosmunda, what brings you out in the street so early, child?" Appel said, her face lighting with a genuine smile. The young woman was about fourteen years of age, with her sandy-blonde braids pinned to her head like a crown of wheat. She had a plain, round face and a few adolescent spots on her chin.

"What a funny question to ask, Frau Appel!" Rosmunda giggled. "You know I am always the first person to wake in my home. But this morning I've finished my chores early. Ma told me to fetch some turnips from the market before the best ones are all sold, but I arrived too late."

"No turnips left at the market?" Appel asked with a raised brow. It was an effort to hide her impatience to continue on her way.

"None. And now what will we have to flavor our supper? We've naught but barley pottage for the whole day until Da is paid his wages for his work at the docks."

Appel patted Rosmunda's crown of braids. "Poor child. Tell your mother I shall be around to see her later this morning when I return from —" She caught herself. "Well, perhaps best not to mention to your mother you saw me. I'll come by later this day."

Rosmunda looked closer at Appel, taking in the basket, the cloak, and the impatiently tapping foot. "Frau Appel, is that your foraging basket?"

"Yes," Appel said quickly. "I'm off for mushrooms before the day grows too warm. Soon it will be the hot season and they will be hard to find until the autumn. Now if you'll excuse me."

"Shall I come with you? I can bring mushrooms for our supper instead of turnips!"

Appel spun and faced the girl. "No! Er...you should return to your mother and say nothing about our conversation. I shall surprise her with mushrooms when I return. Save your strength for your day's labors."

"Don't seem safe for an old woman such as yourself to go outside the walls alone, Frau Appel," Rosmunda said. "I'll come along to raise the alarm if a highwayman tries to ravish you."

"There will be no ravishing. Go along, Rosmunda. I'll be fine on my own."

"But, Frau Appel —"

"Go!" Appel snarled, and Rosmunda jumped back. A few people nearby paused their conversations to stare at her, and Appel's face glowed red. They would talk amongst themselves, for sure. As Rosmunda hurried back toward her mother's house, Appel pulled the cloak closer around her face, hoping to slip away unnoticed. But it was too late. She had been very much noticed after shouting at the girl. Setting her jaw, she threw the hood back, revealing her own braids, iron-gray and pinned around her ears like the horns of a ram. Her clear blue eyes roamed the square, daring anyone to meet her gaze. Let them talk, she thought. *Their own imaginations are far more wicked than I am.* With a swirl of her blue cloak, she marched toward the gate.

Later that morning, after the sun had moved higher in the sky, Appel carefully peered out from the leaves of a hazel thicket. In her green hiding place, she had a partial view of the city gate, but the guards couldn't see her. She watched as a man approached the gate and spoke with the gatekeeper.

Jacques Färber had been her liaison this morning. She allowed herself a moment to feel guilty, for he was Gritta's neighbor, and

Gritta was her best friend. Moreover, she promised her friends, herself, and the church she would stop attempting to comfort the lonely men of Colmar. It was fortunate that the two of them left the gates early enough that no one would notice their absence. She shifted her position in the hazel tree, cursing quietly as she recalled meeting Rosmunda in the street. She hoped the girl could keep her mouth shut.

Jacques turned and glanced back in her direction, and Appel cursed again, this time not quietly, at all. "Don't look this way, dummkopf! You are an idiot, Jacques Färber!" He disappeared within the walls of Colmar, and Appel prepared to follow when she remembered she had promised Rosmunda a few mushrooms for the evening's pottage. If she arrived home empty-handed it would only lead to questions.

She emerged from her shady green lair, swatting the velvety hazel leaves away, and walked – not in the direction of the city, but toward the forest. A few mushrooms, gathered as a peace offering for her friend would suffice, and then she could return to her home. "Efi probably hasn't even stopped snoring yet, the lazy girl," she said under her breath as she picked her way across the forest floor, which was slippery with pine needles. She considered her luck that her housemate, Efi, was such a sound sleeper, or else she would surely have been caught before even leaving the house. She was just forming a rhetorical argument against the imaginary accusations of her friends, when she stopped.

"What was that?" Appel whispered aloud.

Something had thumped. It was a deep resounding thud, strong enough for her to feel through the toes of her thin leather shoes. Looking back, the walls of Colmar were still visible through the sparse branches at the edge of the forest. But she couldn't return without mushrooms! And the longer she stayed away, the less chance the guards at the gate would connect her with the man who had entered inside the walls earlier.

THUMP! THUMP! THUMP!

Appel spun wildly, snagging her braid in the branch of a tree. She shrieked and jumped back. "Footsteps," she gasped. "Those are footsteps!" Something was walking toward her, and quickly. There came a rustling from deeper in the forest, and she thought she glimpsed something large, brown, and hairy moving among the trees. It pushed large branches aside and snapped twigs beneath its feet, like a bear. Stumbling backwards, Appel scrambled on her hands and knees until her skirts tangled and she fell again. Then she opened her mouth to scream.

"Make a sound, and I shall devour you," the beast said in a rumbling, snarling voice. Appel felt her limbs quake. She could barely see it through the trees, but now she made out a tattered cloak, and two ragged ears standing erect on its head. This was no bear, this was something far more terrifying. All sensible thought fled from her mind. She crawled back to pick up her basket, then sprang to her feet and ran to the gates of Colmar and to safety.

Beginnings

In which two young men embark on something called a "holiday"

INSIDE HER WALLS, THE city of Colmar buzzed with life as its residents woke with the sun, fed their animals, emptied their pots of nightsoil into the communal pits, and sent their children to fetch water for cooking and washing. In the houses and hovels from the burghers' quarters to the tannery district, the goodwives roused themselves before their families and began to prepare the day's pottage. The bakers slapped their balls of dough with a vigor implying a personal grudge. And the weary night watchman hung his pole-mounted lantern on a hook near his humble front door and crept onto his mattress of flattened straw and fleas to sleep until sunset.

Ulf sat up on his hard wooden pallet in the novice's quarters of Saint Matthieu's church. He stretched and yawned, running a hand through his hair. He had not taken his orders yet, and so the crown of his head was still wreathed in blond curls, which stood out wildly. For a moment, he scratched his head vigorously. Lice. He could feel them crawling about on his skull all night. It was time to visit Brother Marcus, the apothecary, for some oil of rosemary again. He reached across the narrow space separating his cot from the one next to him and jabbed at his friend, Jean-Louis, who still snored loudly.

Jean-Louis swatted at Ulf's hand. "Go 'way!"

"Wake up! 'Tis time for Lauds!"

"Let the others greet the morning with songs and worship," Jean-Louis grumbled. "I hardly slept all night."

In the room, more young men stirred, greeting the day in the ways of their fathers and forefathers: grunting, stretching, and farting. Jean-Louis turned his back to Ulf, flopping onto his side and pulling his thin wool coverlet over his shoulders. Ulf smacked him again on the back.

"Jean-Louis, it rained last night, and you know what that means, don't you?"

"The horse dung in the courtyard will be even more unbearable when I have to shovel it because Brother Wikerus chooses to punish me today, as he does every day?"

"It's not Brother Wikerus's fault you can't follow orders or remember your lessons, dummkopf. Rain means mushrooms, and today we shall go out to find some."

"I don't care about mushrooms," Jean-Louis slurred as his eyelids slid closed again. "Just let me sleep."

The door to the novice quarters flew open, and a plump friar in a dark-gray robe walked briskly into the center of the room and positioned himself between the cots. Then he began to ring a large brass bell, whose sound reverberated off the stone walls and vaulted ceiling.

"Good morning, good morning! 'Tis another beautiful day of the Lord, and time for us to acknowledge his bounteous glory!"

The novices were so sleep-addled that they did not catch the hint of sarcasm in the friar's voice. He continued ringing his bell, walking up and down the rows, gently nudging the heaviest sleepers with a hand to shake them awake.

"I will acknowledge God's bounteous glory if Brother Wikerus would acknowledge how jarring his bell is before the sun has fully risen," Jean-Louis groaned.

"By the Virgin's teeth, that bell is loud," another novice swore in the semi-dark.

"Shut up, you blasphemous fool, and be glad it's only Wikerus and not Prior Willem here to come wake us!" Ulf hissed. He returned his attention to Jean-Louis, who had reluctantly thrown off his blanket and was knotting his rope belt around his waist.

"So anyway," Ulf whispered to his friend, "I know of a place in the forest where the mushrooms are abundant. Truffles as large as horses' ears. We can eat what we want, and anything else we harvest I can sell to —" He cut himself short, and Jean-Louis narrowed his eyes.

"Sell them to whom?"

"Well, never mind who we can sell them to. I'll get us some coins for our troubles, then we can really have some fun."

Jean-Louis yawned so wide he thought his face would split into two pieces. "We're Franciscan novices and we live in a friary. 'Fun' is not encouraged here," he said. "And besides, when would we ever find time to go to the forest or to enjoy the proceeds of our labor? The brothers keep us busy toiling and praying from before sunup until Vespers."

The sound of a clap interrupted them. Friar Wikerus called for their attention, nodding in appreciation as one eager young novice ran through the door with a smoking oil lamp to illuminate the long, narrow room. "Alright, boys. Now as you have been instructed, you shall walk into the chapel in a single line, heads lowered in humility, and lips sealed. The only sound shall be our voices raised in prayer and song. And besides" – his blue eyes were dark and twinkling in the wavering light of the lamp – "I shall hand you off to the care of the prior after this, who will surely enforce strict obedience. Best to get yourselves in a praying mood now."

Ulf groaned. Willem Wilmer von Stuttgart, the new prior in charge of Saint Matthieu's church and friary, ran things with iron-handed efficiency, and the slightest infraction from a single novice could unleash communal punishment on all the boys. Ulf knew this because he was the one who most frequently required correction. He could feel the warning glares of his fellow novices upon him.

Friar Wikerus smiled – a wide, almost impish grin – slipped his hands into the sleeves of his gray robe, and strode to the door. One by one, the boys followed him, assuming a humble posture and forming a crooked queue. No one spoke. With a quick glance back and a harshly whispered, "Straighten up that line!" Wikerus set off at a slow walk, his leather slippers silent on the stone floor.

The boys both dozed through Lauds, slurring their prayers with drooping eyelids, then they shuffled into the kitchens where they took their meals away from the friars. Jean-Louis could barely find the energy to raise his spoon to his mouth, but Ulf, revived by his steaming bowl of barley pottage and turnip greens, leaned over the table and whispered to his friend.

"This afternoon, Jean-Louis! We can slip out during the hour of contemplation, dash away into the woods, gather our prize, and be back before anyone notices!"

"I'd rather find a place to hide and take a nap during our time of contemplation," Jean-Louis said, yawning again, this time so wide that the whole table had a view of the unchewed food in his mouth.

"We shall return in time for your nap. Come now, aren't you interested in having an adventure? It's been nothing but days of toil, prayer, and boredom in this place since we arrived, and I need a holiday."

"What's a 'holiday'?"

"Like a feast day. A time to do whatever I wish."

"We just celebrated Rogationtide only a few weeks ago. Was that not enough for you?"

The Rogation Day was one of Ulf's favorite celebrations, not because it was a time to fast and pray for protection, but because during the procession the church would display a giant dragon, covered in leather and scales and stuffed with straw.

But now that he was a novice living inside the friary, he was shocked to learn he wouldn't be spending much time watching the festivities and enjoying honey cakes like he did when he was a child.

Ulf snorted. "They worked us even harder on the last Rogation Day, and on all the other holy days, too. The poor are given leave to rest and the rich have permission to gorge themselves, but we men of the church pray harder and bruise our knees with kneeling. No, I'd like a holiday of my own choosing. I want to have some fun."

Jean-Louis pushed another glistening scoop of pottage into his mouth, but Ulf could see his friend was alert and listening. "We will have to keep a wary eye on the sun's position. If we're missed by anyone, we'll be forced to scrub the latrines for a month at least." He lisped his words around the food still in his mouth.

Ulf dropped his spoon and placed a hand over his heart. A few other heads at the table turned to him and quickly looked away. They all knew Ulf's dramatics would only increase if they gave him attention, and what followed was usually collective punishment. There wouldn't be another bite to eat until nearly sundown, and every boy guarded his food like a dog with a joint of meat.

"I swear to you, on the toes of Saint Matthieu, the eyelashes of the Virgin, and on God's elbows, I will have you back to your toil at the friary on time," Ulf declared. "Trust me. No one will ever miss us."

Tryst

In which Lonel Leporteur has several important meetings

Lonel Leporteur crouched low in the shadow of a hazel tree, sweeping a lock of sand-colored hair from his eyes as he squinted at the vast network of fields and canals that hemmed the city of Colmar on all sides. It was still early in the day; the sun had not yet reached the middle of the sky, and its brightness in the cornflower-blue expanse dazzled him. Beyond the fields he saw a line of trees with bright-green leaves, which gave way to the darker pines velveting the slopes of the gently rolling Vosges mountains. His gaze lingered. To the west were Kaysersberg, Ribeauvillé, and more magnificent cities like Troyes and Paris. Beyond them lay a great salty sea, never crossed, or so he had been told.

He had been to Obernai once to visit the nearby shrine of Saint Odille, who legend said had struck a rock hundreds of years earlier and caused water to flow from it. Prior Konrad told his congregation about the waters from Saint Odille's shrine, which could restore sight to the blind, and so his mother took Lonel along on a pilgrimage to try and fix his brother's poor eyesight. His brother was still nearsighted, and they were poorer afterwards than before.

Lonel could work sums in his head when bargaining in the market, scrape a hide for the tanneries, and operate a grist mill (and a gambling scheme or two) but that was the extent of his education. He liked his life, although he had been born poor. But there were days when he looked at those dark mountains and wished he could see for himself what lay beyond them. Life within the pink sandstone walls of Colmar was small and opportunities were few for a young man with big dreams.

But today, he turned his back to the mountains and cities and seas of the west to stare instead at the gates of Colmar, because he hoped to catch a glimpse of someone.

Kamille. Her name sounded sweet to his ears. He wasn't the only young man in town who had an eye for her. Ever since she moved to Colmar during the winter with her widowed mother, she strutted the streets with men and boys circling around her like flies on honey. How her hips swayed when she walked. How her dark eyes flashed, daring each man to come close to her. She moved about with the boldness of a girl who had learned to survive through her own wit and skill. Since her arrival in Colmar, the young men in the city staggered through the streets with tormented souls. And she toyed with them, with furtive looks and smiles that dimpled her plump cheeks. But Lonel felt sure she devoted extra attention to him. After all, there were no other young men in the city who she would agree to meet outside the walls.

He sighed and reached down to the leather strap girding his waist, and from it hung the tools he needed for his day: a sheath for his eating knife and spoon, a small drawstring bag to store coins and other necessities, and a piece of red linen cloth, tied to the belt and on full display. Kamille had given him the little piece of cloth – a 'tissue' she called it, embroidered with a border of roses and vines in black silk thread. Lonel had never owned anything so luxurious in his life. Although he had seen silk on the tunics of rich merchants in the city, he didn't understand the allure until he possessed such a treasure. The glossy threads and the richness of the deep red cloth stunned him only slightly less than the fact that Kamille had favored him above all others with such a prize.

Kamille, whose father had been a weaver in Basel before he died, told him she had dozens of such trifles. Perhaps it was the truth, but even if she was lying about her former wealth, Lonel wouldn't care. Thoroughly smitten, he chose to believe she had given the 'tissue' to him because he was special. The thought filled his whole being with delight.

To help her to sneak away from his rivals, Lonel instructed Kamille to wear a monk's habit and keep her head bowed when she slipped away to meet him outside the city walls. It had worked twice already, and she and Lonel had spent a few merry afternoons in the fields, sprawled on an old horse blanket, working their way through a skin of wine and a loaf of bread she'd purloined from the new communal oven, where she sometimes swept the floors and stoked the fire.

Thinking about the recently rebuilt oven made the scar on Lonel's ankle itch. A new baker and his family had moved to

Colmar from Mulhouse and immediately got to work repairing and reopening the ruined oven. The fire that destroyed the previous bakery burned more than Lonel's ankle, it left an open wound on his soul.

He shook his head as he pondered last four years in Colmar. No sooner had the city recovered from the months of devastating sickness – which everyone now called the Great Pestilence or the Great Mortality – than the neglected crops withered and rotted because there were not enough people still alive and healthy to harvest. Bandits ruled the roads, and travel became hazardous, requiring armed guards who often extorted or even robbed the people they were supposed to protect. He was too young to remember much about life before the disease carried off half of his city's population, but sometimes his parents spoke wistfully of the friends who had died, and of meat on the table every day at supper. The Great Pestilence changed the world, and no one knew how to go back to the way things were before.

Lonel heard a noise behind him and he spun, his heart leaping in his chest as he expected to see his lover's buxom figure. But instead of Kamille's curves and luminous skin, he watched as two pimple-faced young men in gray robes walked furtively through the city gate behind a slow-moving ox cart. As soon as the cart rolled past a coppice of trees, the boys dove into the low shrubbery alongside the road. From his hiding place nearby, Lonel watched as they darted around a briar hedge and into a field, still fallow and soggy with water from a flooded canal. Then they began to argue.

He looked back at the gate. He still couldn't see Kamille, so he walked on his toes as silently as he could to get close enough to hear their raised voices. The two boys looked a few years younger than him. Though they wore monks' robes, their heads were not shaved on top, and their upper lips were only barely beginning to sprout growth. These were novices, who had not yet taken their vows.

"At this rate we're never going to make it to Saint Matthieu's before the next bell. If we're not back on time, even Brother Wikerus won't be able to protect us from a whipping," the dark-haired boy hissed.

"Patience, Jean-Louis," the blond boy whispered back. "Let's move into the trees and then further west. We won't go far from the walls, I promise."

This was annoying. The last thing Lonel wanted were two spectators to his amour with Kamille. He would have to get rid of them. Lonel smirked, for there was nothing he loved more than an opportunity to make someone else feel like a fool, and these two had an air of rash desperation that made them ripe for a little trickery. He slipped further into the shadows of the young forest where he hid and waited.

A short time later, when there was a lull in the traffic of merchants' carts and workers trudging with their tools over their shoulders and their dinners swinging from string bags, the two novices darted from the low shrubs across the road and into the trees on the opposite side.

"I thought we would be discovered for sure!" the one called Jean-Louis said. Ulf just grinned.

"Let's go. Now!"

The two boys pushed their way further into the trees and nearly collided with Lonel, who leaned against the slender trunk of a silvery birch, picking his teeth with a green-leafed twig. "Going somewhere, brothers?"

"I-I..." Jean-Louis stuttered for a moment, but Ulf shushed him.

"The prior of our abbey has commanded us to go out in search of mushrooms for the Franciscans' supper."

Lonel made a great show of looking incredulously to the west, where the boys were heading. "Well, your prior should have sent someone else, for everyone knows the best mushrooms are to the northeast, near the banks of the Rhine." He nodded with his chin toward the dark green line of trees bordering the great river far in the distance, noting the gleam of greed that sparkled in Ulf's eyes. Yes, he thought to himself. This will be easy, and so much fun.

"Indeed so? And why would you share this information with us, friend?" Ulf asked.

"I cannot go there, and someone must harvest to ensure they grow properly." Lonel tossed his twig to the ground and ran his tongue across his teeth. "As a matter of fact, there are more treasures in the north than chanterelles in the woods. Do you see large the road branching off to the north?"

"Aye," Ulf said, his voice taking on an edge of suspicion.

"It leads to Strassburg, and do you know what their problem is in Strassburg?"

"No," the two novices answered together.

"Shoes."

Ulf and Jean-Louis looked at each other, and then back at Lonel. "Beg your pardon?" Jean-Louis said.

"Not enough shoes in Strassburg. But what they do have are men and women who are experts at finding and harvesting mushrooms. If someone were to find say...a dozen pairs of matching leather shoes and sandals, I'm sure a shoe-for-mushroom trade would be amenable to the good merchants of fair Strassburg."

"Where would we get shoes?" Jean-Louis cried. He tugged Ulf's arm. "Come, we must go. This man is trying to swindle us."

But Ulf shrugged Jean-Louis' hand away. "Do they trade other things than mushrooms for shoes, friend?"

"Oh aye," Lonel said with a lazy drawl. "Ropes. Trinkets. Silver coins." He noted how Ulf's eyes blazed at the mention of silver. "And Colmar has an excess of shoes. Why, I heard the Dominican brethren of Saint Martin's have all clad their feet in new leather just this winter."

"No, Ulf, no!" Jean-Louis hissed.

Ulf turned to his friend. "You know who I recently heard insulting our Friar Wikerus? A Dominican friar. And do you know who have more shoes than they need? The Dominicans."

Lonel glowed. Sending these two greedy simpletons on a fool's errand felt to Lonel like doing God's work. For him, a well-constructed bit of roguery was as sublime as an act of worship.

He glanced over their heads. In the distance, a solitary figure in a monk's habit walked on the road from Colmar, with a swaying step.

Kamille. Lonel felt himself grow light-headed.

"Go with my good will, my friends. Bring back riches and fine foods for your brethren, and in your efforts, may God help you provide relief to the feet of Strassburg. There is a secret door to the Dominicans' clothier in their courtyard, near the privies. In there, you will find as much footwear as you can carry" He swept past them.

Jean-Louis was squinting at the figure on the road. "A grayfriar. We've been followed! Quickly, Ulf! We must hide!"

But the greedy sparkle in Ulf's eyes had only grown stronger. "Aye. We can hide in Strassburg – after we've relieved the Dominicans of their sandals."

"Look, I am not opposed to making the Dominicans go barefoot – they could use some additional humility. But Strassburg is too far away!" Jean-Louis hissed. "We must return to the friary at once. We can circle back and enter through another gate. No one will be the wiser."

Lonel stopped his retreat and turned to the novices. "Let me deal with this wandering monk, Brothers, and if he searches for you, I shall…divert him." He suppressed a smile. Oh, he would divert Kamille for certain – straight into his arms. "Godspeed on your quest for the finest sandals, er...I mean mushrooms!"

He strode confidently toward the figure on the road, and the two novices ran into the brush as fast as they could, their gray robes clutched around their waists. Jean-Louis looked back as he ran, and for a moment he thought he saw the strange boy they met in the forest sweep the gray-clad monk off his feet for a kiss.

"Now," Ulf whispered as he rubbed his hands together. "Let us find this secret door to the Dominicans, shall we? I feel good fortune shining upon us today."

The knavish and the vexatious

In which Gritta realizes she has more sons than are necessary

Frau Gritta Leporteur, her hands affixed to her bony hips, stood glaring over her twin sons. They were identical in every way – even down to the matching trails of goo dribbling from the tips of their upturned noses. Living in Les Tanneurs, the most scorned quarter of the city, did her no favors. The families who owned the tanneries that gave the neighborhood its name did well enough for themselves, as did a few merchants who sold dyes and tools to finish the hides destined to become saddles, shoes, bags, and even hinges on doors.

Life in the year 1355 was held together with grit, religion, and well-tanned leather, and the citizens of Colmar knew they relied on the work of these tradesmen. But the stench, oh the stench! When the butcher liberated a cow or a pig of its skin, the hide would spend a full year soaking in a vat of urine, feces, and oak bark before it was removed to be washed, scraped, soaked again, and then stretched on a frame to dry. All in all, a smelly business.

Gritta's family did not participate in the leather tanning trade. Her husband, Jorges, was a porter, lifting baskets of fish and eels at the poissonnerie on the Lauch River, which flowed languidly through the center of town. A notorious drunk, Jorges occasionally missed a step when he tottered across the narrow plank connecting boat to shore, and tumbled into the dark green water. This provided excellent entertainment for the young boys and old men in the city who loitered on the quay with their feet and a fishing lines dangling in the water.

Her assorted sons and daughters found work for themselves according to their temperament; some were apprenticed to reputable tradesmen, and others participated in...less honest work. For her own part, Gritta spent her days overseeing the brewing of ale at her friend Appel's house and trying to keep her youngest children from causing havoc on the streets of Colmar.

Outside, the sun sank low on the horizon – a dying flame in a cloudless blue sky. She had spent the day hard at work washing the linens. After lifting, pounding, and wringing until her limbs and back ached, she was in no mood to appreciate the jewel-tones of a late spring sunset. Although she was a poor woman and her clothes threadbare, Gritta labored hard to ensure no one could claim she and her family lived in filth. But today her hard work had been in vain, for the two messy young boys standing before her had stained more than just their tunics. They had sullied the already precarious reputation of the Leporteur family in Les Tanneurs.

She closed her eyes, took a deep breath, and returned her focus to her twins, Anstett and Mattheus. She heard them shuffling their feet, and their discomfort gave her a small amount of reassurance. Perhaps the boys, who were nearing their tenth year, had finally developed an understanding of shame.

"Why, in the name of heaven, did you think this would be a good idea?" she hissed, her eyes still closed. "And who else saw you? The last thing I need is the sheriff or his men coming around to my house for the second time today." She shot an annoyed glance at the window, where another of her sons, twelve-year-old Urbe, sat on a stool, carefully mending a wool stocking with a large bone needle. Only a short time earlier, Urbe had turned up on her doorstep with the back of his tunic firmly clasped in the grip of Herr Werner, the sheriff of Colmar.

"Frau Gritta, if I have to make one more trip into Les Tanneurs this week to attend to your errant children or wine-soaked husband, I'll toss you in the stocks for not keeping a closer eye on them!" the sheriff had bellowed at her as he shoved Urbe through the door.

Gritta grimaced at the memory.

"First your brother is dragged home by Sheriff Werner for gambling in the wynstube, and now you two wastrels have gone and defaced the edifice of Saint Matthieu's church! And with the new prior only established for a month now! What will he think of us?!"

"Be calm, Ma," Anstett said, kicking the dust with his bare foot. "'Twasn't done in a permanent way. The paint will rub off. We made it from cherry juice."

"Aye, and only the cherries we found on the ground!" Mattheus piped in.

"But you made the paint from cherries from Prior Willem's personal orchard!" Gritta screamed. "And you covered the walls with drawings of pizzles! Of...of...a man's...manhood! Any other building and I wouldn't be so angry, but the church?! We shall all go to hell for this!"

Anstett snorted and giggled, but Mattheus looked serious. "God granted men pizzles, Ma. We are merely glorifying God's creation."

Gritta's face turned the color of a beetroot. "And I am about to destroy God's creation. If the two of you do not go directly to the church and scrub those walls, I shall hang your own pizzles from the city gate, just as soon as I slice them from between your legs!"

The twins scrambled into action, each trying to run out the door before the other, tripping over themselves in their rush. Gritta followed them outside, waving a dripping washrag over her head. "Demons!" she shouted after them. "You're no children of mine!"

None of the people who lived alongside the Leporteurs on Trench Lane even bothered to inquire about the commotion, for it wasn't unusual to hear shouts, insults, and an occasional explosion coming from the old warehouse where Gritta's family lived. What else could you expect from a household made up of twelve children, eight chickens, a drunken husband, and one exhausted woman trying to hold everything together?

In the distance, a familiar silhouette appeared, walking down the lane. Portly, tonsured, and wearing a rough wool robe, Friar Wikerus – Franciscan, advocate for the poor, and frequent visitor, hopped over the refuse-filled ditch running through the middle of the street that gave Trench Lane its name. He stood before her, but he wasn't wearing his usual pleasant smile.

"Greetings, Friar." Gritta bowed her head and quickly resumed her work, plunging a threadbare wimple into the tub of gray, soapy water. "How may I be of service to you today? We haven't any new brews for you to try, but there's a bit of small ale in the cask, flavored with some dried quinsywort for a bit of spice."

Friar Wikerus stepped aside, and behind him stood Lonel, her sixth-born, with a blackened eye and ripped tunic. "I thought it best to bring him straight to you and not involve the sheriff," the friar said, spreading his hands in apology.

Gritta felt her eye twitch, and a storm of anger brewed in her keen gaze – an expression she usually wore when it was time to speak with Lonel. Of her twelve children, none caused her as much grief as this lanky, scheming young man – the one who most resembled his father in looks and character. "Well then, what trouble have you got up to now, eh?"

Lonel shuddered, and he hung his sandy-blond head. "Fightin'. And swearing against the saints, for which Friar Wikerus has absolved me."

Gritta looked at Friar Wikerus, who didn't meet her gaze, and instead made a studious examination of his fingernails. She shook her head. This child would put her in an early grave, if the twins didn't do the deed first.

"And what were you fighting about, my son? Let it not be something that will cost your father money, because I assure you, he hasn't got the coin to pay for it. Come on now, were you messing with someone's daughter?"

Lonel didn't answer but hung his head further.

"Were you drunk? Don't tell me you unleashed my hens inside Frau Lena's cookhouse again because she will never let me hear the end of it. Last time they ate an entire basket of dried peas, and it took a month to harvest and repay her from my own garden."

"No, Ma," Lonel mumbled. "Jarl the baker struck me in the eye because he said you were not comely to look at, and I told him to place his foul tongue in his own oven."

This confession immediately made Gritta suspicious. "Well, Jarl the baker spoke the truth. I ain't nothing to look at. And I have a hard time believing you would damage your face to protect my honor. Jarl has only been baker in this part of the city for a few months since we lost the last one, and it's taken you no time at all to irritate him. Now we shall have to go across town to Frau Ghent's for more expensive bread again." She fidgeted, and everyone grew silent. Only a few months earlier they had lost Hans, who had been the baker for the poorer occupants of Les Tanneurs, in a very gruesome circumstance. She cleared her throat.

"Come now, son, let's hear the truth."

Lonel hung his head further, and Friar Wikerus placed a hand on the boy's shoulder. "This is the same account he related to me, Frau Gritta. Let us assume he angered the baker because he was defending the honor of his mother."

"Aye, that's it. That's what I did." Lonel nodded.

"But, Friar, you do not know my son —"

Wikerus cut her off with his raised palm. "I smoothed things over with Jarl and instructed Lonel on the words of the Psalmist: 'Refrain from anger and forsake wrath! Fret not yourself; it tends only to evil.'"

To this, Gritta responded with an acid laugh. "I've never known my sixth-born child here to fret about anything. But he certainly causes much fret for his parents."

"I spoke to him at length about the bible's command to honor thy father and mother when we walked here from the baker. He is contrite, I assure you. And now, I think a poultice of comfrey and liver on that eye would be well received, wouldn't it, my boy?" Friar Wikerus smiled, and good-natured creases formed at the edges of his large blue eyes.

Still suspicious, Gritta marched Lonel to a bench and made a paste of comfrey leaf with a scant measure of dried sheep's liver, which she applied to his wound with more pressure than necessary. Then she ordered him to take up a needle and join his younger brother Urbe, who continued to mend stockings in the corner. Friar Wikerus moved toward the door, hesitated, then sighed, his shoulders slumping.

"What troubles you, Friar?" Gritta asked, though she suspected he was about to mention the obscene painting on the walls of his church. "I am very sorry about Anstett and

Mattheus. They will not receive any supper tonight until they have erased the damage, I promise you. And I will send them to the friary to clean the privies for a week if you wish."

Friar Wikerus stared at Gritta, his eyes wide. "What have they done today, goodwife Gritta? Have all your children committed crimes at the exact same hour?" He glanced at Urbe, who continued to struggle with his stocking and darning needle. "I heard Urbe cleared out the coins of every patron at Herr Schlock's wynstube this morning. An admirable feat of cunning and skill for a boy not yet thirteen."

Gritta reddened again. "Ah, Friar Wikerus! They um, well..."

"Did Anstett and Mattheus adorn the new walls of Saint Matthieu's church with their favorite body part, perhaps?"

Gritta grimaced. "They spend too much time with their father, Friar."

Friar Wikerus chuckled and shook his head. "They remind me of the trouble my brother and I got up to as boys. All mischief and joy for life – and very little sense."

Gritta's mouth dropped open. She had known Friar Wikerus for a several years now, since he first moved to Colmar, and never in all that time had he ever mentioned his life before he swore his allegiance to God and the mendicant way of life. "Why, Friar, I had no idea you had a brother at all. Was this when you lived in Breisach?"

The smile froze on Friar Wikerus's face and the light in his eyes dimmed. "I am not troubled about the twins, although they do need to make amends for defacing the church. Prior

Willem is in deep prayer and contemplation all day, and he hasn't seen the mischief yet. Anstett and Mattheus may be able to escape unscathed if they scrub the walls before he is done with his worship. No, something else worries me, although I am probably premature in thinking the worst."

Gritta noticed his immediate change of subject and chose not to pursue her curiosity. She gestured to a bench and handed Friar Wikerus a bowl of ale, still cool and sweet from when she drew it from the cask that morning. Friar Wikerus took a long drink and heaved a sigh of contentment.

"You may not be aware, but Prior Willem has placed me in a role of some authority." He grinned at Gritta's shocked expression. "I was as surprised as you. He placed me in charge of the young novices, and I am grateful for his trust. But it seems that, well, I've lost two of them. Novices, I mean. I suppose it is his trust I shall lose next."

On his seat near the window with Urbe, Lonel fumbled with his darning needle and dropped it.

"You lost them, Friar? Well, I'm sure you'll find them in a wynstube or near one of the pleasure houses. You know how young men can be."

Friar Wikerus shook his head. "Indeed, I have already searched all the places where a young man might be tempted to stray, but I've had no success in finding them. It is as if they vanished into the air like smoke."

"And for how long have they been missing?"

"Since after their morning meal. They did not show up for the recitation of prayers or for their daily work in the potager garden. I worry something terrible might have happened to them."

"Ah, Friar, they haven't even been gone for an entire night. Drink your ale and save your worries. They will turn up – possibly inebriated, bloodied, and without their virginity, but I'm sure they will be back at your door as soon as they grow hungry for a free meal."

"Jesu's beard, I hope they have only decided to go adventuring through the water gate and nothing else!" Wikerus said.

Before Gritta could reply, the sound of a young man's pleading voice drifted through the open door.

"Just one chaste kiss, Frau Efi? No one will know about it!"

"Be gone, I tell you!" came a tart reply.

"Come now, Efi. It is a year since you became a widow. Just one kiss!"

"I said no!" Efi responded sharply, and she stomped into the house, her skirts and apron swirling, wimple askew, her blonde hair catching the sunlight like a halo around her head. Her blue eyes blazed, but when they landed on Friar Wikerus they narrowed. Friar Wikerus set his bowl down, winked at her, and strode out the door.

"Hello, my son," the women heard the friar say to the unwanted suitor outside the door. "I heard you speaking of chaste kisses. Perhaps you will kiss my cheek in the spirit of brotherhood and Christ's love?"

A pause.

"Oh, uh...I...must be going, Friar. I am sure you misunderstood." Came a stuttered reply.

"No indeed, I require a kiss from you! In the spirit of chastity and fraternity!" Friar Wikerus cried.

This exchange was followed by the sounds of footsteps running down Trench Lane and across the square. Friar Wikerus returned, shaking his head and laughing. "Far be it from me to assume you need rescuing, Frau Efi, but chasing off your unwanted suitors is quite satisfying. That young man will think twice before he follows you into Les Tanneurs again."

Efi set her basket on the table and twirled until her skirts billowed around her legs like a bell. Young, pretty, and recently widowed, she was an enticing prospect to the eligible young men in Les Tanneurs. But Efi Kleven had no intention of being the wife of a tanner. With her friends Gritta and Appel, she earned a fair profit brewing and selling ale, and the taste of independence put her in no mood to remarry quickly. "I am glad I brought you some joy, Friar Wikerus! To what do we owe this visit?"

"Ah yes, I came by to return Lonel to his home for a little bit of his mother's treatment, and as you can see —" He turned to where Lonel had been sitting, but the seat near the window was vacant. A dark green glob of mashed comfrey leaves and sheep's liver lay discarded on the hard-packed dirt floor next to a half-stitched stocking.

"Now where did he run off to? I didn't even see him leave the house." Friar Wikerus looked at Urbe, but the boy shrugged and returned to his work. Efi began to unpack her basket, pulling out parcels of herbs and a few small loaves of brown bread.

Gritta shook her head. "Knowing Lonel, he's off to no good thing, Friar. No good thing at all."

A necessary journey

In which Father Konrad takes ahold of the ribbons of his own hat

"AND DO NOT FORGET, Brother Tacitus, that although I am placing you in charge of the friary whilst I am away, you are to lead with humility and compassion." Father Konrad, prior of Saint Martin's Dominican church, shot a sideways glance at the tall, gaunt man who stood quietly with both hands concealed in the voluminous sleeves of his black Dominican's robe. Although the man's craggy face remained impassive, the look in his eye made Father Konrad nervous. It was the maniac gleam of a man who was ready to seize an opportunity.

"Of course, Father Prior. I shall lead your flock as if they were my very own children." Brother Tacitus bowed his head slightly, but the pretense of meekness didn't fool the old prior. A lifetime of living among ambitious men granted him a keen eye for ambition.

"Hmmm. That's what concerns me. Remember you have Brother Johannes and Brother Isembard here to provide assistance, and if anything should go awry you can always send someone down the hill to the Saint Mathieu's and the Franciscans to fetch Friar Wikerus for help."

The twinkle in Tacitus's eyes faded, replaced by a glowing coal of hatred. He crossed his arms over his chest. Where there should have been a hand on his right wrist, there instead was a dark iron hook secured in place with leather straps and wooden stays.

"It is not necessary to involve a Franciscan in the affairs of the Order of Saint Dominic," he said with a sniff.

"Nevertheless, Prior Willem of Saint Matthieu's heard of my departure and offered to loan Friar Wikerus should you require him. After all, Wikerus is familiar with our ways."

"Considering this is the second time a Franciscan church has offered to lend Friar Wikerus to us in so many years, should we not question why they are so eager to be rid of him?" Tacitus asked.

Father Konrad responded with a look of reproach and turned to a baby-faced young man who stood nearby. "Is everything packed in the wagon, Brother Tielo?"

Brother Tielo was the newest friar at Saint Martin's, having only taken his vows a few months earlier. Thrilled with his position as servant to the most important man at the church, he nodded with more enthusiasm than the question required, and reached up to straighten Father Konrad's cap.

"All the provisions, and gifts for the archbishop of Strassburg are prepared, including Colmar's finest leathers and skeins of dyed wool. And I've laid aside a packet of salted pork for the road, with hard barley toasts, and eight skins of wine."

Father Konrad swatted the friar's hands away, removed his cap and replaced it, straightening it himself this time so it rested at the perfect angle, where the strings wouldn't choke him when he tied them under his chin.

"Eight skins seem rather a lot of wine for a trip that will only take three days by mule, don't you think?"

"Well, it will be hot and dry on the roads..." Brother Tielo stuttered.

Father Konrad raised an eyebrow but let the matter rest. The young man seemed to think this trip would be as raucous as a pilgrimage to a saint's shrine, but the old prior knew from his own experience that the boy would stay busy working in the grand kitchens of the Dominican abbey upon their arrival. The Bishop of Strassburg was a stingy leader and never resisted the opportunity to utilize free labor.

Brother Tielo proceeded to fluster about the room, knocking over a stack of velum scrolls, and then reached to adjust Father Konrad's robe, wearing thin the prior's already stretched patience.

"Oh, be still, Brother Tielo, and leave me alone! For fifty years I've been fastening my own cloak and tying my own cap. I don't require your assistance now!"

Brother Tielo cowered and slunk from the room, head bowed, his hands clasped in front of him. Father Konrad thought he saw the barest hint of a smile tug at the granite cheek of Brother Tacitus, who had observed the entire scene.

"Something amusing you, Tacitus? Remember what I told you: use a gentle hand, and rule as I would," Father Konrad muttered.

Brother Tacitus bowed but smirked as he spoke. "I apologize for my comments about Friar Wikerus, Father Prior."

"Yes, well see you keep them to yourself next time," Father Konrad replied absently. He leaned his head out the arched window, scanned the courtyard, and narrowed his eyes. Brother Tielo was sitting in the dust next to the laden wagon, his head drooping. The old prior sighed with the weariness of a man who had seen all he wanted of the world and cared nothing for a young friar's injured feelings. Still, the boy would be accompanying him for three days of travel to Strassburg, possibly four. It was best to make amends now. Straightening himself, he marched from the vestibule of his solar and into the nave of the church, stopping before the altar, where he knelt as slowly as his aging knees would allow.

"Holy Father, forgive me for being impatient with the boy. And forgive me for my lack of enthusiasm for traveling with a new friar. My bones and my brain are in no mood for the energy of youth." It would have to do for a prayer. The road and Brother Tielo awaited. Behind him, he heard the clink of an iron hook as it tapped against the wooden cross hanging around Brother Tacitus's throat.

"A lovely prayer, Father. And how excellent that young Tielo will have this opportunity to accompany you on your travels and see more of the world beyond our walls."

Father Konrad turned to his most senior friar. "Tacitus, it was you who suggested Tielo accompany me for his training, and I suspect you did so in order to be rid of him."

But Brother Tacitus crossed himself solemnly with his hook and bowed his head. "Really, Father Konrad, such an accusation in God's house!"

Father Konrad turned his gaze back to the altar. They were not in the small chapel used by the friars for private prayer, but in the towering nave where the public gathered for services and worship. Outside, the church spire speared the sky, dwarfing every other rooftop. Constructed of pink and orange sandstone mined from the local hills and set in place by Alsatian hands, the church glowed when the light struck it. But inside, it was gloomy.

Father Konrad looked up at Christ hanging above him on his cross, face not twisted in agony but in beatific peace, his eyes rolled upwards, looking toward the heavens.

"You're a better man than I," he whispered to the figure on the cross. He didn't mean to speak aloud, but he could see from the surprised expression on Brother Tacitus's face that the words had escaped his lips.

"What did you say, Father?" Brother Tacitus asked.

Father Konrad crossed himself quickly and finished his prayer. "Jesu, let us start this journey now, so it may all be finished as quickly as possible. In nomine Patris, et Filii, et Spiritus Sancti. Amen."

The potter's sons
In which Friar Wikerus braves his own memories

Saint Martin's church stood tall and stately in the Dominicans' square, with a burbling stream nearby. The church enjoyed the high ground – as much anyone could claim, for the city and the valley around it was remarkably flat. But there was a gentle slope in Colmar, and at its top, the church had stood for hundreds of years, its pink and orange stones glittering with mica in the sunshine, its tiled roof streaked with stork and pigeon droppings.

Down the hill stood the newer church of Saint Matthieu, and these two great monuments to God stared at each other as uneasily as Dominican and Franciscan friars did when they met in the street. Friar Wikerus had only just moved into the church of Saint Matthieu, despite having lived in Colmar for almost two years now. He had been sent from his friary in Breisach, lent to the Dominicans to resolve a crime spree and the theft of church property, and continued to live with the black-robed brothers afterwards, which earned him an indifferent reception from other Franciscans in the city.

As a young boy, Wikerus had joined the Franciscans for community and safety but found himself being more readily accepted by the Dominicans instead. This was hardly something to feel easy about, because he'd had his share of suspicion and trouble from the Dominican brothers as well – especially the dour, stern-faced Brother Tacitus.

In truth, Wikerus didn't feel complete loyalty to either Order. His chief motive in joining the Franciscans as a boy was for food, shelter, and protection. It was years later when he realized he had chosen wisely. The life of a mendicant friar suited him. Spending his days cloistered in prayer and silent contemplation might be well enough for a Benedictine in an abbey, but Wikerus enjoyed being out amongst the poor; real people, living real lives away from the incense and ceremony of holy life. Had his childhood played out differently, Wikerus might have been one of those people – living in a house with a wife and children, perhaps occupying a trade.

Pottery, he thought to himself. *I would have been a potter, just like my father before me...* But he pushed the thought from his mind. It served no purpose to ponder the future that had been taken from him.

He hurried through the small square at the entrance of Saint Matthieu's, dodging piles of dung left by a flock of sheep on their way to the slaughterhouse. Old Arne the street sweeper and his son Benno would be along with their two-wheeled cart and spades to scoop up the mess and dispose of it, but until then it was best to keep a wary eye when walking. On this balmy day, the great wooden doors of Saint Matthieu's church were open, and the faint wisp of a chanted song drifted into the square. A few people paused to listen before hurrying on to their work. Wikerus took a moment to dart around the corner and look at the wall near his prior's personal orchard. He smiled. Someone had scrubbed away the obscene artwork Gritta's twins had scribbled on the wall earlier.

Inside, he paused to appreciate the clean lines of the church's interior. The Dominicans had a more ornate interpretation of God's house of worship, but the beauty of this Franciscan building was in its simplicity. The columns of sandstone in alternating shades of cream and pale orange supported tall portals that arched gracefully over his head. The ceiling was ribbed with thick beams of honey-colored oak, and when the brothers sang their prayers, the rich sound of their voices filled the room and overwhelmed the senses.

Standing near the door to one side, Father Willem, the new prior of Saint Matthieu's church, stood with his hands behind his back. Next to him, the sheriff of Colmar picked at his teeth with his fingernails. Friar Wikerus took a breath and braced for the self-aggrandizing and unwaveringly dimwitted sheriff. Prior Willem motioned for Wikerus to approach.

"Ah, Brother Wikerus! I was just speaking to the sheriff about you," the prior said. "Have you met Herr Werner, our esteemed representative of the city council's law?"

Wikerus and Werner regarded each other grudgingly. "Yes, we are acquainted, Father Prior," Wikerus answered.

"Very good," Prior Willem said, oblivious to the glances Wikerus and the sheriff exchanged. "I have asked for the sheriff to help us discipline those two rascals for their flagrant behavior. It really is unacceptable."

Wikerus felt his stomach lurch. Gritta's twin boys, Anstett and Mattheus, were high-spirited and inquisitive, and they certainly deserved punishment for defacing church property, but he didn't believe they were totally incorrigible. He saved that distinction for Lonel, Gritta's sixth-born son. "My lords, their crimes are serious, but I do not believe it requires the intervention of the sheriff. Surely just a stern reprimand and some extra prayers are in order."

"Reprimand indeed," Sheriff Werner snorted. "They should be made to clean the privies until Michael's Mass and wash the brother's clothes with the sweat of their own bodies. Am I right, Prior?"

Prior Willem smiled coolly at the sheriff. Unlike the kindly but often exasperated Prior Konrad of the Dominicans, Prior Willem of the Franciscans was sired by a noble family that claimed a small twig on the tree of Count Eberhard of Württemberg himself. As a second-born son, with one brother inheriting his father's title and another brother serving in the emperor army, Willem was expected to go into the church and find a way to rise in the ranks and distinguish himself. Local nobility in a small city fell beneath him in rank, and in the sheriff's case, in intelligence as well.

"I will determine an appropriate discipline when the boys are returned to me, healthy and alive enough to take their punishment. Novices are always wily and difficult to manage. What word, Brother Wikerus?"

Silently thanking God that the prior was referring not to Gritta's errant twins but to the missing novice friars, Wikerus bowed his head slowly. "No news, I'm afraid. No one saw the two boys leave the church grounds. It is as if they were spirited away by the Devil himself."

Sheriff Werner's eyes grew wide, for there was nothing more frightening to him than the threat of demons, monsters, and the fiery pit of hell. He would rather put up with the wrath of his own wife and his mistress in the same night.

"And this is why I have asked the good sheriff to join us. We must search every home and question every citizen of Colmar. The boys were well fed and cared for here. Nothing could have tempted them to leave our walls except extreme sin or kidnapping," Prior Willem said.

"My lord Prior, it's worth mentioning that young Ulf is a bit of a recalcitrant boy. I think he could have been lured outside our walls using almost no temptation at all. And Jean-Louis follows wherever Ulf goes," Wikerus said. "I don't think it's necessary to go to the door of every home yet. They have only been gone for one day."

"There are dangers about, Brother Wikerus. You may not be aware of them yet, but the dangers outside the city abound."

Before Wikerus could ask, Sheriff Werner cleared his throat. Wikerus recognized the sound. It meant a grandiose speech about the sheriff's own bravery was imminent.

"Several have confided to me about a threat lurking outside the walls, and I can confirm it is true, for I saw the beast with my own eyes."

"Beast?" Wikerus asked, feeling his mouth drop open. "Did a bear or a wolf stray from the mountains?"

The sheriff shook his head. "Nothing you or I have ever seen before, Friar. This is a beast as terrifying as a dragon. Footsteps like thunder. Covered in feathers. Taller than a mill wheel. The claws of a lion and the fangs of a wolf, with a stench as foul and sulfureous as hell itself!"

"Very good, Sheriff, thank you." Prior Willem put a hand on the sheriff's arm. "We do not wish to cause alarm."

"And you worry this monster has taken the boys?" Wikerus asked.

"Taken, and eaten," Sheriff Werner said solemnly. "I am sure we will find nothing but their bones and teeth, young morsels that those boys were. And well fed by the church, too."

"Not eaten. There is no evidence of violence, Sheriff. But if they are still in Colmar, we must find them before they venture outside the safety of our walls." Prior Willem struggled and failed to keep the irritation from his voice. "Brother Wikerus, I wish for you to work with the sheriff until the novices are found. Whatever malevolence is outside the walls, it is unholy. I require a man of God to assist the law."

"But what of my duties with the other novices, Father Prior? What of my ministrations to the poor living in Les Tanneurs? Surely we don't have any other brothers who can be spared at this time. And did you not also tell Father Konrad of the Dominicans I should make myself available to them if they need help?"

"Ah yes, I have come to an agreement with Father Konrad of the Dominicans. In exchange for your assistance while he travels to pay his obeisance to the Bishop of Strassburg, he kindly offered to send a Dominican brother who has worked in Les Tanneurs before to care for your flock if needed."

"Oh no. He must mean Brother Tacitus," Wikerus groaned. Tacitus, whose name was an accurate representation of his demeanor, was an avowed rival, a moralizing, pontificating thorn in his side.

"You have met him? But of course you have – I often forget you lived amongst the Dominicans for so long. I thank God you've rejoined your own brethren. We are blessed to have you with us here in Colmar, Brother Wikerus," Prior Willem said, and Wikerus felt himself flush with delight.

"Now," the prior continued, rubbing his hands together. "You two shall start right away. Find my missing boys, Wikerus. Their lives may depend on you."

A snarl in the dark

In which things outside the walls go bump in the night

THE SUN HAD ONLY just recently set when Arne, the street sweeper of Colmar, tossed his spade into the back of his cart and stretched his aching shoulders. His son, Benno, lumbered toward him in the semi-darkness. Well into his adolescence, Benno was blessed with thick arms like the trunk of a tree, and a low-hanging brow carpeted with a thick, solitary line of hair above his deep-set brown eyes. The boy resembled his mother. By comparison, Arne was scrawny and bent, with only a few white hairs still clinging to his head in a wispy fringe about his ears. A lifetime of shoveling dung from the streets and dragging his two-wheeled cart behind him blessed him with strong, sinewy limbs, but his eyes, set in a deeply tanned face, were so rheumy with age that they could no longer be classified as any particular color.

"Good work, son. No one else is about, and therefore no more horses or oxen will drop their filth. Remember, Colmar will have the cleanest streets and the sweetest-smelling canals of any city in the valley if I have my way!"

"Not Les Tanneurs," Benno said.

"What was that?"

Benno scratched his head, dislodging a few resident fleas. "Les Tanneurs is the smelliest part of city, and there ain't nothing we can do about it, not with shovels or holy water, neither."

"True, son, true. But the tanner's work is important. Softening and preserving the hides requires shit in order to work properly. Why, did you know the tanners will soak a hide in lime and piss for an entire year before it is ready to be scraped and stretched?"

Arne saw his son's attention begin to wander, and he sighed. He had hoped he could apprentice the boy to a higher trade so he could rise in society's estimation – even tanning would do. But sweeping the streets suited Benno. When it became apparent that his son was as slow in mind as he was in movement, Arne had to make backup plans. He thought about the cache of silver coins he had hidden under the wooden planks of his home in the wool dyers' district. Perhaps Benno would always be a street sweeper, but if Arne continued to save his silver, the boy would be the wealthiest street sweeper Colmar had ever known.

"Well, I can see it doesn't interest ye. Now, take the cart outside the walls and empty it into Lord Frider's manure pond, and then we shall be done for the night."

Benno groaned. "Aw, I wish you would let me have one night off, Da. The lads invited me to come to Herr Schlock's, and you know there is a lass who I'm courting."

"I am old, son! The wagon is heavy, and my back is tired."

"Do you want a daughter-in-law to rub your feet an' wash your tunics or not? It's been a whole lot of work since Ma died of the pestilence, and this lass I fancy is a wonder. Let me court her, and when she's my wife, then I'll take the manure to Lord Frider's pond every night."

Arne hesitated. A woman about their little hovel would be a help to him. He smiled, thinking of clean clothes and a bowl of warm pottage waiting each day. Fat grandchildren frolicked through his imagination, while his daughter-in-law planted and cared for a vegetable garden. "Very well. Go to the wynstube and woo your fair lady, son. I'll take this filth outside the walls tonight."

"Thanks, Da!" Benno shouted, and he ran off into the darkening streets, as heavy and clumsy as a young bull ox.

Arne gritted his few remaining teeth and grunted as he squatted down and gripped the long poles of his two-wheeled cart. He heaved the poles to a comfortable position as he stood up and began his slow trudge toward the closest city gate.

By the time Arne made it past the guards, through the gate, and down the wagon track to Lord Frider's château, there was nothing but a deep-blue glow on the horizon from the long-past sunset. The reclusive nobleman didn't enjoy as many benefits as lords who lived in other citiees, but Colmar was free, and Lord Frider was welcome to forfeit his land and leave at any time if he wished, which he didn't. So, he tolerated the fact that the cityfolk could elect their own council and run their city and militia as they pleased. But on one point he was very clear: all manure collected in public places must be put into his fields. And so he maintained his wealth not through taxes and free labor, but through the sale of the sweetest parsnips, the tallest leeks, and the plumpest heads of cabbage in the market, all fed on the droppings of Colmar's pigs, sheep, and cows.

Arne didn't mind dumping his stinking wagon full of soiled straw, animal dung, discarded bits of flotsam, and rotting vegetables from the market at Lord Frider's pond. Were he to dispose of his burden in a canal, he would have to walk much further in order to keep a safe distance from the city. Arne knew his job was lowly in the eyes of some, but he also knew it was important. Some took their clean streets for granted. But the poor folk – those who collected the nightsoil or herded the flocks – were out there working when he was sweeping, and they saw his contribution to Colmar. They saw it, and they honored it.

As he watched the silver of the moon reflect on the rippling water of a small stream, Arne took a moment to appreciate the clear, brilliant beauty of the late spring evening. The air was mild and sweet – save for his load of manure and filth, of course. In a nearby flooded field, frogs sang their longing into the night, hoping to find a mate. He took a deep breath and settled on his back in the tall grass to watch the stars traverse the velvety night sky.

He felt the beast before he saw it.

Thump, thump, thump, THUMP, THUMP! Arne spun around. In his numerous years, he had faced rearing horses, bucking mules, and the angry stamp of his wife's foot during an argument. None of them made the sound like what he heard and felt through the ground. Arne couldn't tell where the footfalls came from, but they drew closer. The light of the long-set sun was now almost completely gone, leaving barely enough of a glow to distinguish the horizon from the heavens, and so he cowered behind his cart and listened.

A figure lolloped between Arne and the rapidly dimming sky, allowing the terrified man to catch sight of its silhouette, and what he saw stole away his breath. A man-shaped form, but larger and thicker, clad in a mane of shaggy fur but wearing hose and a ragged cloak. And atop the body, a dog's head, with a long snout and two ears standing tall. It did not crawl on all fours like a wolf or a lion, and its footsteps crashed to the ground. Arne felt a profound tremor rise from deep inside his belly as he watched the beast slowly prowl around his wagon. The little light that remained was rapidly fading, and soon they would both be in total darkness – Arne and the beast. He was outside the walls of Colmar, and no one knew where he was, save his son who was courting and probably half drunk at Herr Schlock's wynstube.

No one will miss the old man who cleans the streets. The invisible man of Colmar, Arne thought. Until the wealthy burghers step in dung and wonder why it hasn't been cleaned, he added, and the thought gave him some comfort.

The monster continued to slink around the dung cart. Arne couldn't see it, but he could hear its heavy feet as they scraped against the ground. He turned to look back at Colmar. The windows of a few towers and houses peeped above the top of the walls, some lit with candles and lamps. He imagined they were kind eyes in a smiling face. The warmth of those windows gave him some resolve. He would return to Colmar, the city of his birth, or die trying.

Arne sprang to his feet from where he lay in the soggy field. Or, rather, he raised himself at a reasonable pace and listened to the symphony of his joints and bones creaking and cracking. He felt the stiffness of every muscle and bone as he half ran, half staggered toward the city.

Suddenly something grasped him around the hips, dragging him to the cold, damp road, and the monster was upon him. Arne kicked and clawed with his fingernails, and the monster snarled and screamed into the darkness. It was a cold, unholy scream. Grasping a stone, good-sized and smooth, Arne swung with all the force his wiry muscles would allow and heard a muffled thump and a grunt. The creature was on the ground. Arne raised himself to his feet, shuffling toward the gates of Colmar and the warm, smiling eyes of the lit windows. Behind him, the monster moaned.

The gates were locked. Of course they were. After the last light of the sun, the gatekeepers demanded an account for everyone who passed through, and they were rarely willing to open anything larger than the postern – the smaller door that only allowed one man through at a time.

Arne, out of breath and nearly out of his wits with fear, wailed and hammered on the thick wood of the gates with his fists. He dared not glance behind him in case he might see the shaggy form of the dog-beast racing up behind him, ready to pounce and drag him to hell. He pounded the gate with renewed urgency. "Help me, by Jesu's beard!" he screamed.

"Who goes?" a gatekeeper called out from the other side.

"Arne. It's Arne!"

"What's an Arne, then?" the voice responded.

"I am Arne, a man, God damn you and all your sisters! Let me in! I am a citizen! A son of Colmar!"

There was a pause, and then the small postern door creaked open. A smoking oil lamp illuminated the pocked face of the gatekeeper, who squinted into the darkness. "Eh. Are you the street sweeper?"

Arne didn't waste his time on introductions. He shoved his way in, knocking the gatekeeper onto his bottom in the street. "Close it, by the Virgin's pure and holy nostrils, close the door and lock it behind me!" Arne yelled. The pimpled young gatekeeper complied.

Arne sank to his knees, heaving deep breaths while the gatekeeper secured the postern with iron bolts. He was safe, but in the darkness of the gateyard, a few people still walked about, finishing up their tasks before it was time to return to their homes. Somewhere out in the darkness, Joss the night watchman would be patrolling the streets, rapping on doors to remind the goodwives and tradesmen to cover their fires.

Joss must be warned about this monster. And the sheriff, and the council. Prior Konrad should know, too. Arne's thoughts spun. *Everyone is in danger!*

Climbing back to his feet, he grasped the tunic of the gatekeeper, who had approached. "Do not let anyone out, do you hear me? No one must leave the city this night!"

"What scared you, old man?"

"A beast! No, not a beast, a dog-demon! An unholy monster! Something that crawled straight from hell! It smells as pungent and as foul as a refuse pit, and it will devour anyone it sees!"

He could see the gatekeeper was skeptical.

"If you won't believe me, then I shall tell the people myself!" Arne said, and he tottered off toward the Dominicans' square.

The houseguest
In which Appel brings hospitality when Friar Tacitus will not

THE SKY WAS PALE with early morning light when Frau Appel Schneider made her way toward Saint Martin's church for her morning prayers. She was a devout woman, to be sure, although the conspicuous piousness also kept the gossiping tongues of her neighbors at bay. But today she felt a particular need to offer up her prayers and perhaps even speak a confession to a brother of the church. Her encounter with the terrifying talking beast in the forest continued to unnerve her. She couldn't tell Gritta and Efi, her two closest friends, about her encounter, lest they ask too many questions about her business outside the walls. She almost wished she had demanded payment of Jacques, the man who accompanied her that morning, but quickly pushed the thought aside. "I ain't no whore," she said to herself. "And I ain't afraid of what people think."

Because of the early hour, it was still cold, and she clutched her blue wool cloak over her shoulders, passing through thick white clouds of her own foggy breath as she walked. Following the little stream that flowed down the slight incline from the church, she arrived in the spacious Dominicans' square, which was empty save for one other person. The skinny, hunched figure of Arne the street cleaner slumped against a hitching post. It wasn't unusual to see the old man at such an hour. He usually worked until sundown, preparing the streets for the feet and hooves of the following day, ensuring everyone had a clean place to walk.

Poor man, Appel thought. He's so small and slight, it mustn't require much wine to get him into a drunken state. She considered the thanklessness of his job. He was old, and his son was useless. If she was the person responsible for cleaning up after the people of Colmar, she would drink until she fell asleep at the hitching post, too.

Bowing her head in deference, Appel proceeded across the square to where one of the Dominican friars was propping a church door open to welcome the day. Somewhere in the recesses of the building she could hear the brothers finishing their morning songs, only faintly louder than the sound of braying animals from the stable and the rhythmic thwack! thwack! thwack! as a servant struck a stick against a dusty horse blanket in the stable.

"Beware!" a voice croaked at her. "Frau Schneider, be-beware."

Appel turned. Arne tried to stand from where he leaned on the hitching post. His head hung low from exhaustion, and she could see his lips were chapped and cracked.

Taking his arm over her shoulder, she dragged him to the door of the church. "You poor man," she said. "Brothers! Father

Konrad! Help!" On her arm, Arne felt as light as a bird. "Please help!"

A tall, gaunt figure in a black robe appeared at the doorway. Although his arms were folded across his chest, his right wrist ended in a crudely shaped iron hook. He looked at Appel and raised an eyebrow.

"One of your conquests, Frau Appel?" His eyes were cold, and his voice sour.

"Brother Tacitus, please help this man. He is fainting from thirst!" In her arms, Arne groaned. Brother Tacitus looked at Appel steadily for a moment, then snapped his fingers at a nearby friar who was hurrying past with a bowl of spent candle ends, destined for the church chandler.

"You there! Bring this man some water. He clearly drank too much ale last night and has exhausted himself."

"Nay, Brother Tacitus," the young friar said. "That there is Arne, the street sweeper. All night he brayed in the square like a mule, only his voice is worn out now, so you mustn't have heard him."

"Well, bring him water anyway, and be quick about it!" Tacitus snapped. He turned his gray glare on Appel. "Why are you here? Do you not have some tradesman's uncle to seduce or a foul brew to produce somewhere?"

Appel felt her cheeks redden. Brother Tacitus, despite what he owed to her and her friends for saving his life last spring, never ceased to bring his haughty judgment down upon her. "I've come for counsel from Father Konrad, for I do believe I encountered the Devil outside the walls. And I've come to pray, Brother Tacitus, as I do every morning."

"Confessing your sins, which are many, no doubt," Tacitus snorted.

"Indeed, I do have some sins to confess," Appel said, grinding her teeth as she spoke. "Right now I'm fighting the urge to inflict harm upon a holy man."

"Hah! I knew it!" Tacitus said, triumphant.

Arne, still clinging to Appel's shoulder, lifted his head, his eyes wide. "It touched me! It grasped me around my waist with its unholy paws!" He clutched at Brother Tacitus's robes. "Absolve me, for I am unclean!"

Tacitus slapped the old man's hands away. "What are you talking about? Have you completely lost your mind?"

The young friar returned with a pitcher of water and a wooden cup, but Arne pushed them away. "I saw a monster last night. The Devil roams the fields of Colmar, and he touched me. He touched me!" Arne patted his ragged tunic as he spoke, as if he could still feel a searing claw on his torso. Tacitus rolled his eyes.

Appel paled. "Tell me more, Arne. Did this beast have fur? Did it wear a cloak and speak in a man's voice?" she asked as gently as she could. Arne turned his wild gaze on her.

"Thick hair like a bear. Fangs. And a long snout like a wolf, but neither a bear nor a wolf it was! It stood upon two legs, taller than the tallest man. Its footsteps like thunder, and smoke coming from its nostrils! Forks of lightning circled its head, like Beelzebub!" His eyes rolled back in his head, and he swooned.

Brother Tacitus leaned over the old man. He sniffed and then shied away. "Is he dead?"

The young friar with the pitcher of water cleared his throat. "Arne has been yelling all night in the square. I think he is just exhausted. See there – his chest still rises with breath."

"Well, find a layman to bring him to his home, where he can sleep." Tacitus fluttered the fingers of his one hand dismissively.

"You will not let him rest in your hospital? Will you not pray with him? He is clearly very upset." Appel stood, feeling the anger rising in her.

"We haven't any beds available in our hospital. There is a spewing sickness upon the brothers, and many are afflicted."

"Then I shall take him!" Appel turned to the young friar, whose gaze bounced wildly between her and Brother Tacitus as they argued. "Young man, put Arne in a cart and take him to my house on Trench Lane in Les Tanneurs," she said in an imperious tone. "Frau Efi Kleven is there at this moment, and she will receive him."

"Why should you want to take him, Frau Appel?" the friar asked. "I could simply return him to his home in the wool dyer's district."

"He'll need someone to care for him while he recovers, and I doubt his son, Benno, is up to the task. Bring him to my house. I assure you there are two of us already living there. He will be quite safe from harm."

Appel felt sure she and Arne had encountered the same beast outside the walls. But she also knew Brother Tacitus was always looking for reasons to chastise her. She wasn't inclined to explain her presence in the forest, nor did she want to admit she also saw something that terrified her.

The friar looked at Tacitus, who nodded slightly. Then he hurried away to find an unused cart and a man to pull it. Appel put on her severest scowl for Brother Tacitus. He crossed his arms and iron hook over his chest, prepared to do battle with her.

"Well then, Brother," Appel said. "You may have lost a hand, but you're in full possession of your old prejudices."

A crowd gathered outside of Appel's large but shabby house in Les Tanneurs. A cart, pulled by two black-robed friars, had arrived only shortly before, and her neighbors took it upon themselves to investigate. When they saw the cart contained a man, withered and unmoving, several onlookers gasped. Only a few years before, it was not uncommon to see a hay cart laden with the bodies of the recently deceased slowly trundling through the city. Sometimes a smell would follow behind, or a foot would slip out from beneath the straw and bob like a branch on a breeze as the cart bumped over the rutted roads.

Hundreds of people died in Colmar during the Great Pestilence, and thousands more perished all along the Rhine. So, it was no surprise that the sight of a body in a cart could cause alarm. The horrors they endured hovered in the collective memory of the still-fragile population. Some thought the Great Pestilence came on the wings of demons. Some thought it was brought by Jews and other foreigners from the East. Or perhaps it was a consequence of gluttony, or lust, or complacency, or any other sin a person could imagine. The pestilence was indiscriminate in its cruelty. And above all, it was enigmatic. Inclement weather and crop failure were familiar troubles, but disease was a mysterious nemesis. Although the citizens of Colmar tried to move their lives forward and put the terrors of those few years behind them, it didn't take much to shift them from mental fortitude to overwhelming dread.

The friar who pulled the cart cowered slightly as a woman in the crowd, a saddle-maker's wife, wailed and fell to her knees. Appel rushed to comfort her and then, sensing the panic about to erupt outside her door, turned to address her neighbors.

"Do not be alarmed, dear friends! See here, it is only Arne, the old man who sweeps the streets. He's asleep and worn out from a long night. I have asked the brothers of Saint Martin's to send him to my house, where he may rest and find some peace."

A sigh rose from the crowd, followed by some nervous laughter and then excited chatter. How silly they were for being frightened of a sleeping man in a cart! Nothing as terrible as a great pestilence could ever come again to their fair city, for they had taken measures against it – they had burned candles and said prayers, beaten themselves until their flesh hung in raw strips from their backs as penance for sins, and killed or expelled all Jews and Muslims. Yes, effective measures, indeed! They slowly moved away from the house, returning to their tanneries, leatherworks, slaughterhouses, and other trades.

When she turned to her door, Appel smiled. Efi stood there, her feet bare, hands clasped. Her head was uncovered, since she had been working alone in the house, and her blonde curls rose like a tuft of burdock seeds in the damp heat of the late morning.

"Appel? Is everything well? Who is that man?" She nodded her chin toward the cart.

"He is a guest who will stay with us for a few days," Appel replied, reaching out to smooth Efi's hair down. She turned to the young friar, who stared wide-eyed at Efi's uncovered head. "Young man, please put Arne on the bench near the hearth. He can stay there until I prepare a place for him to sleep."

"She looks like the blessed Virgin," the friar whispered, and then blushed when he realized he had uttered the words aloud.

Efi fluttered her eyelashes and tucked her chin in a very un-virgin-like manner, causing the friar to blush even harder, for he had rarely seen a fully grown woman's uncovered hair – besides his mother and sister when he still lived with them. When Appel cleared her throat loudly, he blinked as if emerging from a trance.

"Don't fall for the widow Efi's wiles, unless you wish to defy your vow of chastity for a pretty jar that is completely empty of contents. Now carry Arne into my house and be gone."

Efi, far from being insulted, swayed back into the house and plumped a horsehair-stuffed cushion for Arne's head. When the old man was settled and snoring heavily, Appel gave the friar a mug of ale and sent him back with his cart.

"What are we going to do with a man in the house, Appel? Won't people talk?" Efi asked as she poured an amber stream of fresh ale through a scrap of linen to filter it for the next day's patrons.

"People already talk, Efi," Appel said, her voice weary. "They say that Gritta is a slovenly wife, you are witless, and I am..." She trailed off.

"They say you are a wanton woman of pleasure."

Appel's expression hardened. "Well, I take no pleasure in seeing this old man's mind so troubled. Come, Efi. Let us get him to bed."

She would wait a day and then question him to find out what he knew.

Arne's tale

In which Tacitus uncovers a pungent clue

Arne slept all through the day and into the night. Joss the night watchman had long since passed through the streets seeking hearth fires to smother or drunks to escort home. In the dark, warm top floor of her house, Appel was snuggled beneath her quilts next to Efi's uproarious snores, when she heard a shriek from downstairs that made her entire body tingle with alarm.

"Efi. Efi!" she whispered, shaking the younger woman, but Efi grunted, grasped a handful of quilts in her fist, and rolled over, taking all of the bedding with her.

With a shaking hand, Appel felt around for her rushlight and its heavy iron stand. Fortunately, the moon was nearly full on this night, and she found it quickly. "God's bones," she swore. "I have no coal to light this lamp except the ones in the hearth below." Giving the shapeless lump of Efi's sleeping form a last, baleful glare, she felt her way to the door and down the staircase, which clung to the outside of the house. When she reached the bottom, she pushed gently against her own front door.

It was barred.

Appel put her weight against the door, but it didn't move. The sound of a crash came from the other side, and she pressed her ear against the rough planks. She could hear Arne pleading from within. "Help! In God's name, I am being murdered!" he yelped.

Appel threw her entire weight at the door, but the bar on the other side held fast.

"Only a cowardly burglar squeals like a young pig at the slaughterhouse!" a woman yelled from inside. Appel groaned. She knew that voice. She patted the ground near the doorway in the dark, feeling every sting of pain in her knees. Growing old was painful. When she had found what she was looking for – a bit of sandstone that had crumbled from her garden wall, she hammered on her door with it until her hand throbbed from the effort. The bar was wrenched back, and Gritta's careworn face appeared on the other side. She had Arne captive, held by the scruff of his tunic in an iron grip.

"I always said you needed to remarry, Appel, and this is the reason why. I found this burglar in the house and trapped him inside so as to deal with him myself." She emphasized her point by giving Arne a hearty shake.

"I don't know where I am," Arne whimpered.

Appel gently removed Gritta's hand from Arne's tunic and handed her the cold rushlight she had carried from the sleeping room. "Light this, Gritta, and pour us some ale. Arne is a guest in my house, not a thief."

Gritta's mouth opened and closed for a moment, but she complied, stumbling on an overturned bench as she made her way to the coals, which slumbered beneath their large, clay cover for the night. By the time Gritta coaxed a flame to the rushlight, the dawn sky glowed in the east and a chorus of roosters greeted the day. The three of them each sat at the table with wooden cups of light, flavorful small ale, and Appel explained how she had found Arne fainting with exhaustion on the steps of Saint Martin's church and offered to bring him home before Brother Tacitus threw him out.

"Tacitus," Gritta hissed. "Will that old turnip never leave us alone?"

"Not as long as Les Tanneurs remains filled with sinners like you, Frau Gritta," a stern voice answered from the doorway.

Arne leapt to his feet and crossed himself quickly. "She said it, not I!" he squealed, pointing a knobby finger at Gritta.

"Brother Tacitus, welcome. Can we offer you some refreshment this morning? Why do you honor us with a visit so early in the day?" Appel used her most genteel voice and gave a slight curtsey. Only Gritta understood the danger in it. "Have you come to check on this poor man?" She gestured toward Arne.

"No, I have not." Tacitus swept into the room and settled himself onto a three-legged stool. "I have come to inform you and the other residents of this noisome neighborhood that I will be in charge of your spiritual needs while Friar Wikerus focuses on his investigation."

This genuinely surprised Appel. "What investigation, Brother? Why would he be sent away when he is so badly needed here?"

Gritta handed him Tacitus a wooden cup of ale and he sniffed at it. "No doubt he comes in useful as a willing volunteer to taste every batch of your brew." He set the cup down. "Bring me a cup of good water, not something foul and brown from the canal, but drawn up from a well. And put it in a clean cup, for the love of God."

"All of my cups are clean, Brother, and the purest water in Colmar comes from the stream that runs past your very own church. If you want a drink of clean water, the best way to find it is to return the way you came." Appel flashed her most winning smile.

"Impertinent." Tacitus rose to his feet, attempted to smooth his robe with his hook-hand, but snagged the fabric instead. "After he has found the missing boys, I shall inform Wikerus to give this household particular instruction on how to treat a man of God with respect."

"What missing boys, Brother Tacitus?" Appel asked.

"Two novices under his care and supervision disappeared outside the walls of Colmar, and Wikerus was sent to retrieve them himself."

"Aye, he told me of this yesterday, but I thought they would have returned by now." Gritta furrowed her brow.

"Mmm-mm-monster!" Arne screamed, dropping his cup. "Two boys wandering outside the walls of Colmar? The monster will devour them! It must be stopped before it eats more of our young men!"

Appel and Gritta exchanged a worried look, but Brother Tacitus snorted. "Same thing he told us for an entire day and night in the square. The only monster this sinner should fear is the Devil himself. I assure you, goodwives, there are no monsters in Colmar. I have seen to it."

Gritta arched an eyebrow. "Oh, have you? And how have you kept our city safe from monsters, Brother?"

Brother Tacitus blushed. His bumbling attempts to root out witchery in the past were well known. He had even tried to cast the Devil out of a waystone when he mistook it for an old woman. "Monsters take all forms, Frau Gritta," he said, lowering his voice to a whispered hiss. "Some of them look like slovenly, wicked brewsters."

Gritta slammed her cup on the table, sending a geyser of golden ale into the air. She leaned forward, nose-to-nose with the friar. "The Devil takes many forms, Brother. Some say he walks around as an angel of light. Could he not also take the form of an arrogant Dominican?"

Arne, who had been sitting and clutching his cup, bent his head, sniffing loudly. While Appel, Gritta, and Brother Tacitus looked on in bewilderment, he sniffed the table, and then his cup, then cautiously took a drag of air next to Tacitus's iron hook. Finally, he inhaled deeply in front of Gritta and recoiled. He crossed himself, knocked on the wooden table three times, then tried to stand but stumbled and fell backwards over the bench.

"Poor man!" Appel said, hoisting him to his feet.

"Monster," Arne wheezed. "She is the one. There's a smell about her!"

"Nonsense!" Appel cried. "Arne, you've had too much ale."

"What smell?" Tacitus asked, his eyes glittering.

"Smells like the monster did the night I saw it. A rank scent. Like...like my son under the arms after a day of work!"

"How dare you!" Gritta screamed, but Tacitus held up his remaining bony hand for silence.

"Explain!" he ordered.

"I...hardly remember," Arne stuttered, casting a glance at Appel. "And I'm powerfully thirsty."

"Perhaps another ale would help him to remember more clearly the scent of evil." Tacitus was practically quivering with the anticipation that Gritta could be somehow responsible.

"We ain't running an ale charity!" Gritta shot back.

Tacitus slapped a coin onto the table, and Appel swept it up, replacing it with another cup of ale. Arne took a long drink and sighed. "Ah, now I remember. The monster I met on the road to Lord Frider's manure pond had a smell about him."

"Was it the smell of manure, perhaps?" Gritta asked.

"No. 'Twas something else. It was...it was...garlic! The monster reeked of garlic." He turned to Gritta. "You smell of garlic!"

"I knew it!" Tacitus jumped to his feet. "What mischief have you been a part of now, Gritta Leporteur?"

"None, I swear to you! None at all!"

"Where were you last night, when I was out in the fields, meeting the beast as it devoured my cart as easily as a cat swallows a mouse?!" Arne shouted.

"It ate your cart? You did not mention that earlier. How big was this monster?" Appel narrowed her eyes.

Arne took another large slurp from his cup. "Big."

"Aye. And it seems to be growing bigger with each telling," Appel responded.

"Here now, when you saw this beast, I was inside the walls of the city, and I can prove it," Gritta said. "I was delivering ale to Karl Gasthaus. Appel and Efi came with me, along with my sons, Urbe and Noe, to help unload the barrels. We stayed for a late supper and then collapsed into our beds as soon as we returned. And do I look like I could eat a wagon on my own?"

Arne squinted at her, considering her stature and the soundness of her teeth. "What about yer scoundrel of a husband?" Arne spat on the ground. "I've seen him eat a live fish, still wriggling, when he had drunk too much wine. Wouldn't surprise no one if he ate a wagon, too."

"A whole wagon? The man has an appetite, I'll give you that, but no one could swallow a wagon. And besides, Jorges was in the stocks last night, so he couldn't have been a monster, neither!"

"There was a smell about it, though, and I remember clearly," Arne insisted.

Friar Tacitus smiled and stood to leave. "This does seem like a crucial detail, Arne. I shall inform the city council of your observations." He paused and looked pointedly at Gritta. "And of mine."

After the old friar swept out the door, Appel glanced at Gritta and noticed her friend's pale face. She cleared her throat and stood, handing Arne a bucket. "Since you have slept in my kitchen, perhaps you could be kind enough to fetch the water from the stream today."

Arne snorted. "Water-carrying is woman's work!"

"Very well, but your meal will be late, since it will take me time to fetch the water and return from the stream near Saint Martin's church before I can prepare your food." Appel smiled as she spoke, but the skin around her mouth was tense. With a snarl and a muttered complaint, Arne took the bucket and shuffled slowly from the house. Appel turned to Gritta, who was wringing her hands.

"What is it, Gritta? You look as if you saw the monster yourself just now."

"It's the garlic," Gritta whispered. "Arne said the monster smelled of garlic."

"Indeed. It seems an odd meal for a beast to take, now you mention it," Appel said. When she encountered the terrifying beast in the forest, she never drew close enough to smell its last meal.

"But I fed the children boiled barley porridge with some stewed ramps for their supper last night. The whole lot of us reeked so much of garlic, we could almost forget we live in Les Tanneurs, at least by the smell."

"I don't understand," Appel said. "Do you think the beast came and ate the leftover food from your cooking pot?"

By now, Gritta was on her feet, snatching her basket and flinging a shawl over her shoulders. "No, I think the beast ate one of my children. And as of this morning, all are accounted for, except Lonel."

This had gone too far. It was time for Appel to tell Gritta what she saw in the forest during her tryst with Jacques Färber, and damn the consequences. Being ruthlessly mocked by her friends and despised by her neighbors was better than seeing Gritta's whole body tense with worry. Appel cleared her throat and wrung her hands. "There is something I must tell you."

"Later," Gritta said. "I must go find my son."

Lonel's tale

In which Friar Wikerus attempts to assert his authority

Friar Wikerus considered himself level-headed, and not prone to panic or extreme swings of emotion. His resting state was that of a cheerful, slightly lazy friar, who did what he was ordered by his church superiors – but no more. Of course, he would gladly extend himself if something pleasurable were at stake, such as a crisp, frothy cup of ale, a walk on a warm spring morning, or a plate of steaming kuchen covered with cherries in a honey sauce. But today he felt unsettled, agitated, and ready to flee, for the two novices in his care were still missing from Saint Matthieu's church, and the time to attribute their absence to youthful folly had long passed. Those boys were lost, and it was his fault.

"Stupid!" he whispered to himself as he hurried toward the city walls. He did not wish to alarm anyone else, and so he shuffled his feet with his head bowed and his hands tucked into the large woolen sleeves of his robe, trying his best to look pious and serious, all while his guts churned with fear. As soon as he knew he was alone in the lane, he trotted faster, feeling his jowls and stomach jiggling as he ran. Perhaps, he thought, it was time to drink a little less ale.

He knew the best course of action was to seek out Gritta, Appel, and Efi for help. Their position as sellers of ale meant they were privy to the gossip of the local merchants, innkeepers, and tipplers, and Gritta's twelve children always brought home tidbits of news from their employers and friends. But Wikerus keenly felt the sting of his failure to find the missing novices. Those boys were his responsibility, just as his brother had been his responsibility on that terrible day, when he became brotherless and orphaned between a single sunrise and sunset.

The memory stopped him in his tracks. It was so many years ago, and yet the feeling of it stung sharply as if everything in his life had changed only yesterday. That day, the Rhine raged like an animal – angry brown water carried trees ripped up by their roots, semi-submerged houses torn from their foundations, and the carcasses of dead pigs and oxen, all rushing past as fast as a horse could ride.

In his memory he could still feel the slick surface of the rocks on the water's edge, and he remembered the sound of the muck and stones as they slid from the steep hillsides of Breisach and splashed into the current. For a moment he was back in time, a boy on the cusp of becoming a man, holding the hand of his younger brother and leading them along the bank of the angry river to safety. Wikerus thatched his fingers together tightly inside of the sleeves of his robes, as if to keep his skin, his bones, his soul from remembering the feeling of his brother's wet, muddy hand slipping from his own. The last time he would ever touch the flesh of a family member.

Sploosh!

The sound jolted Wikerus from his reverie, and he felt his heart leap up into his throat. Lonel stood next to the grand canal with his friends, tossing large stones and laughing as the water splashed back and soaked two girls standing with them. The girls squealed but made no attempts to move to safety. One of the girls moved closer and pressed herself against Lonel's arm, and Wikerus noticed with astonishment that the normally shabby young man was clean and wore a red chaperon with an elaborately long hood tailing behind it. Lonel hooked an arm around one of the soaked maidens and pulled her in for a kiss.

Kamille. Wikerus recognized the beautiful young woman who had only recently moved to Colmar. He had encouraged Brother Kornelius, another Franciscan friar in charge of ministering to the wool dyer's district, to visit Kamille and her mother. So far Kornelius had been unsuccessful at coming around when Kamille and her mother were at home.

"Your mouth smells of garlic," Kamille said, wrinkling her nose. "Did you not clean your teeth today?"

Wikerus cleared his throat loudly. Although he hoped this would have an effect on the young man, he knew better. He knew Lonel.

"Oh, hello, Friar Wikerus! Come to find some entertainment of your own, have you?" Lonel called out. He gave the girl a stiff whack on her bottom, eliciting another squeal. She turned and looked at Wikerus, and one corner of her mouth pulled up into a seductive smirk. For a moment, time stood still.

Then Wikerus blinked, and the spell was broken. He had seen enough. His present dilemma forgotten for the moment, he marched up to the group of lads, all of whom towered over him, and planted his feet.

"And what if someone treated your sister Rosmunda in such a manner as you do this girl, Lonel Leporteur? Would you find it funny then?"

Far from being ashamed, Lonel's long face broke into a lopsided grin. "I'd say it was about time someone paid attention to her, Friar. Rosmunda lives a dull and pious life."

"And what if it was your mother treated thus?"

"I think Ma would be glad of some attention that doesn't come from the fingers of my father, Friar."

The other boys snickered at this cheeky response, and Wikerus gave Lonel a flat look. "Leave your hands off that young woman's bottom, or I shall make sure Father Konrad warms yours with a willow switch."

"I'm too old for a thrashing," Lonel said, standing a little taller. "I'm of age to earn my own wage and take a wife now."

"The pillory, then," Wikerus replied. "I'm sure Sheriff Werner would be more than happy to keep you tied up in the center of the city square if it means he will have one less troublemaker to deal with at a time. And of course, there is always public humiliation, which is something our sheriff would enjoy very much, I think." Wikerus allowed himself the indulgence of a wicked grin.

Kamille and the other young woman slowly backed away into the shadows, turned and ran, and Lonel's other companions shuffled their feet.

"Stay a while," Wikerus said sharply. "I am looking for two young men – novice friars. They left Saint Matthieu's friary two days ago, and no one has seen them since."

"We don't usually pay much attention to other boys around town, if you catch my meaning," one of Lonel's companions said, eliciting wolfish grins from the others.

"These two were not from Colmar. They moved here only a few months ago from Ribeauvillé. You would have noticed two new boys your own age loitering about, if only to mark your rivals," Wikerus said. "Now tell me, did you see them? Neither were tall; one had brown hair and another had yellow – their crowns were not yet shaved because they haven't taken their vows yet."

All three boys shook their heads. Wikerus narrowed his eyes at Lonel. His long face wore the same expression as always, but it was usually safe to assume he was up to no good, no matter how angelic his countenance. Wikerus turned to Lonel's two companions.

"It has been a long while since I've seen you three at confession. Now seems a good time. Lonel will go first. You can start by telling me where you procured these fine clothes, when your mother and father work night and day to put food in your mouth."

The prospect of facing their indiscretions and uttering them aloud was too much. The two other boys darted away – not in the direction of the church, Wikerus noted. Fearing that Lonel would also try to make an escape, Wikerus put a hand on his shoulder and guided him to the shade of the city wall. Lonel crossed his arms and leaned his back against the rough, orange sandstone bricks, glaring back.

"I didn't do nothing, Friar Wikerus. I don't know where they went. They're fools to leave Saint Matthieu's."

Wikerus narrowed his eyes. "You speak as if you've met them. What do you mean when you call them fools? Did you speak with them?"

"No," Lonel answered quickly. "I only mean to say that they are fools for…for leaving the walls."

"How do you know they left the walls? Come now, tell me everything, for the lives of two apprentices to the church are at stake, and thus so is your soul."

But Lonel looked at Wikerus with a steady gaze. "You assume much, Friar. I did not speak with them. I call them fools because if they are not in Colmar, they must be outside the walls, and leaving the safety of the city is a dangerous thing. There are bandits outside the walls, and wild animals." He hesitated. "And there's more. Some speak of a mysterious beast. A monster who takes the shape of a man with a dog's head and a wolf's temperament. I heard Arne the street sweeper screaming about it in the Dominican's square last night."

Wikerus felt himself grow cold. He wished this rumor of a monster would go away, but instead it spread through the city, seeping into everyone's conversations. To acknowledge the possibility of a man-eating monster would also mean admitting that not only had he lost two novices, but probably also gotten them killed or, worse, sent to hell.

"And what would you know of monsters, Lonel Leporteur?" Wikerus tried to ask the question casually, but Lonel was no fool, despite what people said about him. His sharp eyes flashed, and then he favored Wikerus with his signature lopsided grin.

"I don't know nothing, Friar. Already told you. It's just things men say when they're on their third glass of Rhenish wine at Herr Schlock's wynstube. Now, you wanted to hear a confession from me?"

"Yes," Wikerus said weakly. He offered up a quick prayer for strength, for he wasn't sure he was prepared to hear about Lonel's many sins.

"Fine. I confess I did think wicked thoughts just now about a man of the cloth who frightened away the woman I fancy."

"And the clothing? Did you steal it?"

"The clothing was given to me. By a friend."

"Nonsense," Friar Wikerus muttered.

"Who gave you your clothes, then, Friar? You have a robe and sandals because your church took money from its parishioners. And seeing as you're not even from Colmar, I reckon you have done less to earn your clothes than the other brothers in the friary."

Lonel looked triumphant, and inside, Wikerus withered. He would never feel equal to these people, being an outsider as he was from Breisach. There were days when he even felt like an outsider in his own church. Wikerus didn't know where he belonged. He didn't know if there was a monster roaming the countryside or not, and most worrisome, he wondered if the two novices had fled the church because of a fault in his own leadership. He cleared his throat, sucked in his stomach as he squared his shoulders, and attempted to look authoritative. "My son, indulging in evil thoughts toward a man of the church is a grave sin. Grave indeed. You must do penance."

"Give it to me then. Reciting prayers? Easily done."

Wikerus set his jaw. "No. Your penance is to help your mother. You will lift barrels, carry baskets of grain, and fetch the water for her ale. You will do this cheerfully and with no expectation of payment, and if I find you haven't done your duty to her, you will not receive absolution."

Lonel's mouth opened in speechless surprise, and Wikerus grinned. Maybe his time with the novices had made him tougher than he thought.

A grudging confession

In which Appel decides to liberate herself of several burdens

WIKERUS HURRIED FROM THE bridge. He had the sensation that he was fleeing from something sinful, but what, he knew not. It was Lonel and the other young people who were carousing, and yet he somehow felt like it had been he with his hands around Kamille's waist. He joined the Franciscans at a young age – just on the cusp of manhood, and unlike many of his brethren, he hadn't taken leave to sample fleshly pleasures. No woman had ever tempted him, neither had any young man. Wikerus found his friendships within the Brotherhood and his companionship with Gritta, Appel, and Efi to be enough.

But even he was not immune to Kamille's seductive charm. And this was why he felt dirty. His admiration for the three alewives was akin to sisterly affection, and it made him uncomfortable to view any woman otherwise. The best remedy was a cup of ale and an evening sitting in Appel's kitchen, listening to the three women chide each other, to reassure himself that women were friendly creatures, and not dangerous, as Kamille's dark eyes and teasing smiles implied.

He was surprised to find the house full of people when he arrived. Gritta loudly scolded her daughter Rosmunda and served cups of frothy, amber ale to a few paying patrons who sat in the corner around a table made from a repurposed wooden cask. Her twins, Anstett and Mattheus, squatted on their grubby haunches at the feet of Arne the street sweeper, listening wide-eyed as he told them a story. Gritta's older son Noe sat at the trestle table across from Johannes Wainwright, both leaning over clay cups of ale and hotly debating each other over which occupation was of more value – crafting barrels or wagon wheels. Wikerus stepped back outside and looked above the door's lintel. Sure enough, a leafy green branch dangled there, indicating there was fresh ale to sell within.

"Figured you be around sooner or later. Have you seen my Lonel? I'm told he was spotted loafing around hither and yon, but I've not laid an eyeball on him yet," Gritta said as she sidled up to him. She held out a small cup of ale, which he accepted gratefully.

"I did see Lonel, and I would have sent him straight to you had I known you were looking for him," Wikerus said between slurps.

"No need. I just want to know he's safe and hasn't been eaten by the Devil," Gritta said, then before Wikerus could ask her more questions, she whirled away when the men in the corner raised their cracked mugs and bellowed to her for a refill.

"'Tis late for you to be here, Friar," Appel said. She smiled, but there was worry behind her eyes.

Wikerus nodded. "Indeed. The night watchman will probably be around soon to tell you to smother your fire and send these men home."

But Appel nodded her chin toward the corner, where sat Joss the night watchman, giggling into a cup. "Joss got distracted."

"Isn't that the butcher's wife sitting on his knee?" Wikerus asked, squinting.

"Aye, but the butcher is off entertaining company of his own, if you catch my meaning."

The two of them sat heavily at the end of the table. Noe stopped his conversation and smiled at them, but Appel noticed distraction clouding Friar Wikerus's face. She scooted closer to him and clicked her cup against his. "Friar, you look tired."

For a moment, Friar Wikerus stared into his cup, saying nothing. He knew he looked tired. His forehead was deeply furrowed, and dark circles ringed his eyes. "The boys are still lost. It has been two days now, and oh, Frau Appel, I fear the worst. I fear they may be dead." He took a sip, his hand shaking. "Every moment I spend not searching for them feels like a weight around my heart, but I have walked every street, inquired at every house, and even borrowed a donkey from the abbey stables to scour the countryside beyond Colmar's walls."

Appel drew in her breath. "Friar, you mustn't venture outside the walls when darkness approaches. I heard more reports of the monster —" She lowered her voice and glanced at old Arne, who was on his feet now, dancing drunkenly. "Can I tell you something in confidence, Friar Wikerus? I also saw this beast with my own eyes. A few days ago, I came upon it while it lurked in the forest."

Friar Wikerus gasped. "Were there any other witnesses?"

"No, and so I left as quickly as I could."

"What were you doing alone in the forest?" Wikerus asked, but Appel shushed him.

"Never you mind. But I know what I saw. It wasn't a bear or a wolf or a dog. It was a demon. A monster."

"Why have you not said anything?" Wikerus asked, but as soon as he saw the deep flush of embarrassment rise in Appel's cheeks, he stopped himself from asking further questions. "Dear God in heaven, what if the boys were attacked?" Wikerus whispered. "I must admit, I doubted Arne's tale, but now I begin to wonder. What if Ulf and Jean-Louis wandered outside the walls and then were carried off and..." He swallowed hard. "And were...consumed."

They looked at each other, their eyes wide.

"Well." Gritta slammed her cup on the table, startling Appel and Friar Wikerus out of their stunned silence. She had tottered over to them unnoticed as they absorbed the seriousness of the situation outside the walls. "You two look as stern as a nun in a whorehouse. Pardon me, Friar." Gritta burped and sat down with a thump.

"Frau Gritta, are you drunk?!" Friar Wikerus asked, shocked.

"Happens sometimes," Gritta said with a giggle. "Appel, you must get rid of that lecherous pig of a street sweeper. He pinched my bottom when I walked past to reach the storeroom!"

Appel smirked. "Nonsense. You don't have enough flesh on your hindquarters to pinch." Before Gritta could defend the honor of her posterior, Appel held up a hand. "Yes, Arne must go. I think I shall let him stay one more night, and then we can return him home in the morning. He should be well enough by then."

"He was well enough as soon as he woke from his stupor if you ask me," Efi interrupted, sitting down next to Wikerus on the bench.

"Well, I didn't ask you," Appel said tartly. "And besides, there are things I need to discuss with him."

"What things?" Gritta narrowed her eyes. "Take the lout home. Ask him your questions when he's scourging someone else's bottom!"

Across the room there came a shout and a crash. Arne's drunken dancing had sent him stumbling across the edge of the hearth and headlong into Appel's little painted cupboard. The door broke open, and the pottery bowls and cups inside fell and shattered. Far from being ashamed, Arne picked himself up, dusted his tunic, and held out his cup.

"Woman! Bring me another ale and then sweep up this mess!"

Appel felt the hotness of Gritta's furious gaze on her. "At first light tomorrow. I promise, Gritta," She said.

Arne tottered toward the end of the table where Wikerus sat with the three women. Ale fumes wafted around him. He lowered himself unsteadily onto a nearby stool, kicked off his shoe, and thrust a smelly foot at Appel's face. "Go on, rub 'em."

"What?!" Appel pushed the foot away and jumped up.

"My hocks is sore. They need rubbin'."

"How dare you presume!" Appel snarled. "Rub your own foul feet!"

"I presume you've rubbed more than just the feet of many a man who ain't your husband, Appel Schneider. Why not me, too?"

Before anyone could stop her, Appel snatched a glazed clay platter of brown loaves and cracked it over Arne's balding head. The little man crumpled to the straw, and the conversation in the room stopped. Appel's ginger cat rose from where he slept in a basket of unwashed linens and curled up on Arne's chest, which Wikerus saw, to his relief, was still rising and falling with breath. The merry hedonism in the room vanished, and suddenly everyone realized they had stayed too late.

"Everyone out!" Joss the night watchman bellowed. "Get to your homes and smother your fires before bed!"

In the distance, the church bells began to ring the hour.

"I've broken the spell," Appel whispered, still holding the two pieces of broken pottery in each hand. The revelers were tipping the dregs of their drinks back into their throats and shuffling through the door, squinting into the darkness outside. Time's passing had escaped their notice. Joss took up his pole lantern, which leaned against the wall, and lit the wick with a smoldering stick from the fire. It did, indeed, feel as if an enchantment had been lifted.

"I am late. That's the bell for Vespers, and so I must leave," Wikerus said.

At her feet, Arne groaned, and Appel's eyes narrowed. "And so must he," she said. "Come Efi! Gritta was right. He returns home tonight!"

Enough is enough

In which Appel and Efi go to great lengths to restore peace at home

THE MOON WAS A sliver as narrow and white as the edge of a clamshell, but despite its size, it provided enough light to navigate through Trench Lane without the need of a lantern. Efi knew it was important to stay out of sight after dark, when drunk and uninhibited men staggered home from the alehouses and wynstubes. She grunted, staggering under the weight of her burden, which she dragged through the darkness with Appel.

"Surely there is no need to be so drastic, Appel!" she hissed as they hurried across the city in the dark. "Surely this can wait until daylight. He is too heavy!"

"There is most certainly a need, Efi! I need Arne to vacate the bench in my kitchen as soon as all haste will allow!" Appel shot back. With one hand she held Arne's wrist to keep his arm across her shoulder. With the other, she clutched at the items dangling from her girdle – keys, a small money purse, and her eating spoon, cursing herself for not remembering to leave them at home as they jangled with each step. "If we can get to his house without being seen by the night watch, all we need to do is force the door open and drop him inside. Let the rats keep him company."

It wasn't like Appel to be so inhospitable towards guests, but Arne had tested all of her ample patience with his constant demands for food, drink, and attention. The last straw was when he ordered Appel to rub his gnarled feet. "Disgusting," she muttered. "Am I his wife that I should be told to touch his vile feet in my own home?" It was a rhetorical question, but Efi tried to answer all the same.

"I don't see why you're so upset about it —"

"Did he try to force you to touch his feet? Does he demand food and then complain about your cooking? He leaves. Tonight!"

They skirted the tower-flanked city gate, keeping to the shadows, for the guards would surely question two unaccompanied women dragging an unconscious man through the streets in the darkness. In their nervous state, it took them a moment to notice the growing commotion in the courtyard near the gate. One of the guards touched a torch to the charcoal brazier at the little gatehouse and ran to unlatch the postern. In the flickering light, Appel and Efi saw the other guards pull a man by his arms through the gate and into the yard.

"Someone fetch the barber-surgeon!" one of them shouted. The injured man groaned, and his head tipped back, a trail of blood glistening black down his forehead. Appel and Efi froze. The guards had dragged the man toward the courtyard wall, and from where the two women crouched in the shadows, they could just barely make out the sound of their voices.

"A b-beast," the injured man slurred. "Took me, took my dog. A monster in the dark!"

"No need for the barber," the guard said to his companion. "Go fetch a priest."

Appel and Efi continued from the courtyard toward Arne's house in the wool dyers' quarter. The scene at the gate had rattled them, the urgency to deposit Arne in his house and return to the safety of Trench Lane growing with each labored step.

"I do not think we should be out of our house past dark, Appel!" Efi hissed. "There's something evil about!"

But Appel was resolute. "The attack happened outside the walls, not from within, and thus we are safe. We finish what we started, return this ungrateful lech to his home, and tomorrow everything will return to normal."

They arrived at the little shack where Arne lived with his son. Raised up on stilts to protect it when the canals flooded, the house was barely more than a thatched lean-to against a larger building. Arne began to stir from his ale-induced stupor – aided by Appel's thump on the head with a bread platter – and so they deposited him on the ground. Appel pushed on the door, but it didn't budge. She tried again, putting her shoulder into it, with no effect. She leaned close to one of the wide cracks in the planks and looked inside. The wood was crude and her cheek prickled with splinters, but it appeared no one was inside the house.

"As I suspected," she muttered. "They say his son left Colmar and hasn't been seen for days. He must have locked up before he went. Efi, hand me the tool!"

Efi looked left and right. The wool dyers' quarter was barely more reputable or sweet-smelling than Les Tanneurs. But the streets were empty and the windows of the houses shuttered and dark. She handed the length of iron concealed in her skirts to Appel. "Can we leave now? There's a beast roaming outside the walls, a stone in my shoe, and I promised Stefan the glover I would come round this evening."

"Stefan who is married to Frau Else and has adult children who are older than you?" Appel answered, her words muffled as she struggled to maneuver the thin piece of iron between the cracks in the door.

"He doesn't love her," Efi pouted.

"Of course he doesn't! Why should he? She gave him sons, and he gives her a roof over her head. That's the arrangement." Appel grunted as she struggled with her work. "Well, this is shut very tightly. Locked and barred from the inside!"

"It's not like you never did nothing rash in your youth, should you even remember what youth is!" Efi grumbled.

"Careful, girl," Appel said. "Stefan is a businessman, and it's good for business to have a pretty woman in his shop. Have you never thought to notice that most of his customers are young men?"

"But we have the most wonderful conversations together, Appel! We have a deeply spiritual connection!"

"Conversations about what, exactly?"

"Just yesterday he spoke to me at length about how difficult it is to sew the smallest finger of a glove just so, especially for a woman's hand. And he told me Brother Tacitus requested a sleeve for the iron hook on his arm. Do you suppose his hook feels cold in the winter?"

"Spiritual, indeed." Appel rolled her eyes and tried with renewed vigor to dislodge the bar over the door, pushing at it through the spaces between the planks with her length of iron. She worked for a moment before she noticed Efi had gone strangely quiet behind her. "Efi, are you still there?"

"Did you say the door is barred?"

"Aye. Firmly."

"Someone needs to be inside the house to set a bar across the door."

They heard a loud thump, and the door jerked back, taking Appel's length of iron with it. On the other side stood Benno, Arne's son, brandishing a spade over his head like a knight's sword. His normally confused expression grew more perplexed as he took in the two women crouching in front of him.

"By God's toes, I thought you were thieves! Are you here to do the washing? Bit late, isn't it?"

Appel stood, brushed the dust from her skirt, and cleared her throat with as much dignity as she could muster. "And what would be worth stealing in your house, Benno? We are here not to steal something, but to put something back."

"Oh aye? And what would you be putting back, then?"

Behind them, Arne groaned loudly and sat up. Benno stepped outside and squinted into the darkness. "Da? Is that you? I heard you'd taken up with a woman somewhere and left."

Appel had never paid much attention to Benno before, except to note that he seemed simple and clumsy. But tonight, she took a closer look at him. He was unusually tall for his age, which must have been close to eighteen years, with powerful arms, a low brow, and a short, thick neck. His tangled black hair was greasy and his hose were covered in black stains. Why had she never noticed before how much taller he was than her, and how his slow movements were like an ox hitched to a plow?

"Something attacked Arne outside the walls. He stayed with us for a few nights to return to health."

Benno looked at his father again, who had a large welt rising on his balding head where Appel had struck him with the plate.

"He has graced our presence for long enough, and it is time for him to go home," Efi said. "And since no one has seen hide nor hair of you for several days, we assumed the house was unoccupied, and we would need to open it and place your father inside ourselves."

Benno looked at both of the women keenly, and a crooked grin spread across his face. "Won't you come in?"

Appel and Efi both took an unconscious step backwards. "No, thank you. Now we know you are home and able to care for your father, you can bring him inside," Appel said. She winced as Efi clutched at her arm. Her skin prickled with unease. Benno took another step towards them. He had been asleep when they tried to open the door and was only clad in a pair of moth-eaten hose.

"I shall come to your house tomorrow and thank you properly," Benno said.

Efi's grip on Appel's arm tightened.

"We require no thanks. Just take him, please," Appel said, feeling her mouth go dry. Next to her, Efi bobbed a quick curtsey, and they backed out of his reach. As they hurried away, Appel glanced back and saw Benno lift his father easily and sling him over a broad, hairy shoulder before disappearing inside the house.

"What happened, Appel?" Efi whispered. "That man scared me."

"I don't know, Efi dear, but he scared me too. There's a miasma about him. A bad spirit."

Efi turned and looked back into the darkness. "I don't think he's following us, but let us hurry home, Appel, and bar our own door. I feel unsafe."

The posse, the priest, and the nobleman

In which one monster attack is a rumor, but two is a catastrophe

"I KNOW WHERE YOU were last night, Wikerus."

Friar Wikerus was walking quickly down the lane from Saint Matthieu's church when the voice of Brother Tacitus stopped him in his tracks. He immediately burned with shame, his mission to visit the tinker who had been attacked outside the walls the night before, forgotten. Wikerus knew it was permitted to visit the alewives during the day as a part of his pastoral duties, but to go there in the evening, intentionally patronizing the establishment, was frowned upon as fraternizing and carousing. And Tacitus was always on the lookout for carousing of any sort.

"Good morning, Brother Tacitus. I see you are out patrolling for someone to condemn as usual," Wikerus snapped. He was in no mood for this delay. Important pastoral work awaited him. "I suggest you look to the riverside, where you'll find a fine crop of miscreant young men who are ripe to do more penance. Good day to you." He hurried on, but Tacitus increased his step and followed.

"There's no use denying it, Wikerus," Brother Tacitus said. "You are trying to undermine my authority, and I will not allow it. As soon as Father Konrad returns from his visit to Strassburg, I shall inform him that it is all your doing."

"What are you talking about?" Wikerus asked. "I haven't thought about you or your authority. My mind is occupied with more important things."

Tacitus twisted his face into a cruel smile. "Ah yes, your missing boys."

Wikerus didn't have time for the usual petty sparring he enjoyed with his rival. Shoving his hands into his sleeves, he stomped forward, his head down against the light mist of rain that had started to fall. Tacitus, who was much taller, strode next to him on legs like a stork.

"If you tell me what you have done with my shoes, I will ignore the whole incident, and Father Konrad will be none the wiser. For my part, I walk humbly barefoot before God, but theft of church property by another member of the clergy is particularly egregious – even for a Franciscan."

Wikerus glanced down. Tacitus stood in the muck, his large, knobby feet bare and filthy. "Where are your sandals?" he asked dumbly.

"Nice try," Tacitus snarled. "I'll give you until sundown to return them to the church – and all the men's footwear. If our shoes are not returned, Father Konrad and your own Prior Willem shall hear of it!"

Tacitus squelched away in a huff, with Wikerus staring after him.

"Why would I steal shoes?" Wikerus called after him, but Tacitus merely swatted the comment away with his hook.

By the time Wikerus reached the barber-surgeon's house, the small main room was crowded with people. The barber was removing a damp cloth from the forehead of a young but haggard looking man who lay on the wooden trestle table in the center of the room. Presumably, this table was where the barber-surgeon trimmed hair, pulled teeth, tended to wounds, and also ate his meals. Sheriff Werner and several members of his posse stood around, trying to decide what to do with their hands. And Lord Frider, who had a physician of his own and would normally never enter the house of a peasant, glowered in a corner, his arms crossed against his velveted chest.

"Greetings, men," Wikerus said with a smile. "I have come to speak with the victim, but I see I am not the first."

"Well, good luck to you," Lord Frider growled. "I can hardly understand a word this man says, his accent is so thick." He jerked a thumb toward the injured man, and Wikerus knelt near the table.

"Friend," Wikerus said, placing a hand on the injured man's arm. "Tell me what you saw, and of your injuries."

The man licked his dry lips and stared up at the ceiling. "Bestia," he whispered. "The Devil come straight from hell to snatch me down to the fire." He struggled to sit up, and Wikerus could see blooms of purple bruises on his chest where the laces of his tunic were undone. "Bestia!" the man cried out. "Hexerei!"

"Well, I understood that!" Lord Frider said. He looked at the faces of the other men. "There is an unholy beast roaming our fields." His face paled and his voice dropped to a whisper. "Perhaps one of the revenant dead, come to torment us and seek peace for its soul. I must move my household inside the walls before nightfall!" He turned and ducked through the doorway.

Sheriff Werner's men shifted and began to whisper amongst themselves, and Wikerus met the gaze of the barber. "Show me his injuries."

The barber gently peeled away the tinker's filthy tunic and the remains of a shredded cotte, revealing deep scratches along his torso, covered in dried blood. "And he also has a growing bump on the top of his head," the barber mumbled. "I've treated his physical wounds, but I am glad you are here, as his spirit has been touched by this devil."

The room grew quiet, and Wikerus glanced behind him. Sheriff Werner had fled, and his men were slinking out of the house. Between their loose lips and the gossip in Frau Appel's alehouse last night, word of this would soon spread around the city, and then panic would ensue. He kissed the plain wooden cross hanging from a string around his neck and pressed it to his forehead, muttering a prayer for courage and safety. Then he said a prayer over the injured man, who had fallen into senseless mumbling, and stood to go. The ceiling of the little house was low, but Wikerus was short and there was no need for him to bend his neck like Lord Frider.

"Do you really think it could be a revenant walking the earth, Friar?" the barber-surgeon asked. "My brother encountered one in his field near Vogelgrun, once. It twisted his ear and demanded his wineskin. But the ghost took the shape of a man, not a dog-headed beast."

"I believe your brother probably encountered a thirsty thief and not a revenant, my friend," Wikerus said absently. He scowled at the man who lay on the pallet before him. Revenants, the unsettled dead who rose from their graves to torment the living until their souls could be released to heaven, were known to change their shape sometimes, but beyond that Wikerus knew nothing about them. It was possible a revenant was menacing the people of Colmar, but something didn't add up. They were rarely violent and mostly relied on fear to control their victims until a priest could properly lay them back to rest.

"I shall speak with Prior Willem," Wikerus told the barber. "My prior is a highly educated man and knows about these things. This city is under a spiritual attack, and it requires a spiritual response."

Wikerus heard the barber-surgeon slide a bar across the door when he left the house, and he frowned. Usually the barber-surgeon took pains to make sure his services were accessible to all who needed help – and a haircut. Several people stood nearby, talking amongst themselves. Word of the injured tinker had already spread, but what was said he did not know. The last time rumors of devils walking the earth circulated was during the worst throes of the pestilence, causing widespread fear and panic. He suspected it would be worse now that people fully understood how much death and destruction could follow an evil spirit. He looked resolutely at his feet and hurried away to find Appel, Gritta, and Efi. Between the missing boys and undeniable evidence of monsters, he knew he needed to call on the alewives for help.

The flames of rivalry

In which Efi feels the uncomfortable burn of competition

Gritta was later than usual coming to Appel's house in the afternoon. By the time she had hopped the waste trench in the lane and breezed through the open door, Appel and Efi were gently scooping dippers of ale from the wooden resting tub and pouring it through a metal funnel into a fresh cask.

"Gentle, Efi, gentle! You go too fast and you're stirring up the muck on the bottom of the tub!" Appel scolded. "That will spoil the flavor in the barrel."

Efi's eyes were hard. She didn't answer, and she didn't slow her work.

"What is your problem, girl? You act as if you personally hate this ale!" Appel yelled.

Gritta set her basket down on the table and took the dipper from Efi's hands. "Go on then, Efi. Go upstairs and weep. I heard all about it."

"Heard about what?" Appel asked. Efi rose from where she sat and stormed out of the house, slamming the door behind her. "Did Arne cause even more trouble today?"

The morning after Appel and Efi deposited him back into his house in the wool dyers' district, Arne had returned, demanding an explanation for his eviction. The women had to enlist Jorges and Lonel to have the man forcibly removed back to his own hovel. Arne complained bitterly, wrapping his arms around a full cask of ale and yelling threats until Lonel pried him away from it finger by finger. That was in the morning, and since then, Efi had been surly.

"You remember Stefan the glover, who was sweet on Efi? He has found himself a new muse," Gritta said, clucking her tongue.

"Someone jilted our Efi?" Appel was genuinely shocked. "Who could possibly tempt him?" Efi may have been poor, but she was also the fairest eligible woman in the city, and everyone knew it.

"The young woman who moved into the wool dyers' quarter a few months ago. Lonel has been swooning over her since she and her old mother came to Colmar last winter. The girl is shamefully unsupervised and is making the rounds about town. She is the new recipient of Stefan's affection, and I am glad of it, for Lonel has been showering her with gifts. I'm not sure where he finds the coin to buy her such finery, but he ought to give it to his family and not some lusty girl from Basel."

Above, they heard a muffled wail filter through the ceiling from the bedroom. "Ah, poor girl will cry herself to sleep tonight," Gritta sighed, gently scooping a dipper of brown ale and pouring it into the funnel.

"Which means I will have no sleep at all." Appel shot an annoyed glance at the ceiling. "Why don't you let her stay at your house tonight? You won't hear her over the sound of Jorges snoring."

"And Lonel. He's outpacing his father. No one in the house can sleep," Gritta groaned.

They worked together in warm and comfortable silence until the tub was empty, save for a pale sludge of sediment at the bottom, which they scooped up and transferred to a clay jar and covered with a cloth. They could put the sediment to use as a leavener for the next day's bread. Then they hammered a wooden plug into the bung hole of the cask and sealed the edges with pitch. The ale was ready for transport to the nearest tavern. As soon as they had finished, they heard a thump overhead and the sound of Efi running across the floor.

"Help!" she screamed. "Fire! There is a fire at Saint Matthieu's church!"

By the time the women arrived, breathless and with their heads uncovered at the courtyard of Saint Matthieu's church, the fire was under control, although that didn't stop an overeager friar from continuing to ring the bell long past the time when help was needed. Peering through the tiny diamond-shaped window in the above-stairs sleeping room at Appel's house, what Efi had really seen were flames licking up the branches of an old plum tree in the church garden, and only a few charred branches and a barrow full of hay had been truly destroyed. Nevertheless, the Franciscan friars were shaken, and they wandered around in a daze, holding the buckets and wet robes they had used to smother the flames. A knot of older friars and Sheriff Werner's guards had gathered around Prior Willem and were engaged in a serious conversation. When he saw the alewives enter the garden, Friar Wikerus broke away from the group and smiled.

"It is well, and we are safe, dear alewives! No lives were threatened or bodies injured. Prior Willem suspects a negligent novice must have left a lantern in the garden and caught the trees alight. Praise Jesu the church building was spared!"

Gritta looked around the churchyard. Prior Willem's face was dark with smoke and soot, and Friar Wikerus had singed patches on his robe. "Seems a bit far-fetched, don't it, Friar? Why would a novice be out in the church garden with a lantern in the daytime?"

"Has anyone found the scorched lamp in question?" Appel asked.

"Yes, we have." Prior Willem had stepped up behind them and, by his tone, was clearly uninterested in the opinions of three women. "Brother Wikerus, I have need of you. We must question the novices. Who else could have caused such mischief?"

Wikerus flushed bright red but held back the defensive retort perched on the tip of his tongue. Dipping his head, he gave the alewives a long-suffering look and followed his prior to the church building. Sheriff Werner sauntered toward them, belly first, and the three alewives looked around, searching for a reason – any reason – to avoid speaking to him.

"Quick, girls! Let us leave before he corners us and finds a way to blame this fire on a member of Gritta's family," Efi hissed.

"How dare you say such a thing!" Gritta snarled, but Appel stepped between them, giving them her most serene, grandmotherly smile.

"Now, Gritta, history proves this will happen. The sheriff is always searching for a reason to lock up a member of the Leporteur clan in the tower. Remember, dear, it was you who he arrested only a few months ago."

The sheriff cleared his throat and appraised the women with as much authority as he could muster, which proved hard, for Appel, elegant and willowy even in her advanced years, towered over him. He chose to ignore her and focused on Efi, the shortest of the three.

"Well then, and where were you women when this fire started?"

"Gritta and I were brewing," Appel said. "And Efi was weeping on the top floor of the house. All of us occupied in legitimate labor."

"Weeping?" the sheriff repeated.

"Yes, weeping," Efi said cooly. "Frau Appel wasn't speaking in Latin, Sheriff."

The sheriff was about to make a comment when Prior Willem hurried over and grabbed his arm, pulling him aside. For a moment, the two of them spoke quietly with their heads close together. Prior Willem raised his voice and pointed angrily at his feet, while Friar Wikerus paled and wrung his hands nearby. Appel started to walk toward her frind, but he shook his head, warning her away. After a some more heated discussion, the sheriff and the prior broke their huddle and went quickly in opposite directions.

"Wikerus! Come!" Prior Willem barked, and Wikerus scurried after him.

Gritta turned to Appel and shrugged her shoulders. "Now what could that be all about?"

Appel frowned. "I don't know. But it's not like Friar Wikerus to conceal things from us. Strange, indeed."

There was nothing else to do but return to Les Tanneurs, which was reaching new heights of stink due to the rain followed by a strong, spring sun, which moistened and then heated the tanning pits and their rotting hides which soaked in a soup of excrement and lye. To the alewives, it wasn't pleasant, but it smelled of home.

Inside Gritta's house, her daughter Rosmunda had swept the dirt floor clean and set a cup of delicate maiblümchen flowers on the table to brighten the dark, low-beamed room. Jorges sprawled in a corner on his pile of straw, snoring and smelling of fish after his day of manual labor at the docks. The twins, Anstett and Mattheus, dandled a dried cherry on a string in front of their baby sister, Wina, who swatted at the sweet treat like a kitten.

Gritta bustled around the room, inspecting the pot of stew on the hearth and the board of clean dishes. "Rosmunda, where is your brother, Lonel? We need his help moving a new barrel of ale to Karl Gasthaus's tavern."

"He went out shortly after you did, Ma, and hasn't been back since." She looked anxiously at the front door and lowered her voice. "Do you think it's true, Frau Appel? Do you think the Devil is walking among us again in Colmar?"

Appel noticed the girl twisting the sleeve of her dress. She looked terrified.

"No, my dear. I am sure there is a mistake. Most likely a bear from the forest wandered too close to the walls, and nothing more."

Gritta sat slowly at the table, groaning as she lowered her hindquarters to the bench. "Appel, I'm falling to pieces, like you. My bones ache from the inside out."

Appel shot Gritta an austere look, but before she could think of a good response, Lonel slunk through the door and darted into the shadowy recess behind the partition where the animals slept in the winter months.

"Ah, there you are, boy! Fetch your brother Noe and help us load a barrel of new ale onto the cart so we can deliver it to Karl Gasthaus," Gritta ordered.

Lonel didn't answer. From the dark, they heard sounds of splashing.

"What are you doing?" Gritta demanded.

Lonel emerged from the makeshift winter stable. His face was pink, and his hair and the shoulders of his cowl were damp from where he had cleaned them with water from the trough. "Just washing my face, Ma," he muttered.

Gritta's eyes narrowed for a moment as suspicious thoughts raced through her head. Then she grinned. "Well then, perhaps you are growing up, my boy! I've never known you to wash your face except before church!"

"And on feast days," Lonel added.

"It must be the influence of young Kamille," Gritta said, turning to Appel and Efi. "Seems all the young men in the city are scrubbed and sweet-smelling these days!" She didn't seem to notice both Efi and Lonel chafing at the mention of Kamille, who was the center of two rivalries.

Lonel shrugged. "Just feels good to wash, that's all there is to it." He hurried outside, dipping his head to fit his spidery frame through the low doorway. Only Appel noticed the faint scent of smoke on his clothes, and the spots of soot he hadn't managed to scrub from his face.

And then there were two

In which Appel and Gritta's social call goes horribly wrong

THE TINKER'S WOUNDS HEALED as he recuperated in the front room of the barber-surgeon's house, although the injuries to his mind appeared permanent. When his frightened dog turned up unharmed and scratching at the city gates, the animal was delivered back to his owner, only to have the tinker start screaming in his thick Flemish accent that the poor creature was a cynocephalus – a dog-headed monster.

The cityfolk discussed the situation at their monthly meeting in the covered wine market. Everyone knew the appearance of monsters foretold the return of the pestilence. Lord Frider, who had heard of the phenomenon before, reminded the assembly that cynocephali were rumored to be strange, but not dangerous.

"They stand on their hind legs, and speak in a barking voice," he told them. "Far less dangerous than a wolf."

After much deliberation, the council decided the risk was too great, despite Lord Frider's testimony. The tinker's dog was likely a cynocephalus in disguise, they said. It could be an agent of the Devil. The sheriff's men tied the animal up in a sack and tossed it into a stream outside the city walls. After all, they told themselves, they couldn't be too careful, and it took a mighty effort from Lord Frider to convince them not to throw the tinker in after his dog.

Their cruel act did nothing to make the city safer, for soon a terrified young Franciscan novice came forward to the sheriff and admitted he thought he had seen the monster lurking about Saint Matthieu's church when the fire started. Someone had also stolen several pairs of shoes from the Franciscans' storeroom. "Perhaps the cynocephali have wet feet," he suggested to the sheriff in a trembling voice.

A few days later, two young girls happened upon the monster lurking in a puddle of shadow as they walked to the privy one evening. Their high-pitched screams frightened it off, and after that, the cityfolk realized no one was safe, outside the walls or otherwise. A rising sense of panic and helplessness – all too familiar from the years when the Great Mortality slaughtered one in three citizens – gripped the city. Long-forgotten tales of revenants and supernatural beings circulated around the hearths of the homes and wynstubes, and even the most plain-spoken and skeptical cityfolk – from the shepherds to the burghers – all seemed to understand there was evil at work in Colmar once again.

The three alewives stayed indoors as much as possible, darting between Appel and Gritta's houses day and night. Although a curfew had not been officially declared, no one was in a hurry to be alone outside the safety of their own homes. Late one afternoon, Gritta trotted across the lane, hopped the trench that shunted wastewater from the street, and dove through the doorway into Appel's house, rolling across the threshold and startling the ginger cat from his slumber atop a pile of un-spun wool.

"Glad you could drop in," Appel said without looking up from her seat near the window. She was carefully picking stitches on a strip of dark-blue fabric with a bone needle. "I don't think it's necessary to launch through the door as if you're trying to grab ahold of a greased pig, Gritta."

"Never know how fast a monster can run," Gritta replied as she brushed dust and straw from her skirts.

"Considering this monster has not been seen for days now, perhaps the problem has gone away."

"Aye, there's no meat for the beast to eat if we're all hiding inside our homes, Appel! What are you doing?"

"Making a hair ribbon for Efi." Appel squinted as she spoke, jabbing the needle through the cloth and then swearing when it sank into her fingertip. "The Devil take this! I always hated sewing."

"Where is the fair Efi?" Gritta looked around. "It ain't safe for anyone to be about on the streets these days."

"She joined the group of women headed out together to take dough to the oven," Appel replied. "Six women and two guards meet each morning in the square, and all go together. You don't know this because you take most of your meals at my house and never bake bread of your own."

"You speak as if I am taking advantage of you, Appel." Gritta crossed her arms and pouted, for she was a proud woman, but in her heart she knew it was true. Despite her earnings from selling ale, money was tight, and she was too exhausted each day to turn up her nose at Appel's generosity.

Appel smiled at her friend, her pale blue eyes twinkling from her pleasantly wrinkled face. "My life is richer for it, my dear. Though I lost my husband, my daughter, and my grandson in the Great Pestilence, I never want for the sound of children in my garden or the help of another woman's hands at my table."

Gritta beamed, soaking up the feelings of love and belonging. Then she cleared her throat. "You know my children all think of you as their grandmother."

"An aunt, perhaps," Appel responded.

"A great aunt. A much older aunt," Gritta laughed.

Appel waved the blue ribbon toward Gritta like a flag. "Someday it will be you sitting here wondering when you became an old woman, Gritta Leporteur. You're so busy with your children that you may not notice the creases deepening around your eyes or the silver in your hair until suddenly you look like me."

"There's no harm in praying I never will look like you, Appel!" Gritta laughed and jumped from her seat, dodging as Appel snatched a willow basket and threw it at her. There came a tapping at the door, and Gritta opened it. Outside, one of the city guards stood awkwardly, fidgeting with his tall spear and holding up his oversized helmet to keep it from slipping down the bridge of his nose.

"Fair women! I am here to ask if you require escort!" he bellowed before Gritta could properly greet him.

"You're louder than a flock of geese, young man. Who sent you here and why?"

"Lord Werner wishes his men to be ready to escort the public to and from their places of work and worship so the city may continue to be prosperous!" the young guard said, just as loud as before.

Gritta looked back at Appel. Appel shrugged, set her sewing down, and tied her straw sunhat over her wimple. "Friar Wikerus has been strangely absent these last two days, and if he doesn't return, we shall have to suffer the guidance of Brother Tacitus once again. Let us call on him, for I feel as caged as a cow in a milking shed. Oh, hold your tongue, Gritta!" The glee in Gritta's eyes was so bright that Appel could recite the rude comments her friend wanted to make before she even spoke them.

A few people hurried through the square outside their homes – mostly tanners' wives who went to fetch water in the clean streams or who had missed the escort to the market or the bakery. They swiveled their heads, looked over their shoulders, and avoided the shadowy nooks and alleys of the crooked streets. As they approached the church, they passed through finer neighborhoods, where not a soul was to be seen and all the windows in the two- and three-level homes were tightly shuttered. It was a scene eerily familiar from only a few years prior, when disease ravaged the city and people hid in their homes, praying for God to spare them from death.

The Great Pestilence left its mark on everyone. It was a deep wound that healed into a thick scar on their minds and hearts. When the foul plague of buboes and fevers finished killing half the citizens of Colmar, the shattered survivors attempted to resume their lives, but they did so in a state of disbelief. Those who couldn't find the strength in them to carry on as reputable members of society took to the highways to rob and kill for their survival, or drown themselves in drink, or they simply wandered into the wilderness and were never seen again.

Appel glanced at Gritta, and she saw from her friend's distant gaze that her thoughts had turned just as darkly introspective. This would never do. Keeping despair at bay was the key to survival. She cleared her throat loudly.

"Young man!"

The guard jumped. He was walking awkwardly in front of them in a flimsy cuirass of ill-fitting boiled leather and a ridiculous set of round wooden poleyns strapped to his knees, despite the lack of protection anywhere else on his legs – armor more suited to crawling on all fours to dig for turnips than for fighting monsters. Unable to turn his head, he instead turned his entire body toward them.

"How many of you patrol these streets?" Appel asked.

"I don't rightly know, madame. Lord Werner only brought us lads in from the fields yesterday and told us to guard Les

Tanneurs and the wool dyers' quarter. There were seven of us tending the sheep, and many more come from the ploughing."

Appel's face softened. The boy was young and simple – he must be, for he called her "madame," which no city boy would have ever said. "And how old are you?"

"Don't know, madame. I s'pose I am young, athough my Ma always said I had a pair of old eyes in my face."

"How can you see his eyes beneath that water pail on his head?" Gritta leaned over and whispered into Appel's ear.

"Young man, when we reach Saint Matthieu's, come straight to the kitchens with us. We shall find you something good to eat and a warm fire to sit at while we visit our friend, Friar Wikerus."

The boy grinned and pushed the helmet away from his eyes. They were quiet, pale gray, and wise. Appel decided she liked this youngster.

When they reached the pink stone edifice of Saint Matthieu's church, the guard tapped on one of the great wooden gates with the butt of his spear. After a very long wait, not one but three gray-robed friars appeared. One cracked the door open, and the other two stood behind him, holding spades above their heads as weapons.

"Fear not, men! 'Tis only two women and a boy who threaten your gates." Gritta laughed and pushed her way past the quaking friars. Inside, the church was dim. Several friars knelt at the altar, praying fervently. A door in the vestibule slammed open and Prior Willem strode out, his robes flicking his ankles, annoyance radiating from his body.

"Goodwives?" he said. He held his posture straight, looking at them only with his eyes, down the length of his well-shaped nose. "I assume you are here because there is some trouble. Do you require spiritual assistance?"

Gritta and Appel both curtseyed, exchanging a panicked look while their heads were lowered. They hadn't expected to meet the prior, only to see their friend. Perhaps it was not such a good idea to visit Friar Wikerus, after all.

Appel spoke first. "My lord Prior, we came to inquire after Brother Wikerus, who ministers to our part of the city. It has been several days since we saw him, and we wished to know if something was amiss."

Prior Willem eyed them silently until Appel and Gritta began to squirm with discomfort. "Allow me to understand you correctly. You came to call on a brother of this church? A social call?"

"No, m'lord, it is a charity call. We came to see if he is sick," Gritta said quickly, for it suddenly occurred to the both of them that Prior Willem of the Franciscans was a different and more severe ruler than the beleaguered but kindly Prior Konrad of the Dominicans. Neither of them had considered how their actions could get Brother Wikerus in trouble.

"If Brother Wikerus were ill and unable to perform his duties, another brother of the Order would be dispatched to care for your community. As such, I know your district is being served by the Dominicans as well. Your request to see him is highly unusual and inappropriate. He shall be punished."

Appel and Gritta exchanged horrified looks. Behind them, the young shepherd-turned-guard quaked in his wooden poleyns. Prior Willem was handsome and fierce in his anger.

"I realize now we should not have come, my lord," Appel said, keeping her eyes downcast and her posture as humble as possible. This was the exact opposite of what she had wanted!

The guard stepped forward. "Please, your highness," he stuttered. "These two women just wanted to leave the house for a bit. They only wanted to get about, since everyone is locked inside, and I offered to escort them."

"Who are you?" Prior Willem demanded.

The guard startled, and the helmet slid down over his eyes. He pushed it back, but before he could speak, there came a cry from the back of the church, an anguished wail echoing around the high ceiling of the nave. The sound was so heart-wrenching that Gritta thought her blood would curdle like milk in her veins. Those wails, those cries of absolute devastation, brought back chilling memories of the months when they endured the Great Pestilence. It was the sound someone made when they discovered their loved one dead.

A figure staggered into the room, and the alewives gasped. Brother Wikerus was doubled over, clutching something to his chest, weeping. The friars at the door dropped their makeshift weapons and rushed to him, just in time to catch him before he fell to the stone floor. Prior Willem ran to him and grasped

Brother Wikerus's head in his hands, looking intently into his face. "Brother, are you hurt? Are you in mortal danger?"

Wikerus tried to shake his head, but the prior still held his face. "No...no, I am not hurt in body, but my heart, my heart will surely break!" Tears spilled from his large blue eyes, and he held out the bundle of rags clutched to his chest.

"The guards brought these." Brother Wikerus held the rags in trembling hands. Prior Willem held them up to the light, and the other friars and the two women gasped. The remains of two tattered gray cowls with stiff black patches of dried blood could only mean one thing: they belonged to the two missing novices.

Once he recovered from his surprise, Prior Willem narrowed his eyes. "Where did you say the guards found these robes, Brother?"

"Just outside the wall nearest to Saint Matthieu's, my lord. Two of Sheriff Werner's guards discovered the robes and brought them here. I was giving instructions to the cook in the kitchens, and the men came to the postern at the back of the courtyard."

"And you believed this story immediately?"

"Brother Tacitus of the Dominicans was with the men to provide spiritual protection if the monster attacked on their watch. Despite my personal opinion of Brother Tacitus, I believe what he and the guards told me. These belonged to my novices, Ulf and Jean-Louis. They are...they are dead." He dissolved into shuddering sobs again. "They were my responsibility," he wailed. "They were mine to protect!"

"What were the two fools doing outside the walls in the first place?" Prior Willem growled. "Had they stayed in the friary, they would still be alive and causing mischief. This is not your fault, Brother Wikerus."

"P-put me in charge of the postulates, my lord. Send me to shovel the soil from the privy. I do not deserve to have responsibility for the children of other men!"

Prior Willem's face was grim. He turned to one of the other terrified friars. "Go at once and gather the novices. Count them all, and ensure no one is missing."

"Shall I also count the robes in the storerooms, my lord?" the friar asked. "Perhaps this monster is responsible also for stealing the brothers' shoes when the orchard caught fire."

Prior Willem's expression managed to look more annoyed than before. "No. Monsters do not bother stealing shoes when there are souls to drag to Hell instead. Someone else is stealing shoes from the Dominicans and the Franciscans. Now go and count the novices. When you have finished, report back to me." He snapped off the order, and the friar took off running.

Gritta looked at Appel and mouthed the word, "Shoes?" Appel shrugged in response. They and their young guard had been forgotten after Wikerus made his anguished entrance into the nave of the church. The three of them slowly backed out of the candlelight until they were hidden in the dark aisle, then began to creep toward the doors. They felt like trespassers viewing something not meant for the eyes of laypeople. Seeing their beloved Brother Wikerus – whose easy nature and gentle humor so often calmed them when they were fearful – lying prostrate on the floor, howling with grief, filled them with dread. If Brother Wikerus was scared of this monster, then nowhere was safe.

In the shadowy recesses of the aisle, Appel guided Gritta and the young guard back toward the narthex. They had nearly reached the little vestibule when a smaller door in the aisle burst open and a young friar fell through it, gasping and crawling on all fours in the dark.

"Heavens, what has happened?" Gritta cried. She and the guard attempted to lift the poor man to his feet, but his legs were like ropes and wouldn't hold his weight. His entire body trembled, and his face was beyond pale; it was gray, like the dead. Prior Willem and his brothers still attended to the weeping Friar Wikerus and didn't notice the commotion at the back of their church.

"Brother," Appel said, grabbing the man by his shoulders and shaking him gently. "Young man. Are you hurt?"

The young friar tried to speak, but no words would come from his mouth. Appel saw in the gleam of the candlelight a puddle spreading from underneath his robe. He had wet himself out of fright. She knelt down and looked into his dark eyes. "Brother, what frightens you?"

"Mmm-mm-MONSTERS!" he screamed. Once the word finally came out, he couldn't stop. Jumping to his feet, he hurtled into the nave and toward the altar and Prior Willem. "I saw them! Run! Flee, unless you wish to be ravaged like Ulf and Jean-Louis!"

For want of a helmet
In which tragedy strikes in Les Tanneurs

Everyone in the nave of St Matthieu's church stood in silent shock as the words of the terrified friar echoed around them. Wikerus had stopped crying and was holding his breath on the stone floor, Prior Willem and two other friars kneeling near him. Appel, Gritta, and the young guard were frozen with horror. For a moment, the only movement in the room was the slow slide of the young guard's helmet as it lowered itself over his eyes.

"What do you mean when you say you saw them, Brother?" Gritta asked. But she knew the answer in her body, for she could feel herself growing cold as the blood drained from her face and hands. "Do you mean to tell us there are two monsters inside the walls of Colmar?"

The terrified friar blinked up at Gritta. "Indeed, two of them. I saw one creeping through the hall near the novices' quarters. Tall it was, with ears and a snout like a dog. And teeth! Ohhh, those teeth!"

At the mention of the novice quarters, Wikerus struggled to his feet, still clutching the bloody clothes. "Did the beast not see you, Brother Kornelius?"

"I was only passing by the hall, and I did not know if it saw me, but I didn't want to take any chances. I hid in the storage room where we keep the vestments, quaking like a leaf, praying to Jesu that the door, which I had barricaded with a chest of spare robes, would not open."

His audience were waiting with their breath held, so Brother Kornelius continued. "When I finally ventured out, I sought the prior immediately, but oh, what horror! As I hurried through the garden, what did I see but a second monster! I caught sight of it as it climbed over the wall and disappeared. That was when I turned and ran, thinking to take refuge at the altar, so my last act upon this earth would be to prostrate myself before the cross in supplication and worship."

"How can you be certain it wasn't the same monster you saw, gone off to the gardens after stalking the novice quarters?" Prior Willem asked. Appel felt a grudging appreciation for the man. She didn't care for his arrogance, but he asked the right questions. She could see why he and Friar Wikerus admired each other so.

"Different," Brother Kornelius whispered. "The first beast was black all over with the teeth and ears of a wolf. It had shaggy fur. But the second monster was thicker and even larger, and in the place of fur it wore brown leathery skin. Shaped like a man it was, but with tatters of bone and blades hanging from its arms, like the wings of a bird that had been scorched in a fire. And on its hands were claws, nay, talons as long as a fishmonger's knife and twice as sharp! Terrible to behold, my lord! And oh, God help us all, it is loose in the city now!"

A loud crash interrupted Brother Kornelius. The young guard who had accompanied Gritta and Appel to the church had thrown his ill-fitting helmet to the ground and gripped his spear in both hands. "If there are two, then they will be getting at the sheep as well as the people." He strode briskly toward the door.

"Young man, where are you going?!" Wikerus called after him.

"I am a shepherd, Brother. I defend my flocks from wolves, dogs, and when necessary, monsters, too."

He was out the door before anyone could stop him.

"There is still a second beast unaccounted for in the church," Brother Wikerus said, looking down at the bloody robes still clutched in his hands. "If that young man is brave enough to face the monster alone with just a spear to save his sheep, then I shall confront the remaining demon with my crucifix and my prayers. I shall protect my novices."

"Friar Wikerus, don't!" Appel pleaded, but Wikerus didn't hear her. He turned and marched toward the door that led to the men's living quarters. Prior Willem set his jaw and grasped the plain wooden cross at his throat.

"Come," he commanded the other friars. "We shall help Brother Wikerus defend our own flock." The friars swallowed, took up their own crosses, and followed behind him. The door slammed shut with a loud boom. Appel and Gritta looked around. They were all alone in the church nave, with only a few guttering candles to illuminate the room, and twilight darkened the colorful glass in the windows. Gritta snatched one of the tapers from a nearby candle stand.

"Gritta!" Appel hissed. "Put that back at once! You must not steal from the church!"

But Gritta was resolute. "To protect my life and yours, I would steal the habit off a nun. Now stand behind me, Appel. It's a long dark walk back to Les Tanneurs."

It took twice as long for Appel and Gritta to return to Trench Lane than it normally should. Without their guard escort and all the friars in the friary chasing monsters, the two women moved cautiously, creeping through the rapidly darkening alleys and avenues, their backs pressed against the rough garden walls and crumbling wattle and daub houses. There was no one on the streets, and because of the expense, few people kept candles or rushlights burning for long after the sun set. Even if a flickering flame were glowing inside of a house, it wouldn't matter, because every shutter and door was tightly closed against the evils of the night.

By the time they stumbled on the trench that ran down the middle of their street in Les Tanneurs, the sun was resolutely set, and there were no sounds other than a few dogs who barked and yipped at each other, and occasionally joined their voices together, enjoying the primal sound of their howling songs rippling across the stillness of the night. The two women could feel the small hairs on their arms and the backs of their necks raise at the eerie chorus.

Gritta went straight to her home and was greeted by a few of her younger children and Jorges who, far from appearing concerned, simply asked her when she would be ready to serve them their evening meal. Appel found her own door firmly barred, and pounded on it, her ire rising.

"Who goes?" a muffled voice trembled from the inside.

Appel glanced toward her front window. The shutters were wide open, and inside, she could see Efi holding a rushlight in one trembling hand and a hot poker from the fire in the other.

"It is me, Appel Schneider, the owner of this house, and if you do not open the door immediately, I shall be more formidable than any monster the Devil could conjure, Efi Kleven!" She was tired, hungry, and ready to put her feet in a bucket of hot water and sip a cup of strong ale.

It took longer than expected for Efi to open the door. First, Appel heard a bang as Efi lifted the wooden bar from its brackets, followed by a the ponderous scraping sound of Appel's painted cupboard as it was shoved out of the way.

"Oh, Appel, I thought you had been eaten!" Efi cried, flinging her arms around Appel's neck as soon as she had the door open. She set the rushlight stand on the broken cupboard, but the poker she had dropped hastily on the ground, and the straw on the floor quickly began to smoke.

"By Mother Mary's teats, girl, are you attempting to turn my house into a torch?!" Appel yelled, snatching the poker and dancing about the floor to stamp on the smoldering straw. Efi scooped it up with a spade and tossed it into the hearth. As it flared to life, the bright orange light revealed the young woman's haggard face. Dark shadows smudged the delicate skin under her eyes, and it was clear she had been crying.

"I was just so worried, Appel. I thought I had lost both you and Gritta. And what would I do if I were to suddenly become the mistress of an aleworks and of Gritta's twelve children? How would I cope without you two?"

"You would have to marry Jorges to become mistress of Gritta's children, and even you are not as desperate as that, Efi."

While Efi contemplated the horrors of marriage to Jorges Leporteur, Appel dragged her broken chest back to the wall where it normally stood. Nearby, the large washbasin and the shelves of herbs, brown and green-glazed crockery jars of food stores, and a few iron and wooden cooking tools made up her kitchen. Then she pushed the shutters closed and barred them against the night. If Efi noticed the gaping window next to the door she had barred and blockaded, she said nothing.

"There are two monsters in Colmar."

Efi's hand flew to her mouth, and she drew a sharp breath. "No," she whispered.

"Yes," Appel whispered back. There was nothing else to say. For a moment, the two women each retreated into her own thoughts. Appel sat heavily on the bench at the large table, and Efi poured her a bowl of ale, rich reddish-brown in color and redolent with herbs and honey. Appel drank deeply and sighed. She then proceeded to tell Efi about their strange and terrifying experience at the church of Saint Matthieu. Efi listened without interrupting, her chin in her hands, until Appel reached the part where Friar Wikerus left the nave and ran off to face the monster and protect the novice friars.

"He ran off, even though he knew you and Gritta would be all alone?" she asked, her sky-blue eyes wide.

"Gritta and I can fend for ourselves. But those boys, well, they are young and senseless. Much like you," Appel said with a smile. "Friar Wikerus made the right decision to protect them. Besides, I am too bony and stringy to be an enticing meal for a monster, and Gritta would taste far too bitter." They both laughed until their sides ached.

"Wait!" Efi held up a hand and sat perfectly still. "Do you hear something?"

Appel listened, and indeed, outside she heard the unsettling rumble of a mob. She unbarred the door and peeked outside. To her left, orange light flickered along the walls of the narrow portion of Trench Lane.

"Is it another fire?" Efi whispered.

"I think not," Appel said. From across the lane, Gritta's bony figure trotted toward them, clasping a moth-eaten shawl around her shoulders. She greeted them with a serious face. "Something has happened, and I intend to find out what."

"And I," Efi said, but her voice trembled. "Though I am frightened."

Gritta nodded and took Efi's hand. Appel slammed her door shut but left it unbarred so her friends could return. She set two more bowls of strong ale on the table and covered them each with a piece of stale bread to keep the flies away. Then she waited.

Appel woke with a start. She had drifted off to sleep in the dark warmth of the house with her ginger cat curled on her lap, purring luxuriously. She stretched her shoulders and groaned. If she slept for an entire night or only as long as it took for a loaf of bread to cook in an oven, it didn't matter – she always felt stiff and old when she regained consciousness.

Efi and Gritta had just returned and were removing their wraps near the door. They sat and each took up a bowl of ale without speaking. Gritta stared into her bowl as if looking for answers, while Efi drained hers in a single gulp, her head tilted back until her curls touched the small of her back.

"Well?!"

"The guard is dead," Gritta said. Next to her, Efi looked at her hands.

"The kind, simple young man who protected us today? Dead?" Appel could feel her eyes burning as tears rose. No. It wasn't fair. It wasn't fair! "I never even learned the boy's name."

"His name was Helmut. One of Sheriff Werner's men found him lying next to a canal."

They sat in silence for a moment, then Gritta spoke again. "It was strange though, the way he died." She rose and began to pace about the room. "Yes, something about the manner of his death was very strange, indeed! Appel, do you recall how Brother Kornelius at Saint Matthieu's described the two monsters he claims he saw?"

"Aye. The first was black and covered in shaggy fur, with a dog's snout and teeth, and the second had brown, scaly skin."

"And claws as long and sharp as a fishmonger's knife. Those were his exact words. That was the beast Helmut chased into the night. So how do you suppose Helmut was killed?" Gritta asked.

Appel swallowed hard. "I suppose he would have been slashed to pieces. I do not wish to think of it, Gritta. It is too terrible!"

"But he wasn't cut to pieces. There wasn't a scratch on his body. Efi and I saw as the sheriff's men removed his body from the canal, didn't we, Efi?"

"Yes," Efi said, shuddering. "No scratches, and no blood."

"Could he have fallen in the water?" Appel asked. "It was dark, and he was more familiar with the fields and the hills than the city. Few people who live outside the walls ever learn to swim."

"It's possible, but there is only one way to know for sure," Gritta said. Appel and Efi looked at her blankly. "We need to go see the body for ourselves."

Clues

In which Friar Wikerus provides an important piece of information

THE DAY AFTER HELMUT'S body was discovered next to one of the canals, the three alewives stood in the cemetery near the church of Saint Martin, staring at a fresh mound of earth. Several other cityfolk, mainly thrill-seekers, wandered among the mossy gravestones, stealing glances at the newest addition to the neighborhood of dead relatives and deceased friars.

"If they think the rotting body of Helmut the shepherd is going to come crawling out of the ground like a revenant, they are mistaken," Gritta snarled.

"Hush, Gritta! Don't speak of the boy that way," Appel scolded.

Gritta prepared to lash out with an even more visceral response but held her tongue when she saw the tears running down Appel's face.

"I am glad they put him to rest so quickly," Appel whispered, "but now we may never know what really happened to him. Are you sure you saw no blood on his body? No cuts or slashes in his clothes?"

"It was dark," Gritta responded. "I saw no blood, but it was difficult to see at night. We need to find the person who prepared the body. And we need to speak with the man who found him. Something about this doesn't make sense." She turned and walked briskly away from the graveyard.

"But Gritta, what do you suspect?" Efi asked, trotting alongside to keep up. "I heard one of the men say that Helmut appeared to have been bludgeoned over the head."

"But with what? How?" Gritta said. "Do monsters go around hitting people instead of devouring them? No, it doesn't make sense at all. But before I tell you my suspicions, let us hear what the sheriff and his men have to say."

Sheriff Werner lived in a large house on the highest ground of the city, in a stone building with a walled yard for his stables, gardens, and other outbuildings. The men who worked for him and the city militia lived nearby, but spent an immense amount of their time loitering in his spacious courtyard, where they could cajole free scraps of food from the kitchen and drink wine around a fire to avoid their wives. The alewives went to the courtyard expecting the gates to be open as they usually were, to let men come and go on their duties for the sheriff. But today, the gates were firmly locked, and even the small postern door was shut and barred.

As soon as Gritta pounded on the gate, the sound of scuffling came from the other side. Two guards, fully armored, appeared at the wall with bows and nocked arrows aimed at them.

"If you are monsters, revenants, mermaids, infidels, or other such monsters from hell, prepare to have your guts spilled by our arrows!" one of them called out in a trembling voice.

Gritta crossed her arms and looked up at the guard. "Are you blind? Lower your weapon, or the next time you come to buy ale from me I shall toss you out on your arse!"

The guard lowered his crossbow and squinted. "What are you doing here, Gritta Leporteur? We don't even have your husband in the stocks today."

"Just as well," Gritta called back. "Although, could you take him soon? He has been home every evening after his work at the docks these days, and I'm not used to having him around so much."

The old gatekeeper pulled the postern open on loudly screeching iron hinges, and he pointed a gnarled finger at Gritta. "That one always brings trouble, she does!" he crowed.

"Oh, tell it to the birds!" Gritta snarled back at him.

A tall, stern-looking man strode up to them and blocked their path. "I am Dorian, Sheriff Werner's new chief of the guard. What do you want? You had best tell me quickly and then be off before his lordship returns from his meal."

Efi stepped forward, twirling the edge of her sky-blue wimple between her fingers. "Why, thank you for asking, Herr Dorian. We would like to speak to the man who discovered the body of

Helmut the shepherd near the canal last night. May we?" She fluttered her eyelashes and looked at him coyly.

Dorian was unmoved by Efi's flirtations. "No, you may not. Is there anything else you require before you leave?"

Efi, unused to having her charms rebuffed, stood in shock. Gritta pushed her aside and planted her own feet, facing the hulking guard stance for stance. "The shepherd was bludgeoned, or so we were told. Were there any other marks on his body? Cuts or wounds of any kind?"

"There were none, not that it is any business of yours. The boy died because his skull was cracked in two. And now you should leave. Go back to your homes and your families."

"Wait, I have more questions!" Gritta shouted, but the chief of the guard gripped Gritta's wrist and put a hand on Appel's back, walking them forward against their will. Efi followed meekly behind.

"Good day to you, goodwives. Do not return here," he said, and slammed the postern shut.

"Well! If I didn't know any better, I would suspect he killed our young shepherd!" Gritta roared at the gates. "What are you hiding in there? How dare you treat us so rudely!"

"Oh, Gritta, Dorian didn't kill Helmut. He looks at us and he sees three people with no power or authority, and so he doesn't care about being kind or polite," Appel said.

As they walked home, Gritta's thoughts grew increasingly murderous, and she muttered curses and slanders under her breath. They had just turned to walk down Trench Lane when they saw a figure running toward them from the other side of the square.

"Why, it's Friar Wikerus!" Efi exclaimed.

"Friar, whatever is the matter?" Appel asked when they reached him. Friar Wikerus leaned against the crumbling yellow plaster of her house and gasped for breath. The alewives hustled him inside, stoking the fire and seating him near it with a bowl of hazy golden ale and a knitted blanket across his knees. After he took a long drink from his bowl, he sighed and motioned for the three women to sit.

"After I so foolishly ran off and left you two in the nave of the church completely unprotected, I took a count of my novices and found they were all accounted for. Same for the rest of the brothers in the friary. Only after I had ensured their safety did I realize I abandoned you, Appel and Gritta. I apologize."

"We understand, Friar, and we hold no contempt for you," Appel said, placing a hand on his arm and giving it a squeeze. For a moment, Friar Wikerus flinched, then relaxed, closed his eyes, and smiled.

"My mother used to do that when she spoke with me," he said. "She was a kind woman, just like you, Frau Appel."

"Did anyone find Helmut's mother to tell her of his death?" Gritta asked.

Friar Wikerus shook his head. "The boy's entire family perished in the pestilence. He lived in a shack with several other shepherds out in the fields and moved into the city during the winter."

"How do you know this about him?"

Wikerus set his bowl of ale down and dragged his fingers over the shorn tonsure on the top of his head. In the several days of chaos and fear at the friary, he had neglected to run a blade across it, and a stubble of brown fur tickled his palms.

"I know this because after I heard about his bravery and death, I insisted on preparing the body, and his fellow shepherds joined and helped me. Together we dug his grave, and I prayed for his soul's safe passage to heaven. It was a way to atone, since I could not bury the two boys I lost in the novitiate." His eyes grew large, but he shed no tears. He had none left.

"Thank you for honoring him, Friar Wikerus," Appel said.

Gritta rose to refill his bowl, but Wikerus held up a hand.

"No more, please. I must return to the church soon, but I have been looking for you all morning because there is something you must know. I heard the sheriff's men complaining about alewives from Les Tanneurs asking questions about Helmut, the shepherd. The boy was poor and had no family, and I am afraid if we don't seek justice for him, then no one else will."

"Well then, what do you know, Friar?" Gritta asked.

"It was no monster that killed Helmut," Wikerus said. "It was a man."

"Same difference," Efi snarled, but she stopped when she saw the hurt look on Friar Wikerus's face. "Pardon me, Friar. Please continue."

"When I first looked at the body, nothing appeared strange. He was bludgeoned over the head with something heavy. But then it seemed odd. True, there was a swelling on the skull, but I perceived no bleeding or breaks in the bone. There was no blood coming from his eyes or mouth, either. None of this proves the bump to the head didn't kill him, of course. Men have died from simply hitting their heads when they fall over, drunk."

Gritta leaned forward. "But in order to hit a man with an object, the monster had to be able to pick it up with its hands, and we know this monster didn't have hands! Brother Kornelius described the monster that escaped over the wall as having claws or talons as long and sharp as knives."

"Exactly." Brother Wikerus stood, the blanket slipping to the floor, and began to walk around the room.

"As I washed and dressed poor Helmut for his burial, I got a good look at his body, and there were no cuts, not even a scratch from a twig. Wouldn't a beast with claws use those to lash out at its prey? But then I did notice something on Helmut's throat."

The three women waited in suspense. Wikerus looked at each of them in turn. "Finger marks. The skin on the boy's throat was purple and black, with clear finger marks around his throat. He wasn't bludgeoned by a monster, he was strangled. By a man."

"Or a woman," Efi said solemnly. When three sets of incredulous eyes turned on her, she shrugged. "It crossed my mind to put my hands about the throat of Stefan the glover yesterday. Just because I am a woman doesn't mean I am incapable of strangling someone, and neither is any other woman here."

Appel returned her attention to Friar Wikerus. "So, he wasn't killed by a beast with claws, but that doesn't mean he was killed by a man. It could have been a different monster. It could have been the first one, with the head of a dog." She paused and lowered her voice to a whisper. "It could have been a third."

"Oh, stop!" Gritta jumped to her feet. "Don't you see? None of these beasts are monsters! They are all men! Whether they are two, three, or three hundred, there are no monsters! The whole time, it was men who killed."

Appel scowled. "But what about Arne the street sweeper's account? He said the monster ate his cart."

Gritta took three furious strides across the room and snatched up a broomstick. Without another word, she sank her teeth into it and shook it, snarling like a dog at a bone.

"Gritta!" Appel said, aghast. "Stop this at once!"

Gritta tossed the broom to the ground. "Why should I?"

"Because it's...well..."

"Monstrous?"

Appel, Efi, and Friar Wikerus all looked at their hands while Gritta surveyed them triumphantly.

"Anything that seems strange, out of the ordinary way, or uncomfortable could be called a monster, Appel. Perhaps I know this better than the rest of you because I am married to Jorges."

"But this monster doesn't look like a man, Gritta, it looks like a wolf. It has ears that stand up on its head," Efi said.

"Trickery. Monsters ain't real. That's what I'm telling you." Gritta stomped her foot and glared.

Efi shook her head. "Gritta, devils walked the earth during the pestilence, and you know this as well as the rest of us. My sister, may her bones rest peacefully, told me that a cynocephalus appeared at our garden wall and tried to bark at her. Two days later, she was dead of pestilence. How can you deny such obvious truth?"

"And if monsters are here again...does that mean the pestilence has returned?" Appel's face paled as the implications dawned on her. She turned to Friar Wikerus. "Friar, could Helmut have been struck down by disease?"

The very idea that the pestilence might have returned was too terrible to consider. Appel, Efi, and Gritta all looked at each other and then to Wikerus. He heaved a deep breath, then shook his head.

"Jesu be praised, no. Helmut had a wound on his head, and it's clear that someone had their hands firmly around his throat, too. But Gritta's assertion that these so-called 'monsters' could actually be men in disguise intrigues me."

Efi refilled his dish of ale, and despite his earlier protest, Wikerus grinned, took a long drink, and continued. "Assume the first monster sighting by Arne and the second attack against the traveling tinker were both acts of man not demon, then the next question is why," he said slowly. "Why would someone do such a thing? Who has the time and wherewithal to do something so insidious?"

"Could it have been mischief?" Efi asked.

Appel, tapping her chin in thought, turned to Gritta. "Where was Lonel last night?"

Gritta bristled. "Why do you ask?"

"Well...I have not seen him around much lately, that is all." Appel knew her excuse was weak, and the look on her friend's face told her Gritta knew it, too. Gritta rose to her feet, her whole body shaking with rage.

"To suggest my boy could have done something so, so...evil! To suggest that he killed someone! And Lonel, who has always looked to you as his own grandmother!"

"Please, Gritta, I only meant to say he might somehow be involved, but not directly responsible." Appel held out her hands to soothe Gritta's wrath, but nothing could placate her. Gritta's temper, more formidable than any monster known to heaven or earth, was unleashed.

"You meant to say nothing of the sort! It is clear you think he's more than just an accessory to this mischief. And what's worse, you made this assumption based on absolutely no evidence at all!" Gritta snatched her shawl and stomped toward the door. But before she left, she turned and pointed a shaking finger at them. "In here, I see three monsters. And all of them are wearing sheep's clothing!" She turned and ran. A few of Appel's chickens trotted eagerly after her.

Appel looked at her hands, feeling the red-hot gaze of Friar Wikerus on her. "I am fond of the boy, I really am. But he does find himself in the middle of trouble more than anyone else I know." Her words sounded lame and pathetic in her ears.

"All the more reason to take the time to speak with him and learn the truth before casting accusations," Friar Wikerus said, standing. "I must return to the friary. Prior Willem is holding a service in Helmut's honor this evening." He paused in the doorway, then turned back to Appel. "Lonel was at Herr Schlock's wynstube last night at the same time Helmut met his demise. He was crying into his wine because he discovered his lover with another man. He couldn't have been the murderer. I think you owe Gritta an apology, Frau Appel."

Monstrous accusations

In which Sheriff Werner and Brother Tacitus attempt to teach the alewives how to behave

GRITTA DIDN'T SHOW UP the next morning to scour the cauldron and fill it with fresh water for a new batch of ale, so Appel and Efi labored in silence with a cloud of sadness hanging over them. Efi stole glances at Appel as she poured a measure of malted barley into the pot with her mouth set in a thin, angry line. She would not apologize. Caught in the middle, Efi grieved over her friends' argument, but she knew from some experience that the women would resolve their differences in time.

They had just finished straining the ale through several layers of cloth tied over the top of a large tub to filter out any remaining herbs and grains when Brother Tacitus strode into the house, followed by Sheriff Werner.

"Greetings, Frau Efi. Frau Appel," Brother Tacitus said solemnly. He had his left hand and hook tucked into the sleeves of his dour black robe. "I am here to provide counsel on a grave issue."

Appel dropped the cloth bundle of soggy grain and herbs. It hit the ground with a wet thump, and several chickens rushed around the men's legs to have a go at the sudden wealth of wet barley. "Something has happened?" Her face was white with worry.

Sheriff Werner stepped forward. "Indeed, something has happened. My men told me you were at my home asking questions about the murder of Helmut the shepherd. I have warned you before not to meddle in my business or bother my men, and yet you continue to flagrantly defy me. And so, I have brought Brother Tacitus here to help you understand the impropriety of your actions. Not only are you an insult to women everywhere, you are an insult to God." His countenance grew red and then purple with rage as he blustered at them.

Brother Tacitus cleared his throat with the gravitas of a judge. "Indeed, for it says in the scriptures that older women are to be reverent in behavior, not slanderers, or slaves to too much wine." He glared pointedly at the tub of freshly filtered ale on the table as he spoke. "Frau Appel, you corrupt this younger woman with your meddlesome actions. And as for Frau Gritta, well, where do I even begin?"

By now, the color had returned to Appel's face. "I thought you had come to tell me that someone had been killed, that something had happened to Frau Gritta or one of her children. Instead, you come here to shame me because I showed concern for a brave young man who died." She lifted a hand, trembling with indignation, and pointed at the door. "Out! Get out of my house!"

Sheriff Werner crossed his arms and gave her a wicked smile. "No."

"Help! Help! Sheriff, please help us!" came a cry from the street. Brother Tacitus and Sheriff Werner turned and ran to the doorway. Outside in Trench Lane, Gritta stood, her head uncovered, pointing to the canal and the tanning pits. "I saw it! Horned beast stalking about near the pits! Oh, it shall bring another great mortality upon us! Call the militia! The beast is inside the walls, and you can go kill it!"

Brother Tacitus snarled, grabbed the wooden cross hanging about his throat, and stormed outside, prepared to do spiritual battle with the monster. But Sheriff Werner hesitated, then backed a few steps further into the house. Appel crossed her arms.

"What's wrong, Sheriff? Frightened of the monster, are you?"

"Come, Sheriff!" Gritta screamed. "Quickly, before it gets away! Now is your chance to save Colmar!"

The few people who were out in the square scurried into their homes and slammed their doors and shutters. Appel pushed at the sheriff from behind. "It says in the scriptures that a man is to be brave in all things. Remember the proverb that says, 'the righteous are as bold as a lion'? Go on then!"

She shoved him across the threshold, and Gritta darted inside, slamming the door shut and sliding the bar firmly in place. Then she leaned her back against the wood and cackled.

"Quickly! We must close the window shutter as well or the monster will crawl inside!" Efi said.

But Gritta waved her away. "There is no beast at the tanning pits, unless you count the beastly smell. I saw that those two windy fools would not leave your house and so I drew them out."

Appel smiled and sank into a chair. "I am so relieved! I thought we were about to be under attack – by those two."

"Will you take back what you said about my Lonel?"

Appel squirmed where she sat, as her reluctance to admit she was wrong battled with her affection for her friend and ale-making partner.

"Well, you will take it back when you hear what I have learned. I know who the murderer is," Gritta said. She wore a smirk on her face.

"Wait a moment before you tell us," Efi glared at Appel, crossing her arms across her bosom. "Appel, don't you have something to say to Gritta?"

"Don't speak at me like I am an errant child, you harlot!" Appel snapped back at her.

"What do you have to tell me?" Gritta asked.

"Friar Wikerus confirmed that Lonel was at the wynstube on the night of Helmut's murder, lamenting the loss of his beloved Kamille, who was apparently out cavorting with yet another man that evening." She said it, but it stung Appel to admit she falsely accused Gritta's son.

"She is the harlot," Efi hissed. "Kamille is working her way through every man in Colmar. Well, at least she is finished with Stefan the glovemaker now."

"She hasn't messed with my Jorges yet," Gritta mused, not noticing the pitying looks Appel and Efi cast in her direction.

"So." She rubbed her hands together. "It weren't my Lonel. Now are you ready to hear who it was?"

"You are ready to tell us. You're as proud and puffed up as a cock among his hens." Appel grinned.

Gritta cackled again. "Well then, who was it claimed to have seen the second beast at Saint Matthieu's? And who was the last to run off after Friar Wikerus, Prior Willem, and the other three friars in the nave who raced to confront the first demon still roaming the church? Who was the only witness?"

"Brother Kornelius? You can't be serious, Gritta!" Appel was aghast. "The poor man was so frightened when we saw him that he pissed himself."

"Piss? That could have been anything. Water. Ale. If he spilled a little ale down his leg before running into the nave, it would be the most convincing thing in the world."

"But why would Brother Kornelius do such a thing?" Efi asked, her forehead scrunched into an unfamiliar map of thoughts and questions.

"Who knows! Does a man always need a reason to do anything at all?"

"Well...yes!" Efi said. "'Tis a mortal sin to kill, and a holy man never murders without a good reason."

"I would hope a holy man never, or rarely, murders at all," Appel said. She had recovered her surprise at Gritta's accusation and was on her feet. "Gritta, you are right to suspect him. In the back halls of the church, Brother Kornelius could have dressed as a monster, frightened Friar Wikerus in the courtyard, then diverted to another room or even out of the building easily without anyone noticing. In their panic, the other friars would be thinking they had already seen him and he would be above their suspicion."

"He could have removed his costume in the cloakroom, where he claimed he hid from the monster—" Appel said.

"And then removed the disguise while everyone was in a panic," Gritta finished Appel's sentence for her. "Let us go get Friar Wikerus and Prior Willem now, before this horrible man, this tonsured monster in a gray robe, strikes again!"

"Not so fast, Gritta. It is a serious thing to accuse a man of murder," Appel said.

Gritta's expression darkened. "You had no qualms about casting accusations on my Lonel only yesterday."

"And I have learned from my hasty mistake. Before accusing anyone, we should speak directly with Brother Kornelius. He may have a perfectly reasonable explanation for himself. Besides, we are behind in our brew and must spend this day preparing a new ale for tomorrow. By the time we are finished, the brothers will be at Compline and preparing for sleep."

Gritta sulked. She felt so sure of her theory, but Appel was right. They were woefully unprepared to serve ale to their customers unless they spent the day in preparation. She could wait one more night. And if the foul man struck another victim after dark, Gritta would be justified in her suspicions. Thinking of how good it would feel to be absolutely, infallibly right – to have

Appel, Efi, and Sheriff Werner prostrate themselves before her with apologies sounded just fine to her.

"Very well then." She smiled. "But bar your door tightly tonight. Tomorrow, we shall find Brother Kornelius."

Sheriff Werner's suspect

In which Lord Frider receives a shock in his own home

L ORD FRIDER HATED LIVING in the city. Although he knew life within the sandstone walls of Colmar was safer, it was far less extravagant and much smellier than his grand château in the foothills of the Vosges mountains. When he was in his castle, there were no squeaky cartwheels and bleating herds of sheep to wake him in the morning, no incessant church bells from the competing Dominican and Franciscan friaries, no eyes peeping at the cracks in his shutters, and best of all, no stench from the filthy leather curing pits of Les Tanneurs.

He kept a steward and a full staff working at his fortress outside the walls. Even though the house was empty, there were women who washed already clean linens, men who shoveled the manure of horses that went unridden, and cooks who prepared meals for workers but no nobles. It never occurred to Lord Frider to ask or even care if his employees were also afraid of living outside the walls when there were monsters roaming the countryside. And it wouldn't really matter, for now the demons were inside the walls of the city, too. Or so the rumors claimed.

Another thing he disliked about living inside the walls was that Sheriff Werner, the red-faced, pot-bellied, self-aggrandizing rule-enforcer of the city, clearly thought the two of them were on equal footing. Never mind that Lord Frider was a cousin five-times removed from Emperor Charles IV himself, and that his great grandfather had once kissed the ring of King Henry of Luxembourg. Lord Frider had married Lady Margueritte, whose ancestry could be traced all the way back to Charlemagne, whereas Werner was merely the grandson of a pikeman who made his fortune in the Holy Land a hundred years earlier. It was insulting, but unavoidable. The holy wars in Jerusalem were an equalizer – an opportunity for a man to change his station in life, and for people with low pedigree, like Werner, to receive a title they didn't deserve. Lord Frider didn't like it one bit.

He slouched in his large wooden chair at the high table, which stood upon a raised dais in his long, narrow hall, thinking ill thoughts about life in town and the constant presence of the insufferable sheriff. The other men in the room, mostly the city council and the wealthy burghers, grew rowdy and inebriated from wine provided by Herr Schlock. It might be more interesting if there were women about, but his wife, Margueritte, and her ladies took their meals in her own quarters, as they often preferred to do when the house was full of drunk men.

Living in the city was dull indeed. There was nothing to do but drink, gossip, attend church services, and promenade on evenings when the weather was mild. In the foothills of the Vosges mountains he could hunt in his forests and watch from his tower as the fields flourished and his animals grew fat. He could see his profit growing before his eyes! He was lost in these thoughts and in his pewter cup of wine when there came a roar of astonishment among the men. Lord Frider looked up and caught his breath.

A monster pranced in the middle of the room.

Covered in dark fur, horns on its head, standing tall on two legs as a man did, it reared up and let out a roar and a snarl, then proceeded to climb atop one of the tables, overturning cups and stepping in bowls of cabbage soup. The shouts of surprise from his guests turned to screams of terror.

"It is the beast!" Lord Frider shouted. He looked around for the other able-bodied men in the great hall, and spotted Sheriff Werner, who jumped to his feet and darted from the room. In truth, fleeing the room had been Lord Frider's intention, too, but when the sheriff ran, all eyes turned to their host, and so he unsheathed his sword with a shaking hand, his arm feeling like jelly. Can a demon even be killed with a humble sword?

He heard a giggle and a few snorts, and then several of the men exploded with laughter, holding their sides and slapping their thighs. The monster pulled on its horns and off came its head – or rather, off came its mask, which was nothing more than a hollowed-out stag's skull covered with a moth-eaten pelt. The man in the monster suit dipped an elaborate bow, and the men cheered, clashing their copper cups together and sloshing ale and wine on the stone floor. Lord Frider felt his rage boiling over.

"Lock this man in my cellar and throw away the key!" he screamed. The jollity died down immediately. The other guests looked uneasily at each other.

"My lord, 'twas done in jest," said Herr Heinrik, a merchant from Strassburg. "This man meant no harm meant in it."

"No harm?" Lord Frider's voice grew low and dangerous. "The people in this city are terrified. People have died, Herr Heinrik! You apparently don't know the danger because you're merely a visiting merchant." He stabbed a finger at the offending man, who stood perfectly still, clutching the mask of his monster costume to his chest. "This fool almost lost his life at the tip of my sword. I won't hesitate to kill the beast if it presents the opportunity!" Now the room was completely quiet, save for the popping and hissing of the flaming logs in the hearth. Lord Frider surveyed the assembled men with disgust. His city house was small, the room hot and crowded. Were he back in his château, he would be able to take up his bow and ride out to hunt and cool his temper.

"You may stay here if you wish and continue with the feast. I am finished." He stomped from the room and made for the door. All he wanted was to go above stairs and rest in his bed, but he saw the rotund figure of Sheriff Werner lurking near the doorway and he stopped.

"What an admirable display of bravery, my lord!" Sheriff Werner said.

"And where were you?" Lord Frider snapped.

Sheriff Werner widened his eyes with feigned innocence. "Why, I was hurrying to assemble the militia, for it would take more than one man to subdue that beast."

Lord Frider sniffed. "Doesn't seem as if you even left the house, Werner. Take care not to cross me, or the whole city shall know of your cowardice at the next citizens' meeting."

"My lord, wait!" Sheriff Werner hurried after Lord Frider. "I have received some information about the beast that may be useful."

"Oh? Out with it, then." A sharp ache was beginning to stab between Lord Frider's temples, and the siren song of his feather mattress and the warm arms of Lisette, his favorite washerwoman, grew louder.

"I believe the creature received assistance from Lonel Leporteur."

"Who?"

"Surely you remember the son of Jorges, who was locked in the tower a few months back?"

"Jorges Leporteur, the local drunk? His son always seemed a decent young man to me. Makes a mighty fine wine cask. I have several in my cellar." Lord Frider felt his mouth begin to water at the thought of a nice, undiluted cup of wine.

"Not that one, my lord. You are thinking of Noe, one of his older brothers. Lonel is the sixth-born son of Jorges and Gritta, and a wastrel if I ever knew one. He's going to be just like his father someday, mark me."

"What evidence do you have that he is in league with the devils haunting our city? This is a serious accusation, Sheriff."

"Lonel was seen outside the walls when the two novitiates at Saint Matthieu's friary went missing, and he was also nowhere to be found inside the city when the first attack happened to the street sweeper, Arne."

"And how do you know this?"

"He was seen by Herr Furman, the carter, and also by Kamille, the pretty young pauper who lives in the wool dyers' quarter, my lord."

"So, the boy is a layabout. This doesn't mean he's an assistant of Satan."

"When Saint Matthieu's church went up in flames, I heard one of the tanner's wives in Les Tanneurs telling a neighbor she saw Lonel run to his house covered in soot, and then emerge scrubbed clean and looking guilty. He was near the fire but didn't want anyone to know about it," Sheriff Werner continued.

Lord Frider frowned. "Now that is a bit strange. Perhaps he was merely battling the flames?"

"No one saw him attempting to quench the fire. He was missing until after the friars extinguished the flames, returned to his house with face and clothes blackened by smoke, and emerged clean. The goodwives asked him if he had battled the flames and he said he knew nothing about a fire at the friary. He lied."

"Very well, Werner, you win. He may not be guilty of letting demons in the city gates, but there does seem to be plausible evidence he was near the fire and didn't want anyone to know about it."

"Shall I look into it more, my lord?"

"Might as well." Lord Frider shrugged. He didn't care much about what happened to a lazy boy in the tanners' quarters, but a fire-setter roaming about was a serious problem that needed to be addressed quickly.

"I will need your help, my lord."

"Oh, what now, Sheriff?!" The aging nobleman's patience finally snapped. "How could I possibly be a help to you? This is a civic matter. If this were any other place and not one of the emperor's ten free cities, I could assert some authority, but that was stripped from my father and me as well." The bitterness in his voice was unmistakable. Lord Frider maintained his title, his wealth, and his land, but he had no ability to compel tenants to work his fields without pay or to collect taxes from the citizens. Colmar was a free city, run by a council of upstanding citizens and guildsmen. In exchange for a donation of able-bodied men when the emperor felt a need to attack a neighboring territory, the people were left to govern themselves.

"Summon the boy's mother to you, my lord. Tell her that she and her friends should cease investigating the murder of Helmut, the shepherd boy found killed by the beast a few days back. Tell her the case has been solved and the murderer apprehended."

"Why?" Lord Frider demanded.

"Because if Lonel is guilty, his mother will tell him my men and I are looking into it and will hide her son from us."

That seemed reasonable to Lord Frider. "Very well, I will send word to her." He had edged out the door and around the building with Sheriff Werner following alongside. Now he put a foot on the first step to the second floor of the house.

Sheriff Werner bowed low – lower than necessary for a fellow member of the gentry. "And if Lonel Leporteur should come to trial, you will assist me and hold my position?"

"Yes, yes." Lord Frider would say anything at that moment to escape the sheriff.

A cask full of Kornelius

In which providence presents Gritta with an opportunity

GRITTA ROSE LATE THE next day, stretching stiffly on her straw mattress. Rosmunda, her daughter, had already fetched water from the well and set Anstett and Mattheus to work plucking weevils out of the grain for the morning's pottage. Even Jorges was gone, off to the docks on the grand canal to carry willow baskets of fish to and from the boats at the bidding of the city's ferocious fishwives.

"Heaven and hell, I've overslept," Gritta groaned, staggering to her feet. She splashed a bit of icy water on her face from the basin, plucked the straw from her hair and clothes, passed a damp cloth across her underarms and between her legs, and cleaned her teeth with her willow twig and a pinch of salt. She had just finished plaiting her hair when a firm knock on her door startled her. When she opened it, a herald stood before her, wearing the colors of Lord Frider's house. The herald took in her uncovered head and the shabbiness of her house, and his lip curled.

"I bear a message from Lord Frider. He commands you to cease your meddling in the investigation of the shepherd's death. The boy died of natural causes."

"What?!"

He continued. "If you do not stop pestering the sheriff and his men, Lord Frider has given his blessing to put you into the tower." Then without so much as a farewell, the herald turned and stomped away from her door, muttering to himself about the indignity of being sent to Les Tanneurs on such a fool's errand.

"Well!" Gritta said to herself. "If either of those old goats think I am going to just let that boy's death pass on by without any more attention, they are mistaken!" But she knew the alewives should exercise more caution from now on. She needed to tell Appel and Efi what had happened before they endangered themselves.

By the time she had eaten a piece of brown bread with butter and pinned her dingy white wimple on her head, the sun was transiting its way through the sky, and she hurried across the street, hopping the trench and pushing her way into Appel's house.

"Sorry I'm late!" she shouted. The room was empty, and so she ran up the crooked stairs that clung to the outside of the house, leading to the second floor where Appel and Efi shared a large, sagging bed. No one was there, either, but the bedclothes had been smoothed and the horsehair-stuffed bolster pillow was arranged neatly on top of the straw-stuffed mattress.

"Huh," Gritta commented to the empty room. "That looks pretty." Perhaps she should try to smooth her blankets every morning as well. Then she shrugged the idea away. The children would only mess it up.

Back in the great room of the house, Gritta sat for a while, waiting. When the women didn't appear, she put herself to work. "No sense being idle when there is money and ale to be made," she muttered. It was nearly the hour of Terce, and the unmarried men would arrive soon to take their morning portion of small ale before they set off to work. Gritta swept the floor with the twig broom, stoked the smoldering coals into a fire in the hearth, and hung a leafy oak branch on the peg next to the door – a sign to people that she was open for business and had ale to sell.

Soon, masons, glovers, plowmen, blacksmiths, and tanners walked inside, exchanging a copper coin for a pitcher of ale. Sometimes they drank it all down, but most of the men quenched their morning thirst, then poured the rest into their leather flasks to save for later. Women came too, the wives of the field workers, who would join their husbands weeding and tending to the rows of turnips and cabbages growing in neatly planted fields outside the walls. Shepherdesses, wool carters, bakers' wives, and embroiderers all came, because in Colmar, and in every city, women worked just as hard as men.

By the time the morning rush of people slowed, Gritta had collected a reassuring weight of copper coins in the cracked pottery jar they used as their bank. But Appel and Efi were still not at home. She picked up her last jug of small ale, dismayed at how light it felt. She was nearly out, and there would be another rush when the midday meal came.

In the lean-to at the back of the house, a shallow earthen ramp led down to a cellar where more barrels kept cool. She walked among them, looking at the scratch marks Appel made on the barrels with the charcoal end of a burned stick. Three marks meant strong ale, two meant medium, and one mark meant small ale – so weak and crisp that it was fit for morning consumption by men, women, and children. When she arrived at a barrel with one mark, she smiled and popped the lid off with an iron bar.

The barrel was large and only had a shallow puddle at the bottom. She scowled at it for a moment, trying to decide if it was best to sample the ale and make sure it was still fresh before going to the trouble of scooping it out, or if she should open a fresh one, when she heard someone call out in the front room.

"Hello? I say, is anyone here?"

Gritta emerged from the storeroom and froze. Standing in a shaft of light from the open door, hands tucked into his voluminous sleeves, was Brother Kornelius, the friar who discovered the second monster, and the very man she suspected of killing Helmut.

"Greetings, alewife!" he said cheerily. "I was sent here to see if you have any small ale available to sell to the friary. We discovered this morning that our stores were spoiled by worms." He wrinkled his nose. "Disgusting creatures, though God made them. The brothers drank water when they broke their fast this morning, but they will complain bitterly if there is no ale at the evening meal as well." He smiled, and Gritta narrowed her eyes at him. And then, like a bolt of lightning, an idea came to her. She curtseyed with as much deference and balance as she could muster.

"Of course, Brother. But the barrels are heavy, and I will need your help. Can you assist me? Everything is in the storeroom."

Brother Kornelius nodded and followed Gritta down the ramp into the cool, earthy-smelling room. "Ah, it is dark in here, Brother Kornelius. If you wait a moment, I will bring a rushlight." Leaving him in the cellar, she hurried out and touched the tallow-soaked end of a wheat straw to the fire and placed it in the iron holder as soon as it flared to life. Then she undid her girdle and removed her plain wooden rosary beads from where they usually hung ignored and unused. When she returned, Brother Kornelius was where she had left him, and looking uneasy.

"There now, this is much better. Hold the light, will you, Brother? I need to open this barrel and confirm the contents." She held out the rushlight, careful to make sure he could see she held her rosary in her other hand.

Brother Kornelius was clearly growing annoyed. He nodded, took the rushlight, and held it aloft while she pried the lid from the barrel. Then she let the beads slip from her grip, and they fell with a wet plop into the shallow pool of ale.

"What was that?" Brother Kornelius asked.

"Oh no, I've dropped my beads!"

"Silly woman," Brother Kornelius snorted. "Why did you not hold them tighter? Why were you holding them at all if not in prayer?"

"Ah, I am a godly woman. Always praying. Will you please get them for me, Brother? I am short and cannot reach them in the barrel."

Brother Kornelius frowned. On the one hand, he wanted to be out of this storeroom as quickly as possible, for if someone was going to accuse him of impropriety, he preferred the accusation be cast against him and the fair Frau Efi Kleven. To be accused of fornicating with the scrawny, world-weary Gritta Leporteur was an insult. On the other hand, to have prayer beads marinating in a barrel of ale was an abomination.

"Very well, but I am not much taller than you, Frau Gritta. Please hold this." He handed her the light and reached into the dark, pungent blackness of the barrel.

"Can you please hold the light higher, Frau Gritta? I cannot see anything in here," he called back. But instead of light, he felt someone lift his legs and heave him headfirst into the barrel. He heard a cackle, a scramble, and loud thump! Thump! as Gritta slammed the lid on the barrel, slipped the iron ring over the top, and pounded it into place with a wooden mallet.

"Hi! Wait! Wait, what are you doing?!" Brother Kornelius screamed.

"I know about you, Brother Kornelius!" Gritta grunted as she smacked the hammer and wooden wedge on the iron ring, pushing it down until the staves were so tight the man couldn't force the lid off from the inside.

"Frau Gritta, stop!" Brother Kornelius's voice garbled as he wiggled and squirmed, trying to right himself. The barrel was a tight fit, but he was a small man. After a few maneuvers he managed to wedge himself sideways, his neck twisted at a right angle. It was blacker than night inside his wooden prison, and he remembered with a sudden drop of breath that ale barrels were sealed with pitch, and the staves were fitted to be perfectly watertight. He began to pound on the curved walls with his knuckles, knees, elbows, and any other part of his body with enough space to move.

"I shall die! I shall not be able to breathe!" he screamed. He heard a rasping sound, and then a dim light opened above him. Gritta had augered a hole into the barrel's lid.

"There. Now stop your screaming, or you shall fall asleep and never wake up. I will be back soon with the sheriff, and your reign of terror will be over."

Brother Kornelius muttered a prayer of thanks for the hole in the barrel. "What are you talking about?" he screamed. "Whose reign of terror?"

But there was no answer. Gritta had gone.

The street sweeper's secret

In which Lonel makes a discovery, and so does Arne

Lonel kicked a stone and watched as it skittered across the dusty lane and bounced off the ankle of a finely dressed merchant who had just emerged from his shop.

"Urchin! Rabble! Go back to the reeking tanners' quarters where you belong!" the man shouted, flinging an angry gesture with one hand and clutching his knobby ankle with the other. Lonel grinned. Nothing brought a smile to his face like angering members of the privileged class.

His joy was only temporary, however. All week long his mood had been foul. His mother delighted in his efforts to help her around the aleworks, and whenever he made up his mind to simply walk away and shirk his promise, Friar Wikerus always seemed to appear, smiling and ready for an ale. But the biggest source of his annoyance was a rumor going about town that Kamille, the fairest, whose body he worshipped, whose smile he revered, was not only openly cuddling and kissing Stefan the glover but also Benno, the street sweeper's son, of all people! Just thinking about that great lumbering ox of a boy made Lonel's whole body heat with rage, until sweat pricked the skin on his back and his hands squeezed into fists.

If Lonel were a more mature young man, perhaps he would understand all this hopping from man to man as a fault in Kamille's character. But to him she was perfect, and somehow the warty old glove merchant and the bear-like street sweeper's son were fully to blame for her roving eye. He kicked another stone. Ever since Kamille moved to Colmar with her mother, Lonel had been able to do nothing else but think of her. He haunted the lanes and little squares around the wool dyers' quarter where she lived, oblivious to the people around him, thinking of her face, her body, and the feel of her sweet, plump lips pressed against his.

He adjusted the hempen sack slung over his shoulder and continued his march toward Les Tanneurs. The sack was stuffed with fragrant curls of wood shavings gleaned from his brother Noe, who was an apprentice to the cooper and always willing to set some of this woody prize aside for Lonel to sell in the market as a filler for mattresses and cushions, or as fire starter.

He let his feet carry him along for a while as his mind churned. Then he looked up, and for a moment he was confused. He stood at the entrance of a little lane that wound a crooked path to the city wall. His heart lurched. It was as if his feet had carried him to the wool dyers' quarter on their own. This part of the city was downstream from Les Tanneurs, and although the stink wasn't always as terrible, the water was far worse, for it carried the filth from the leatherworks, the dyers, and the butchers' shops through the last few feet of the city before it swept in a brown torrent through the watergate, under the wall, and out of sight.

The narrow lane was enclosed by homes – some nice, some shabby, and each with an assortment of shelters and lean-tos hanging from them like barnacles. The poor lived cheek by jowl in the windowless buildings, sleeping crammed together on the floor at night for a few coppers a month. The poorer draped old hides or panels of moldy thatch against the buildings, and they slept in the mud and standing water during the wet season and with the flies and rats during the summers.

Lonel turned to leave, ducking into a lane almost completely covered by the overhanging floors of two houses that leaned into each other as if they were trying to share a secret. A sharp, high-pitched mewling echoed in the empty lane, followed by another and another.

Kittens!

Lonel looked around. Some believed monsters brought the pestilence to Colmar, and others thought it was Jews or witches, or even cats. Lonel didn't know which was true, but he did know his mother complained mightily about mice chewing holes in the bed linens.

"A good mouser would sort us out," he whispered, "and absolve me from Friar Wikerus, no doubt." He followed the sound until he found himself standing in front of the small shack where Arne the street sweeper and his son Benno lived. Because the nearby stream often took to flooding during the spring thaw, most of the homes on the street were built above the ground on stilts. The meowing came from the inky, garbage-strewn darkness of the cavity beneath Arne's house. Lonel looked left and right. Although it was midday, there was no one around in this corner of the city. In the wealthy burgher neighborhoods, fearful residents hid, because monsters portended another wave of pestilence. But the poor who lived in the wool dyers' quarter couldn't afford fear. Men, women, and children worked in the fields, begged in the busy squares, picked rags, shoveled the public privies, or swept the streets.

Lonel dropped to his hands and knees, leaning in for a closer look, then shimmied on his belly until he was halfway beneath the house. Two iridescent orbs blinked at him in the darkness. The mother cat hissed and hunched her back over her offspring.

"Let's see them, then," Lonel grunted, reaching into the squirming nest of warm, furry bodies. "Ow!" He pulled his hand back, feeling a warm drop of blood as it dribbled to his wrist. He plunged his hand in again and was met with more stabs along his palm. "Is there one mother cat in there or three?" he growled.

Reaching in one last time, his hand closed around something hard and sharp. He squinted, and in the barest bit of daylight, he saw the glimmer of a knife. The kittens now forgotten, Lonel carefully tried to pick it up. It wasn't a knife he saw, but a cluster of them – or rather, pieces of sharpened and polished bone inexpertly sewn onto a shabby old leather hide. With a mighty heave, he pulled the hide from beneath the house, scooting his body backwards until he emerged, covered in mud and cobwebs. When he finally got a good look at what he had found beneath the house, he dropped it as if it were a hot coal from the hearth. In his mind spun all the names of unholy beasts he knew. Manticore? Revenant? Cynocephalus? Dragon? He didn't know which demon skin he held in his hands, but it was immediately obvious to him that the monster terrorizing the city was nothing more than an infidel piece of costumery.

Looking around again and seeing no witnesses, Lonel picked up the costume and inspected it. Poorly constructed and shedding bits of flotsam, the costume wasn't convincing in the daylight, but with its spikes and terrible horns he could see how it had frightened men senseless when they encountered it in the dark. He looked up at the house on stilts, and a wicked thought played through his mind. All his intentions of bringing home a kitten to catch mice for his mother vanished. Lonel was always interested in a good trick, after all, and this was by far the best bit of mischief he had ever seen.

"Whoever has possession of this disguise would have immense power over the city indeed," he whispered to himself. "Wouldn't matter if that man were rich or poor."

A short time later, he emerged from the dark street, sack slung on his back, whistling, and greeting one of the young Franciscan friars who hurried toward someone in need. For the first time in many months, he felt light. As if he had done the right thing, finally.

Arne trudged back to his shabby house in the wool dyers' district, his back and limbs aching. He dragged his cart, emptied of filth but still smelling foul, behind him. His spade, fork, and collection of willow-twig brooms rattled as he pulled the wain through the rutted streets and across the wastewater ditches.

Benno was supposed to help him; supposed to do the shoveling and cart-hauling so Arne, in his old age, would only need to pass his broom across the streets and doorsteps, exchanging gossip with the tradesmen and smoothing the dust, which always made everything look clean and neat.

"Obsessed with that woman, he is," Arne muttered. "But no marriage prospects unless he tidies up. Messy hair. Filthy clothes. The boy needs to learn how to care for himself!" he shouted the last part aloud. A nearby door opened, and a wet nurse with a baby on her hip peeked out.

"What are you staring at, ya milch cow?" Arne yelled, and the girl slammed the door shut.

He picked up the two wooden shafts and heaved, dragging the cart behind him. In the narrow lane, the wooden sideboards scraped their way across the houses, sending showers of plaster to the ground. A faint track ran across the front of all the houses on either side of the road, etching a little deeper each time Arne went by. When he arrived at his little hovel, he shoved the cart against a wall and stashed his tools in the space beneath the house where the wooden stilts elevated it from the street. A sharp yowl rose as he disturbed a mother cat and her nest of kittens.

"Take yer cat family elsewhere if you don't want to sit with my brooms, you pest!" he hollered. All he wanted was a bowl of pottage in one hand and a cup of ale in the other, and hopefully a fire to warm himself. If Benno was out carousing with his friends and that loose woman, he probably came home so drunk he couldn't cook, and this thought made Arne even angrier.

He slammed the door open. Inside, it was dark and damp. No fire burning, no smell of food cooking. "The Devil and his demons take the boy," he snarled. "Don't know why I save my silver for such an oaf."

The coals of the fire were still covered with stones from the river to keep any stray embers from sending the whole building up in flames as they rose through the hole in the thatch. Newfangled hearths and their associated chimneys were a luxury Arne didn't need. A fire circle and smoke hole had been good enough for his father, and so it was good enough for him.

For a moment his thoughts drifted to his brief stay at Frau Appel's house. She had a hearth and chimney, and a large iron pot hanging on a hook that could swing over the flames. She didn't have to put her cookpot directly on the coals, as he did, and therefore she made a fine pottage, not blackened on the bottom. He sighed, remembering the soft knitted blanket he slept under on the bench near her window.

And then she unceremoniously evicted him.

"That old widow didn't know a good thing when she saw it," he grumbled. "Could have had me as her husband and never had to worry about not having a man about the house again."

He groped in the dark for the twisted length of iron they used as a shovel to pull the rocks from the fire. Then he tossed some straws onto the coals and blew on them gently until they flickered and burst into flame.

In that brief moment of light he saw Benno's lifeless face, eyes staring up at the ceiling.

Accusations

In which a basket of turnips facilitates an escape

Sheriff Werner marched through the streets of Colmar, navigating his way toward Trench Lane in Les Tanneurs with an uncharacteristic spring in his step. Next to him, Brother Tacitus glided on long legs, his black robes swishing. On his feet he wore makeshift sandals of straw and hemp rope. Two guards with helmets and spears marched behind, and taking up the rear trudged Brother Wikerus, his head down and his hands clasped around his plain wooden cross. Although many Franciscan shoes had also been stolen from the friary at Saint Matthieu's, Wikerus was still in possession of his simple leather slippers, and with them, he dragged his feet.

They followed the trench until they reached the tumbledown home of the Leporteur family. The door stood wide open, and inside, a girl of about fifteen sat on a bench near the window, humming and knitting a stocking from a skein of undyed wool. On the floor, a dirty-faced toddler played at her feet with a few extra balls of yarn. Brother Tacitus cleared his throat loudly and the girl jumped, dropping her work. Brother Wikerus pushed his way through the guards and elbowed the sheriff aside to stand next to Brother Tacitus.

"Oh!" the girl sighed. "Brother Wikerus, it's you. I thought we were in trouble for some reason. Because, you know, there are some men in this city who will always accuse Ma and Pa of crimes they didn't commit." She shot a pointed look at Sheriff Werner, who didn't seem to notice or care about the scorn of a teenager.

Well done, Rosmunda, Brother Wikerus thought. You're finally starting to show some spirit. His blue eyes, earlier so sad and downcast, twinkled at her. He spoke.

"Rosmunda, is your mother around?"

"What Friar Wikerus meant to ask is whether your brother is around," Sheriff Werner corrected him.

"Depends," Rosmunda shot back. She did not elucidate what it depended on, forcing the sheriff to ask, his voice dripping with impatience. "What does it depend on, girl?"

"Well, I have eight brothers. Do you mean Michel? Noe? Or do you mean Geld, Urbe, Egilhard, Anstett, Mattheus, or Lonel?"

"I think you know that if the sheriff comes looking for one of your brothers, it is always Lonel he seeks," Brother Tacitus commented dryly. "Since Lonel is not reliably employed, we thought we might find him here."

"Lonel only takes his meals here and spends the rest of his days out of the house, as he should." Rosmunda sniffed. Then she marched back to her bench and took up her knitting. "My mother is across the lane. You can speak to her about it."

On the other side of the trench, in Appel's low-ceilinged front room, Gritta was humming a tune and slowly stirring the gruit herbs into a very large pot of boiling wort. She sat on a three-legged stool with a dreamy look on her face, which promptly turned to a scowl when Sheriff Werner and Brother Tacitus darkened the doorway.

"What do you lot want? The last time I saw Jorges you had him tied to the pillory for public drunkenness, and he can't have done anything too terrible with both his arms trussed over his head, now, could he?"

"It is Lonel we seek, Frau Gritta," Sheriff Werner told her.

Gritta nodded, her shoulders slumped in resignation. "So it begins," she said. "What has he done? Put honey on the privy seat? Tied all the city cats together by their tails? Or perhaps you're here because you suspect he is the one who stole the shoes of all the Dominican friars?"

The last comment brought a deep frown from Brother Tacitus. His makeshift sandals of straw and hemp left a trail of debris wherever he walked. "I knew it!" he hissed. "I had no proof, but I just knew it was he who stole our shoes from the friary. And from the Franciscans, too!"

"Well, don't get too excited, Brother, for I've seen no shoes near my house, so if Lonel took them, the secret of their location will go with him to his grave."

"Frau Gritta, Lonel is closer to the grave than you may think. Please, we must find him," Brother Wikerus pleaded with her.

Gritta dropped her mash paddle. As it slipped beneath the roiling brown liquid, she clasped her hands at her heart.

"Something has happened to him! Did someone hurt him? What happened?"

"It's not a question of someone hurting him, Frau Gritta," Sheriff Werner said, his close-set eyes glowing with triumph. "It's a question of him stabbing and murdering Benno, son of Arne the street sweeper."

Gritta's mouth hung open in shock. Then she threw her head back and laughed. "As if my Lonel, who doesn't have the stomach to slaughter a chicken for the pot, could kill a man! Ah, Sheriff, there are days when you do give me a good fright. You really had me worried for a moment! Go on and seek someone who thirsts for blood. The only thing Lonel thirsts for is a full cup of wine and a plump fraulein on his knee."

"This is no laughing matter, Frau Gritta. A young man is dead, and your son is the most likely killer."

"What proof do you have that Lonel is involved in this? How dare you cast accusations at my son!"

Sheriff Werner reached into his leather purse and drew out an object with a flourish, his excitement barely concealed. It was the scarlet handkerchief bordered with black embroidered roses that Lonel always wore at his belt, given to him by his faithless lover, Kamille. Gritta recognized it and felt her heart sink. Brother Tacitus watched impassively, and Brother Wikerus hung his head.

"Ah," the sheriff said, "you've seen this before, have you? Lonel's useless friends tell me he wears it on his belt and never removes it. So how did this handkerchief end up inside the house of Arne the street sweeper, next to his dead son?"

Outside, a man whistled a jaunty tune, and as the song drew closer, Gritta realized with rising panic that it was Lonel's voice. She opened her mouth to shout out a warning to him, but Sheriff Werner clapped a meaty fist across her lips and wrapped another arm around her chest before she had a chance to scream.

"Oh no you don't," he snarled in her ear, his breath so hot and rank she could have sworn she smelled it through her eyeballs. "I'll not have you giving the warning shout."

Lonel appeared, carrying a large basket of vegetables. He stopped in the doorway, taking in the sight of the friars, the city guards, and his mother struggling in the arms of the sheriff. But one glance was all Sheriff Werner needed. As soon as he looked at Lonel's belt and saw the handkerchief was missing, he knew it was as good as an admission of guilt. "Take him!" he screamed at the two guards.

Lonel didn't waste the blink of an eye. He tipped the basket of vegetables, sending turnips bouncing and rolling in all directions. One of the guards slipped and fell on a root, which was woody and hard from its long stay in the ground over the winter. The other guard, standing inside the house with the sheriff, leapt into action, but tripped over Friar Wikerus's foot as he tried to run through the door. Lonel was off as fast as a rabbit, hopping stone fences and darting around the corner of a stable with the efficiency of a boy who has spent many of his days picking pockets and stealing pears from stalls in the market.

"Well, we'll never see him again," Brother Tacitus drawled. He had watched the clumsy acrobatics of the guards with an expressionless face. "I must return to the friary. The brothers of Saint Dominic are under my supervision while Father Konrad is away, and as their spiritual leader it is my duty to ensure they follow God's law at all times."

Sheriff Werner and the guards looked at Brother Tacitus with a renewed sense of awe. None of them noticed Friar Wikerus rolling his eyes. Then the sheriff turned to his guards and scowled. "I asked you two to accompany me because I thought you were the least likely to cock it all up, but since neither of you can stand on your own feet, I now see it would be better if I asked for help from a band of minstrels!"

"He tripped me!" one of the guards shouted, pointing at Brother Wikerus.

"True, you fell across my foot, but as a man of God I would never dream of intentionally doing anything to hinder the investigation into a murder such as this," Wikerus said.

Sheriff Werner shoved his sullen guard through the door. "Get out," he growled. "Frau Gritta, we will search your house for the weapon used to kill Benno the street sweeper's son."

Gritta smothered the fire while Friar Wikerus waited. She tied her wimple over her head, closed Appel's door, and called out to a young boy who was skipping down the lane.

"Young man, please find Frau Appel Schneider and Frau Efi Kleven and tell them to come home at once. Seek them at the grain merchant. Tell them Frau Gritta sent you and promised you would receive a copper for delivering the message."

The little boy scampered off, and Gritta stepped over the trench toward her house. She gave Brother Wikerus a sidelong look. "I know it was you who tripped the guard, Brother Wikerus," she said under her breath.

Brother Wikerus maintained his straight face, with only the slightest hint of a smile at the corner of his mouth. "I did nothing of the sort, Frau Gritta," he muttered. "But 'tis true, the man fell over my foot, and perhaps, as I think back on the situation, I should have stepped back a little further to let him through."

"Well, I thank you all the same. It gave Lonel a chance to make his escape."

Brother Wikerus turned to Gritta now, his blue eyes serious. "Frau Gritta, I can attest, as others have, that Lonel's been acting strangely lately."

"Lonel is always strange, Friar. He's a strange young man indeed," Gritta shot back. "Too much like his father."

The sheriff and his two men were not inside the Leporteur house, but Rosmunda was there, her arms crossed, staring angrily from her chair near the fire.

"Well, girl, did three men come here to search for your brother?" Gritta asked.

"Yes, Ma, they went out behind the garden," she said. Brother Wikerus could see her eyes were red from crying.

"Whatever is the matter?" Gritta asked. Her Rosmunda was always calm and kind, not like this angry young woman she saw sitting before her.

"Oh, Ma, what do they want? Why do they not leave us alone?!"

"Peace, Rosmunda. I am sure they will find nothing of interest to them," Brother Wikerus said. Before Rosmunda could answer, they heard a cry from outside the house. Gritta, Rosmunda, and Friar Wikerus hurried to the back door that led through the stable, with little Wina toddling after them on chubby bare feet.

Sheriff Werner's two guards crouched on their hands and knees, rooting around through a pile of straw that Jorges had put up for the goat. Sheriff Werner was bending over, examining an object on the ground.

"What news, Sheriff?" Brother Wikerus called out, and then he stopped, the color draining from his face. Sheriff Werner hefted the object and held it aloft. Dozens of blades, some dull and carved from bone, others glinting in the sun, tinkled against each other. It was a cloak of leather and blades with a skeletal head and rotting antlers on top. They had found the second monster.

Strange brew

In which one mystery is solved

Friar Wikerus hurried through the winding streets of Colmar from Saint Matthieu's friary to Les Tanneurs. Before the horrific and unholy murders, these avenues and squares would be clogged with throngs of people – women on their way to market with their children in tow, girls with long willow switches herding flocks of geese to the banks of the streams, wooly barricades of complaining sheep on their way to the slaughterhouse, all greeting each other, squabbling, laughing, and making a general noise. That lively chaos was only a memory, now.

News of Benno the street sweeper's murder quickly swept through the city, and once again the avenues and alleys were empty, save for a few souls who walked quickly, glancing behind them as they traversed the city on essential errands. The horrors of the pestilence haunted the people of Colmar. Their city suffered as much as any other in the green valley between the Rhine and the Vosges mountains, but the mystery, the unknowable source and then disappearance of the disease was like an illness of its own. Suspicion and fear ate at the minds of the survivors, and they continued to quest for a reason to explain what had happened. Monsters. Witches. The consequences of their own sin. Any could be true, and so all should be believed.

Wikerus felt his own mind was haunted, too. Amidst the death from the unseen pestilence that spread from home to home, taking some to the grave and leaving others, his younger brother had drowned in the Rhine. Drowned. A life untouched by the pestilence, but lost nonetheless.

He shook his head. Why this memory of his brother's death had plagued him so much lately, he didn't know. As he drew closer to Les Tanneurs, the presence of people in the streets increased, which brought a small smile to his face. Hiding from monsters behind closed doors was a privilege of the wealthy. Here, there was work to be done – hides to dye and tan, bread to bake, alms to be gathered. He heard snatches of gossip from the men and women who gathered to talk in small clusters.

"Did you hear about the street sweeper's son?"

"They say the old man is mad with grief."

"...had a body covered with blades, and tall antlers on its head, it did! This is a different monster! A second one!"

Well, thought Friar Wikerus. *At least the news about Brother Kornelius hasn't gotten out yet.*

When the young monk didn't show up for the evening meal, Friar Wikerus and the other brothers found it suspicious. Prior Willem paced the length of the dining hall and wrung his hands, snapping at people. But it wasn't until Brother Kornelius failed to appear at Vespers that the prior demanded a search of the entire friary. By that time, it was late in the evening, and they couldn't go out into the streets to search for their missing comrade until the next morning. The sheriff was summoned, and his men spread out through the city, knocking on doors and searching in stables. Although they maintained an optimistic tone, everyone knew without saying it aloud that they were most likely searching for a body. The friary had lost two novices and now a friar. It was a sobering mystery, and secretly every man wondered what sin had been committed by one of their number to incur such wrath from God upon them.

Friar Wikerus found it quite amazing that news of Brother Kornelius's disappearance hadn't spread further, for no one could rely on the sheriff or any of the men working for him to be discreet. He pondered this as he entered the square in Les Tanneurs. He stood still and scanned the faces in the sparse crowd. Mostly goodwives were out and about, assisting their husbands in the family business, minding children, or gathered on benches in front of their homes to stitch or knit and talk with neighbors – but always near their open doors, should they need to flee inside. There were no other friars present – not even Brother Tacitus.

He went from door to door for a while, visiting the occupants of each house under the guise of checking on their physical and spiritual health. He prayed with a few frightened tanner's wives, heard three confessions, and boiled some broth for an old man afflicted with swollen joints. He dandled babies on his knees and rolled up his sleeves to help a woman lift baskets of clean wet linens, ready to hang in the sun. All the while he casually asked after Brother Kornelius, but each person told him he was the first friar to visit them that day. He supposed Brother Tacitus was staying away until he could find replacement footwear.

Friar Wikerus saved Gritta and Appel's houses for last. As usual, Gritta was across the street in Appel's larger, cleaner home. All her younger children were there with her, getting underfoot while the three alewives attempted to brew a small ale.

"Honestly, I am surprised," Efi said as she poured malted grain onto a large cloth so she could scan it for grubs and rodent droppings. "With so many people staying in their homes, I thought we would sell less small ale, not more."

Appel grunted a response. "Could be because it's harder to find grain and gruit. No one is malting. We were lucky to get this malt, for it was the last in the malting house and it came at a dear price. We shall have to charge twice as much for small ale until it is safe for people to go out of their homes again." She looked up when Friar Wikerus walked into the house, and smiled. "Good morning, Friar!"

"Greetings, alewives! I had come for a drink, but it sounds as if you have nothing left but strong ale, although I admit it would be nice to forget my troubles, even at this early hour."

"All our customers today have demanded strong brew to ease their minds, but I think there's still a finger's worth of small ale in the cask. What troubles you, Friar Wikerus? Unless it is merely the same threat of monsters and demons worrying all of us. The news about Arne's son is tragic, indeed, though it is vexing that Lonel is blamed for it," Appel said. She paused as an enormous yawn passed across her face. Nearby, Efi also yawned.

"Well! Was it a poor night's sleep for the two of you?" Friar Wikerus asked.

Appel nodded. "Noises all through the night, Friar. Efi and I were above stairs when we heard all manner of poundings and knocking. We thought it was a demon trying to get into the house, as if it hadn't taken its fill of evil out on Benno. But we couldn't find anything wrong in the house, and so—"

"The tanner's assistant who lives next door just got married!" Efi chirped. "And Appel said she knew the sounds of a new married couple when she heard them."

Gritta, who had been wiping dirt from little Wina's face, stopped to looked at Efi, her eyes wide.

"Hush, girl, you're being crude!" Appel snapped at Efi. "Gritta, what is wrong with you? You are as pale as a bowl of milk."

"Nothing," Gritta muttered.

Brother Wikerus was blushing from the bottom of his throat to the top of his shorn head, and he dearly wanted to change the subject. "Perhaps I will have a bit of that small ale you have in the cask. I suddenly feel very thirsty indeed."

"I'll get it," Efi said, picking up a stoneware pitcher.

Gritta jumped to her feet. "I'll take care of it, Efi." At her ankles, Wina screamed and raised her arms for her mother to pick her up.

"It's no trouble, Gritta. You have your hands full," Efi said, and she turned and skipped to the storeroom.

Gritta followed, grabbing her by the elbow. "It's just that the ale remaining in the cask is spoilt. We didn't sell it fast enough."

"Oh dear," Appel said, rising to her feet. "We shall have to scour the cask before we can reuse it." She began to walk to the storeroom after Efi.

"No!" Gritta shouted, and everyone stopped to stare at her.

"Whatever is the matter with you, Gritta?" Appel demanded.

"Wait," Friar Wikerus said. "Did you hear something?"

They all stood perfectly still, listening. All except for Gritta, who bustled around the room, shoving her shawl and Wina's wooden toys into her basket. "Well then, I think it best that the children and I return to our home now," she said loudly.

"Why, it's the same sound we heard last night. I wish those two newlyweds would find some other ways to fill their time," Appel said with a smirk.

"No," said Friar Wikerus. "It's not coming from outside the house." He began to walk around the room, listening at the walls.

"Friar, would you mind joining me across the lane? I need to talk to you about, uh...spiritual things," Gritta said, again louder than necessary.

But Friar Wikerus didn't appear to hear her. "Do you hear someone singing?" he asked.

"Friar? Friar! I must make a confession! Please accompany me to my house so I may confess to the unbearably heavy sins weighing upon my soul!" Gritta was shouting now.

Friar Wikerus continued to move around the house, and Appel was staring at Gritta, a frown on her face, her hands on her hips.

"It's coming from here," said Friar Wikerus, pointing to the lean-to door that led to the storeroom.

Appel marched to the door and wrenched it open. Sure enough, they heard banging coming from the darkness below. And the muffled sounds of a tavern song.

"Bring us in no bacon, for that is passing fat,
But bring us in good ale, and give us enough of that;
And bring us in good ale, good ale, and bring us in good ale,
For our blessed Lady's sake, bring us in good aaaale!"

Friar Wikerus hurried down the gangway and called for a light. Efi brought a rushlight from the fire, and they crowded into the little earthen hole where they kept the cheeses and the ales cool.

"Why, it's coming from a cask!" Efi gasped.

"Quick! Bring me a pry bar!" Appel called to Gritta. But Gritta was paler than ever. She stood frozen in place at the top of the earthen ramp to the storeroom, wringing her hands. Appel located her hammer and a wedge of iron, handing them to Friar Wikerus, who quickly pried the lid from the large cask. "By God's toenails!" he shouted. "Brother Kornelius!"

"Bring us in no butter, for therein are many hairs. Nor bring us in no piggies flesh, for that will make us bears; but bring us in good ale, good ale, and bring us in good aaale!" Brother Kornelius sang out. "'Tis lovely to see your face, Brother Wikerus," he slurred. "Has anyone ever told you that you have very fine eyebrows?"

"Help me lift him," Brother Wikerus said, grasping Brother Kornelius beneath the arms. He and Appel heaved, but Brother Kornelius was floppy from drink, and he tipped the entire barrel on its side, spilling himself onto the ground. A small trickle of ale came out after him.

"How much of my ale did you drink, Brother Kornelius?" Appel said. "There should have been at least two pitchers' worth in there still!"

Brother Kornelius struggled to his feet, groaning as he stretched out his cramped limbs. "I drank the perfect – hic! – amount, Frau Efi, er, Frau Appel," he slurred. "Where is the fair Efi? I would like to plant a kiss of friendship upon her mouth."

"Brother Kornelius," Efi gasped. "How did you get inside our ale barrel? And so tightly sealed!"

Brother Kornelius was struggling to keep his gaze straight. He lifted an unsteady hand and pointed at Gritta, who remained rooted to her spot above them at the storeroom door. "Wench that she is! But I cannot be too upset. I slept as much as I pleased, and I had a fine amount of ale to soothe my worries. I shall be glad to come and stay in one of your ale casks another time soon, Frau Gritta!"

"Please take him back to the friary, Brother Wikerus," Appel said, and she turned a furious gaze on Gritta, who suddenly found her feet and began to dart about the room.

"Come, children!" Gritta said. "This is not a sight fit for young 'uns!"

Appel charged up the earthen ramp and stood at the doorway, barring the exit. "Just you try and leave my house without telling me why you sealed a Franciscan friar into an ale cask, Gritta Leporteur!"

Gritta hung her head. "I thought him guilty of impersonating a demon."

"And you never thought to tell any of us? This man could have died in my storeroom!"

"Ah, but I would have died with my belly full of your delicious ale, Frau Gritta!" Brother Kornelius called out, followed by a flurry of hiccoughs and belches.

Brother Wikerus slung Brother Kornelius's arm around his shoulder and escorted the inebriated friar from the house. As they walked away, the women could hear Brother Kornelius chattering. "Has anyone ever told you, Wikerus, that you have a nice pair of ankles?"

"Truth is, when news of Benno's murder got out, and with Sheriff Werner chasing after my Lonel, I forgot about Brother Kornelius," Gritta said, hanging her head. Appel had never seen her old friend look so contrite.

"This is bad, Gritta." Appel felt hopeless. "Why can we not go more than a few weeks before you or your family do something to break the law? When Prior Willem and Sheriff Werner hear about this, you shall be placed in the stocks."

"Ah well, Jorges is sure to be in the stocks, too, as he is every week. Maybe I'll have some time to spend with him. Have a real conversation, you know? Without all the children around."

"Oh yes, just like the time the two of you were locked in the tower together!" Efi said. "It was a nice break for the both of you."

Gritta beamed.

Mummery

In which it's finally time to take a close look at the monster

Brother Kornelius stared at the monster costume laid out on the table in Sheriff Werner's great room. Somehow, in its shapeless form without the structure of limbs, it looked even more terrifying than the last time he beheld it as it stalked the halls of Saint Matthieu's friary the night when the shepherd was found dead. He frowned deeply. It had been one day since Brother Wikerus freed him from the ale cask in Appel Schneider's storeroom, and his head still ached from the quantity of ale he had drunk from the very same barrel. He closed his eyes for a moment, hating the memory. He drank ale that he had been sitting in, and all because of this piece of badly sewn mummery set out before him.

"Well, Brother Kornelius? Do you recognize this or not? Have you lost your power of speech?" Sheriff Werner asked.

Brother Kornelius jerked his eyes open. "Indeed, it looks like the monster, but how can it be? What I saw stood on two legs and scaled the wall of the courtyard as easily as if it were climbing an apple tree. This is merely the husk of the beast."

"A husk indeed. It is a mummer's trick, also known as a disguise. What you saw at Saint Matthieu's was no demon, it was a man wearing the skin of one," Lord Frider said. He also looked at the disguise laid out on the table and shivered at the very malice of the thing.

Brother Wikerus examined the costume, feeling the crackling stiffness of the poor-quality leather and squinting at the bits of twine that fastened the knives, shards of bone, and other flotsam at the sleeves. "The skin of some poor beast, perhaps a pig, who gave up its life only to have its carcass badly tanned. This isn't even good enough to be used for sandal leather."

"Considering the time you spend in Les Tanneurs, I suppose you would know, wouldn't you?" Brother Tacitus said acidly. He had also been summoned as an extra spiritual layer in case the inanimate cloak suddenly sprang to life and required the strength of three holy men.

"Prior Konrad assigned you to minister to Les Tanneurs since I left Saint Martin's, Tacitus. Surely you took the time to understand the details of the tanners' work, as I did when I started ministering to that neighborhood, yes?" Brother Wikerus said as he leaned in for a closer look at the cloak's hood. A hollowed-out stag's skull, complete with a pocked set of antlers, topped the spiky cloak. Harmless the disguise may be, but it certainly looked unsettling.

Tacitus sniffed, and Wikerus spoke quickly so his rival wouldn't have an opportunity to follow up with another critical speech about Les Tanneurs. "This leather is unevenly tanned and scraped. It's stiffer in some places than others, and see here

– some bits of hair still cling to the hide. It was not done by one of our tanners, that is for sure."

"So it was brought into Colmar from the outside?" Lord Frider asked. "Where would Lonel Leporteur get his hands on something like this?"

"Lonel is a resourceful ne'er-do-well, who is frequently seen outside the walls, and even in other cities. He could have obtained this at any time in the last year," Sheriff Werner responded. Brother Wikerus despaired, as he also knew this to be true. Although no one had yet found Lonel, it was only a matter of time. The guards had been put on alert at all the gates, and extra men patrolled the posterns that punctuated the walls. In order to spread te word, the sheriff dispatched several of his men and the city herald to remind everyone to be on the lookout for Gritta's sixth-born son. The boy couldn't stay hidden forever.

Sheriff Werner dismissed Brother Kornelius, who crossed himself and whispered a prayer as he walked from the room. He was the third witness they had seen that day. Earlier, they met with two goodwives from the slum where Arne and Benno lived, who both claimed they saw a young man of about eighteen matching Lonel's description slinking around with a large sack over his shoulder. Large enough to carry a cloak with a stag's skull inside.

"What will happen to the boy when he is found? Will you place him in the tower to await a trial?" Brother Wikerus asked.

Sheriff Werner shrugged. "I suppose he does need a trial, but I will insist it happens quickly. We all know Lonel Leporteur to be a trickster and that you are his mother's friend, but this is serious, Brother. Between the multiple witnesses who confirmed they saw him loitering around Arne and Benno's house, the red handkerchief given to him by Kamille, the discovery of the monster disguise in the pile of straw in Les tanneurs, and the fact that he ran from me...well, I think it is clear to everyone that Lonel is guilty of murdering at least one person, if not more. After all, there's still the mystery of Helmut the shepherd...and the two dead novices."

"Lonel was at Herr Schlock's wynstube the night Helmut died. And perhaps Ulf and Jean-Louis survived. After all, no bodies were found, only their cloaks," Wikerus whispered, but Lord Frider shook his head.

"If two naked novices were tramping around the roads, we would have heard about it. Prior Willem tells me you searched night and day for those boys, and you are to be commended. But they are dead, Friar. Their families have been informed."

Brother Wikerus felt his heart sinking. He still dared to hope that Ulf and Jean-Louis escaped somehow, but Lord Frider's stark words stung. And to think that it could have been Lonel who killed them! Despite Lonel's mischief, Wikerus liked the boy. He was a scoundrel, like his father, but a lovable one.

"Well, I must go. After all, there are other novices in my care, and they need guidance and protection more than ever," Wikerus said. He wanted to be as far away from Brother Tacitus and the menacing monster disguise as possible.

He wandered the streets for a while, barely looking up as people called out their greetings to him, until he realized his feet had walked him to Trench Lane and the threshold of Frau Appel Schneider.

"Hello?" he asked, peeking through the open door. Appel and Efi both stood at the hearth, hovering near a large black pot which stood on iron legs over a roaring blaze. They each had their skirts tied up around their knees, wimples off, and took turns pushing the contents of the pot with a long paddle.

"Ah, greetings, Friar," Appel said, but her voice lacked its usual cheerfulness. "If you seek Gritta, she is at home right now with her children. The evidence of guilt against Lonel has hit her hard, Brother Wikerus, and she grieves even though Lonel is still alive and at large in the city somewhere. And, I suspect she may be feeling guilty and ashamed about her treatment of Brother Kornelius, too."

Friar Wikerus sat heavily on the bench at the table. "If Lonel didn't kill Benno, he will have a hard time proving it wasn't him. Witnesses have come forward, and the handkerchief found near Benno's body is like a damning mark upon his face. Frau Appel, we should have listened to you. All along you suspected Lonel."

Appel stopped her work and wiped at her damp brow. "And I have hated myself for even uttering my suspicions out loud. Gritta has rekindled her anger at me."

"Gritta is angry at everyone, Appel, not just you." He sniffed the air and screwed up his face. "I say, what is it you're brewing today? It smells as foul as a vat of boiled hop flowers."

Efi plunged the paddle into the pot and strained to lift something out. Her face flushed from the exertion, and her lovely golden curls clung to her neck in damp tendrils. Appel hurried over and helped, and together they heaved something dark and dripping from the pot. "Today, Friar Wikerus, we brew laundry. 'Tis time we wash the linens and stitch up all the holes now that spring is well upon us."

Brother Wikerus grinned. "Of course! I forgot you also must take time from your work as Colmar's most talented brewsters, to do mundane tasks like laundry."

Appel and Efi didn't share in his mirth.

"And we cook our meals, distribute the leftovers to the poor, change the straw on the floors, soak some of those straws in tallow for rushlights, weave cloth and knit blankets, grow vegetables, tend to the hens, and milk the goats. And across the lane from us, Frau Gritta does all those things too, while mothering twelve children and her drunk husband."

For a moment, Brother Wikerus felt his ire rising. A scripture verse or two, admonishing women to be cheerful in their work, rose and then died on his lips. At the friary, the brothers shared the labor, and their servants took care of everything else. "It is immense, the work you three must do every day, Frau Appel. You have my respect and admiration. You too, Frau Efi."

Outside they heard the tromp of many booted feet and saw some of Sheriff Werner's guards walk past. With their heads high and chins jutting out as they strutted, they looked like a gaggle of geese.

"Searching for Lonel," Appel sighed. "They have been at it all day. I doubt the lad would be foolish enough to return to his own neighborhood after all that's happened."

They watched as the men followed the trench and disappeared around the corner, their spear tips flashing in the spring sun. Brother Wikerus looked across the street at the shabby sloping walls of Gritta's house. The door and the shutters were firmly closed against the neighborhood. Normally, Anstett and Mattheus, her twins, would be playing or causing mischief somewhere nearby, the door would be open, and the sound of Rosmunda's singing would drift from inside. Brother Wikerus thought it looked as if someone had died.

The church bell at Saint Matthieu's rang out and kept ringing with increasing urgency. Friar Wikerus felt his scalp prickle. People emerged from their homes and shops, all with their faces turned in the direction of the church. Friar Wikerus scanned the sky but could see no plume of smoke rising and he heard no screams.

Appel and Efi walked into the street and looked toward the sky too, and Gritta's door creaked open. Jorges shuffled outside in his stockinged feet, squinting toward the church. People were beginning to hurry now, closing their doors, grabbing shawls, and a few took buckets with them in case there indeed was a fire that required attention. Appel saw her neighbor Frau Lena bustling past, holding the hem of her skirt to keep it out of the dust.

"What news, Lena?"

"They've found him! Lonel, the murderer of Colmar, was apprehended, and they are calling everyone to a public hearing."

Efi gasped, covering her mouth with her hands, and Appel looked up at Gritta's house. Gritta stood in the doorway, hands braced against the lintel, looking for all the world like she would collapse. For a moment, the two women stared at each other. Then Gritta retreated into the darkness of her home and shut the door against the sound of the bells.

Les Tanneurs on trial

Where a pattern in Sheriff Werner's accusations emerges

THERE WAS EXCITEMENT IN the air at the great wine warehouse that also served as a community gathering place in Colmar when a large crowd was expected. Sheriff Werner had dressed smartly this evening, in a dark brown velvet cotte with a braided leather belt girded low about his waist. His hands were sheathed in calfskin gloves of dyed red leather that matched his point-toed shoes. Standing next to him, Lord Frider looked almost shabby, for his velvet cotte hadn't been brushed and had bits of white hair from the coat of his horse stuck to it. The fact that the nobleman looked insufficiently grand next to the sheriff vexed him, and he had turned his mouth down in a deep frown, which hid behind his gray-flecked beard.

A large crowd of cityfolk faced the two men, and the mood in the room was as tense as a lute string waiting to be plucked. Word had spread that one of the demons was nothing but a ruse, and by Lonel Leporteur, son of the town inebriate, no less. The fear of stepping out of their homes had cost them time, productivity, and money, and the irritated and embarrassed citizens of Colmar were prepared to take justice into their own hands. They wanted as much revenge as the law would allow.

Sheriff Werner observed their unrest, heard the buzz of angry chatter in the room, and smirked. He turned and grasped a nearby rope and pulled. Earlier in the day he had tossed the rope over a high beam in the warehouse and tied the antler-headed demon costume to one end. As he hoisted it up above the crowd, it swung like a man hanging from a gallows, and the room roiled. Some screamed and others tried to run for the exits. But many shook their fists and demanded Lonel's neck be placed in the noose instead.

These theatrics did not impress Lord Frider. He raised his hands and signaled for quiet. As the din slowly died down, he arranged his features into a stern mask of rebuke and condescension.

"Well, here we find ourselves once again, and in the presence of the very monster you all feared," he said, glancing up at the costume swinging over his head with its many sharp objects tinkling. "I hope you have learned at last that you need not trust every rumor you hear."

His comments were met with hostile silence. If he expected to receive affirmation for telling the people of Colmar they were foolish for believing in monsters, he was wrong. Any hint of a supernatural beast capable of dragging a man to hell, or acting as a herald of another great mortality, would be taken seriously.

Lord Frider didn't much care what the people of Colmar thought about him, but he greatly disliked having his fatherly admonition fall flat. He cleared his throat. "Well then, bring out the accused and let the jurors question him."

A guard brought Lonel into the room with his wrists bound behind his back and his eyes blackened. Gritta, who had been standing in the front of the room with Efi's and Appel's arms around her, cried out when she saw her son. Lonel gave her his lopsided smile.

"It's nothing to worry about, Ma. I gave 'em a good fight and bruised their knuckles something terrible with my face."

Gritta hid her own face in her hands.

"Lonel Leporteur, are you accused of deceiving the people of Colmar for days, causing malicious mischief and mayhem. Moreover, we charge you with the murders of Helmut, son of Harmut the shepherd, and Benno, son of Arne the street sweeper. What do you have to say for yourself?" Lord Frider asked.

"I have not done any of the things you say," Lonel replied calmly. Around the room, the crowd murmured.

"Insolent beggar," Sheriff Werner grumbled.

"I am no beggar, my lord. But you may call me an insolent thief if you like, for that is true." He turned and faced the room. "I have stolen many loaves of bread from your ovens and buttons from your cottes, have I not?" A few tradesmen and women who sold wares in the markets nodded to each other. Lonel was notorious. He grinned again.

"You see there, Sheriff? I'll admit to my sins. But I won't admit to false accusations from anyone, and least of all from you."

Sheriff Werner turned and struck Lonel in the stomach. Lonel doubled over, gasping for a moment. Seeing his mother's tears, he smiled again. "There, you see, Ma? I'll wager you didn't know I could hit a man's fist so hard with my belly, did you?"

A faint chuckle rose from the onlookers, and Sheriff Werner grew visibly annoyed. "Quiet now, quiet, all! Let me lay out what this jester has done to deserve my accusations. First, he was seen fleeing Saint Matthieu's friary with soot on his face and clothes on the day the orchard caught afire. He did go into his mother's house and wash himself clean before emerging and pretending nothing had happened."

"And why would he set a fire at the church?" Jorges shouted, jabbing a scrawny fist into the air. "Ain't no crime for a lad to wash himself." Jorges screwed up his face and looked at his son. "Though it is mighty strange. Surely, I never taught you to wash your face."

"No, you didn't," Lonel agreed.

"Shut up, Jorges!" Sheriff Werner snapped. "He did it in order to burn down the house of God, because your son has no respect for anything holy or earthly." He cleared his throat and continued.

"Secondly, you left Herr Schlock's wynstube the night that Helmut, son of Harmut was found murdered next to the canal. Witnesses who were drinking with you that night attest to this."

"After all that wine, do you think I wouldn't need to relieve myself?" Lonel asked, and a few members of the crowd chuckled. "Although there is another thing I am guilty of."

Sheriff Werner and Lord Frider leaned closer. "Well?" Lord Frider demanded.

"I chose to relieve myself against the south-facing wall of your house, Herr sheriff," Lonel replied calmly.

"You wretch!" Sheriff Werner snarled, but Lord Frider put a hand on his arm.

"Leave it, Werner. Carry on with the trial."

Sheriff Werner took a few deep, steadying breaths, and continued. "Third and finally, two witnesses saw young Lonel creeping about the dark alleyways in the wool dyers' quarter with a sack slung over his shoulder near where Benno the street sweeper lived. Undoubtably, this sack contained the disguise of the monster, which he later hid in a pile of hay behind his home."

"Now wait," Lonel interrupted, his good-natured expression now changed to an angry scowl. "True, I had a sack over my shoulder, and true that I did see the monster costume, which was hidden beneath the house of Benno and Arne the street sweeper." He paused as the people in the crowd began to chatter. "But I left itI there. Didn't touch it. And how can your witnesses know for certain what was inside my sack? I could have been carrying off your own wife, Sheriff, and they would be none the wiser."

Sheriff Werner purpled with rage, and Lord Frider again placed a hand on the man's shoulder to calm him. "Blatant lies!" The sheriff shouted. "I have one more piece of proof it was you who murdered Benno. Inside the boy's house, I discovered this." He produced the red embroidered handkerchief from his money pouch with a flourish. He held it up for a moment while the nearsighted people in the crowd leaned forward, squinting.

"What is it?" someone from the crowd shouted.

"Why would a poor boy have something so fine?"

"This is a token, given to Lonel Leporteur by a woman he courted. He wore it tucked into his girdle to taunt his rivals, but he hasn't had it on his person for days. Not since the murder. And it was I who found this token inside Arne's house when Benno's body was discovered," Sheriff Werner declared loudly, basking in the attention.

A hum rose in the room as the onlookers whispered and debated with each other. The five jurors who had been chosen from the city council sat on a bench nearby, stroking their beards or, if they had none, twiddling the strings of their felt hats, and doing their best to look grave.

"That is not my handkerchief!" Lonel shouted. "'Tis another! Mine had a different type of flower embroidered."

A few women shrieked with laughter. "As if any man not a tailor or a draper would know the difference between one type of embroidery and another," one of them giggled.

From the back of the room came more loud whispers and gasps, and the people parted to let a young woman walk through the crowd to where Sheriff Werner stood. Kamille curtseyed and turned to face her peers. Her dark hair was braided and tied back with a kerchief of palest pink, which revealed her elegant, slender throat. Standing next to the sheriff and to Lonel, who was filthy and bruised from his imprisonment, she looked like a painted statue of the Virgin. Without asking permission, she took the handkerchief from the stunned sheriff and examined it. Then she shook her head sadly.

"This is the handkerchief I gave to Lonel Leporteur," she said. "But it was not a token of love. I merely requested he use it to wipe the drips from his nose. When I asked for it back, he put it in his belt and told me he would only return it if I...if I..."

She drifted off, and a chaste flush rose to her cheeks.

"Are you telling me this young man tried to extort pleasures from you in exchange for that pretty thing?" the sheriff growled.

Kamille, too ashamed to look at the sheriff, kept her eyes modestly downcast. "I am sure I am not the only woman in Colmar to receive this treatment from him."

Gritta's heart sank. Lonel loved women, and although he could be free with his affections, she couldn't believe he would ever extort favors or force himself on a woman. But then again, how well did she really know her son? The dreadful possibility that Kamille could be telling the truth sank like a stone in her stomach.

"Well, there you have it," the sheriff said, speaking louder. "And the fact that he kept the handkerchief with him is proof this young maid did not sacrifice the most precious thing her father owns: her virginity."

"She ain't no virgin," Lonel said, and the sheriff turned to sink his fist into Lonel's gut once more.

"It is clear to see!" Sheriff Werner now spoke to the assembled jurors. "Lonel Leporteur, a known mischief-maker, either obtained or crafted a suit of knives and leather in order to terrify the population. He attempted to seduce this young woman, who stayed true to her virtue. Frustrated, he resorted to smaller crimes, such as setting the church afire. When that failed to thrill him, he turned to stalking the streets, making people think there was a monster inside the walls. He murdered Helmut the shepherd and got away with it, because we all still believed the monster to be a citizen of hell. But when he also slaughtered Benno the street sweeper, he was scared off and had to hide his costume quickly. In his haste, he chose to bury the offending costume in a pile of straw outside his mother's house. And to further implicate him, he nailed poor Friar Kornelius into an ale cask!"

Friar Kornelius timidly raised his hand to correct the sheriff but was drowned out by the outraged roar of the crowd.

"Lonel Leporteur fled when I confronted him with this handkerchief!" the sheriff screamed. "Would an innocent man flee? No! He would stand his ground and defend his reputation! Lonel Leporteur is a coward, a liar, a thief, and a murderer!"

Oh, how they yelled! How they shook their fists and stamped their feet until the walls of the great wine warehouse trembled and sent a shower of plaster upon their shoulders. Sheriff Werner looked at the assembled jury, who spoke in a huddle with their heads together, and smiled. Finally, Herr Arno, the oldest man on the jury, rose on shaky legs to speak, and the room quieted.

"Will none vouch for this lad?" he wheezed. "By this account his guilt appears overwhelming, but let us hear from someone who will speak in his defense!"

For a moment there was silence. Lonel looked out from where he stood, with his hands bound behind him. He saw his friends, Franz, Johann, and several other lads he often sat with beneath the bridge, sharing a skin of sour wine between themselves as they watched the water of the grand canal flow lazily past. None of them would meet his gaze. And Kamille, his angel who had betrayed him, turned and crept away through the crush of spectators.

"Ah well, if the rest of you cowards will say nothing, then I shall stand for the lad," said a voice. "Move! Let me through, I say!"

Appel elbowed her way through the people, saving an extra jab or two for her neighbors in Les Tanneurs who had watched Lonel grow up. She cleared her throat and adjusted the wimple on her head. "Standing here and giving testimony for my neighbor Gritta and her family is becoming a regular occurrence, Sheriff. How shall I find time to do my work if you are always attempting to execute them?"

"Perhaps it wouldn't be as tiresome if they spent less time engaging in criminal activity and more time being valuable citizens of our city?" He turned and waggled a finger at Gritta and Jorges, who both clung to each other. "Fortunate you are that you live in Colmar and not in Speyer or a manor in England!

Here, you are free! And you use your freedom to birth criminals!"

Appel stepped forward. "Well, Sheriff, as I see it, Gritta and Jorges are valuable citizens. Without Jorges, the salmon and eels you like to import from the Rhine would rot on the boats before they could make it to your table. And I know you think Gritta's ale is the finest in the land. I heard you say it once, and in my alehouse, too. Their children are hard-working members of this city. Noe is a cooper's apprentice, Michel's work with the chandler ensures you have candles to light your banquets, and Lisette ensures Lord Frider's um...laundry is clean." A knowing chuckle rose from the crowd, and Lord Frider blushed as red as a cherry. It was an open secret that Lisette was his favorite mistress.

"Now Lonel may have a streak of mischief, but there is not a bone of outright malice in him. In my opinion, I am standing before you and defending the reputation of my neighbors yet again because you prefer to implicate them and the other residents of Les Tanneurs above the burghers and the wealthy in the city."

"Do you accuse me of bias, Frau Appel?"

Appel turned to face the crowd. She pointed at an old man with a humpback. "Joseph Scherer. Only recently you insisted he was responsible for setting a herd of pigs loose in your fields, even though he can barely walk that far even with a stick and plenty of time to rest."

She pointed at a middle-aged woman. "Widow Schwartz you put in the pillory for selling you a basket of apples with worms in them, even though the real reason was because she laughed at you and called you a stinking lard-dollop one day in front of Lady Margueritte."

"That hog-swine didn't even put me in the good pillory!" Widow Schwartz called out, shaking a skinny fist above her head. "He put me in the old, stinky stocks!"

Sheriff Werner could feel the crowd's sentiment turning against him. "The evidence I have against Lonel Leporteur is overwhelming," he sputtered.

"Oh, is it?" Appel taunted. "The boy had soot on his face and he decided to clean himself up. Not a crime. He had a red handkerchief and now he doesn't. Also not a crime. Multiple drunken men saw him at the wynstube on the night of Helmut's murder, and he was only out of their sight long enough to take a slash against your wall, which wouldn't be enough time to run to the canal, intercept Helmut, bang him over the head and kill him."

"But he ran away from me like a guilty dog who has stolen food from its master's table. What do you say to that, ha!" the sheriff shouted.

"Yes, Sheriff, he ran," Appel said. "And who wouldn't? Everyone from Les Tanneurs knows they are likely to be locked in the tower if they see you marching toward them."

"Aye, the tower, which is exactly where Lonel will spend his night. This meeting is over. All of you, go to your homes and let the jury decide in peace! If any of you are caught outside your houses past curfew, Joss the night watchman has my permission to lock you up in the same room as this young miscreant." The sheriff turned and stomped from the building, trailed by two of his guards, who dragged Lonel with them by the ropes around his waist. Lord Frider gave the crowd one lingering glare and followed.

People mingled for a little longer and then wandered home in small clusters. The trial had been mighty fine entertainment. The alewives in Les Tanneurs could always be relied upon to provide a good show, and they did not disappoint on this night. As the three women walked arm in arm back to their neighborhood, a few of the burghers called out congratulations for being set before a jury once again.

"How long has it been?" asked one man, a wealthy silk merchant. "I believe someone from Les Tanneurs has been put to trial once a week since Michael's Mass. Excellent show!"

"Let's see how entertained you are when I come in the night and pour tanning water down your chimney, you bloated coxcomb!" Gritta yelled back. The merchant chuckled, shaking his head, and returned to his house, where a warm hearth and a joint of roasted lamb awaited him. When Gritta returned to her house, it was filled with her children, ready to console her. All but one. Lonel was sleeping in the tower, and she would not rest until he was released.

The verdict
In which the jury reaches a conclusion

"Sheriff Werner is a foul knave and a vicious perverter of justice!" Gritta said, swiping angrily at the tears trickling through the lines on her face. "Why won't he leave my family alone, Appel? Why?!"

The women had regrouped at Gritta's house to discuss the trial, and – in Appel and Efi's case – to ensure Gritta did not do anything hot-headed to the sheriff. Her promises to pour tanning water down the silk merchant's chimney were not just idle threats, and whatever punishment she was secretly planning for Sheriff Werner and the jurors would be far worse.

The five younger children were all in the house, sitting at the long table, their frightened faces illuminated by a single, smoky pine knot which had been stabbed into a piece of stale bread to hold it upright. Immediately, the three women got to work. Appel stoked the fire and replaced the stinking knot of flaming pitch with a rushlight. Efi poured Gritta a cup of ale, then stirred a handful of barley and a measure of water into the porridge pot. Tossing in a bunch of fragrant herbs and a stick of dried mutton for a little flavor, she lowered the pot over the coals on its iron stand and set it to boil. Gritta pulled Wina and Egilhard on her lap and rocked them back and forth, her face vacant.

"Ma," Rosmunda said. "Ma, what will happen to Lonel? Where is Da?"

"Your father is probably off at a wynstube to drink away his sadness, my dear," Gritta answered with a hollow voice.

The front door creaked, and the women all jumped like startled colts. "Which one of you fools left the door unbarred?" Efi hissed as she took up a stick of firewood in two hands, prepared to wield it as a weapon. But it was only Friar Wikerus who poked his head inside, then pushed the door open wide. Two men staggered in after him, carrying the limp body of Jorges between them. Gritta jumped to her feet. "No! Tell me the true murderer in Colmar did not get him, too! Dear God!"

"He is only asleep from too much wine, Frau Gritta," Friar Wikerus said. "I wanted to bring him back here as fast as I could, and to tell you the jury's verdict before the sheriff's man arrives, for he is finalizing a few arrangements and will make his way here next to speak with you."

They all waited in silence, but by the ashy color of Friar Wikerus's face and the way he twisted the frayed end of his rope belt in his hands, they knew the news wouldn't be good.

"Additional evidence was brought forth after the crowd dispersed for the evening. Apparently, Prior Willem suspects Lonel is responsible for the disappearance of Ulf and Jean-Louis, the two missing novices from the friary. He spoke with a witness who claims to have seen Lonel talking with the two boys the day they vanished. As you know, Sheriff Werner's men found their bloody garments in a nearby field a few nights later."

"Well, they could have been mauled by a bear! They could have been attacked by bandits! Why would Lonel kill two novice friars?" Gritta shouted. "How can these dullards simply believe everything they hear? Are they incapable of questioning the word of others?"

"It is one thing to question the word of a bystander in the poor neighborhood near where Benno was murdered. But it is another situation when the evidence is presented by the prior of the Franciscan church, and a member of the nobility. Prior Willem is the third-born son of Lord Hubert of Waldensheim."

"And Lonel is the sixth-born son of Gritta and Jorges, who hold no power and have no money. Therefore, your prior's word is worth more than my son's," Gritta said bitterly. "Whether Lonel is guilty or not, it doesn't matter, does it?"

A flicker of light shimmered through the cracks around the door. Appel peeked out, and then pulled the door open wide. Dorian, Sheriff Werner's chief of the guard, stood with two other men at his side. He held a lantern aloft on a short pole, much like a night watchman, and wore a grim expression.

"Frau Gritta, where is your husband?"

Gritta glanced at the pile of straw where Jorges lay, snoring. "Here in body but absent in all other ways, sir."

Dorian strode into the room and looked around, clearly unimpressed with what he saw. He snatched up Gritta's half-finished cup of ale and sloshed the golden contents on Jorges' face, but the sleeping man did not stir.

Friar Wikerus shuffled his feet. "Jorges sought comfort at the bottom of a pitcher of wine at Herr Schlock's wynstube, Herr Dorian, and will probably not rouse until the morning."

"Foul churl," Dorian muttered. "Very well then, Friar Wikerus, I'll deliver the news to you in the presence of these women. The jury has come to a decision. Lonel, son of Jorges Leporteur, will hang tomorrow morning for the murder of the Franciscan novices, Ulf and Jean-Louis, of Benno the street sweeper, and for attempting to set fire to Saint Matthieu's church."

Rosmunda screamed and Gritta dropped to her knees, too overcome with shock to speak.

Dorian's lip curled. It was a cruel shape to an otherwise handsome mouth. "Please calm these women, Friar, and when you have finished, make your way directly to the gate tower. Lonel has requested you come to hear his last confession."

"Sir, please wait." Friar Wikerus followed the guard as he stomped out of the house. "We need more time. Please delay the boy's execution for a few more days."

"He hangs tomorrow, Friar. There's nothing you can do to save him, unless you can produce irrefutable evidence that he's innocent, and we all know Lonel Leporteur is usually guilty of something."

Just a glance

In which Friar Wikerus endeavors to gather clues

It took a good deal of strength to restrain Gritta, who raged and lunged at Dorian as he left her house. Wikerus and the two men who had helped carry Jorges home from the wystube held Gritta's arms, while Appel barred the doors to the house and Efi kept watch on Anstett and Mattheus, who vowed to break into the tower to free their older brother. Although he felt uncomfortable treating his friend and her children roughly, Friar Wikerus knew the consequences of an outburst of temper and rash actions could mean more than one Leporteur would hang the next day.

After everyone was calmed and secured, he hurried to the tower through the darkened streets, the light of a full moon in the cloudless sky showing just enough detail to keep him from twisting an ankle in the rutted roads. A few houses had a candle or a rushlight burning inside, although when he passed the entrance to the wool dyers' quarter, the dark and twisted alley looked like a yawning, toothless mouth. Few who lived in that part of the city could afford to light their homes after nightfall.

Friar Wikerus was usually safe and warm inside the friary at this time of night, singing, praying, or instructing the novices on the toils of Franciscan life. He had food for his belly, light to see his books if he wished to read, and the company of his fellow brothers. When he looked at the dark alley in the wool dyers' quarter – the disintegrating houses and the people so desperately poor – he shuddered to think about how close he came to being an occupant of such a neighborhood, had he not chosen to join the protection of the church.

There was some activity outside the gate tower, and Wikerus hung back in the shadows for a moment to watch. He blinked against the darkness, because although he thought he saw the lithe shape of a young woman, her head bare and her hair loose, he couldn't be sure he trusted his own eyes. A man walked out of the tower with a lantern on a short stick. It was Dorian, the tall, stern captain of the guard who had brought the awful news to Gritta earlier that evening. The light from his lamp illuminated the glossy dark hair and elegantly arched brows of a familiar face.

"Kamille," Friar Wikerus whispered as he resumed his approach. "She must be here to see Lonel before his execution."

Kamille's flirtations distracted the other men, and no one noticed as Friar Wikerus approached and stood nearby with his hands tucked into his sleeves. The girl did have her head brazenly uncovered, and her girdle was wound several times around her midsection, showing off her slender waist and the roundness of her hips.

"Fraulein Kamille, you must be here to see young Lonel in his time of fear and loneliness," Friar Wikerus said with a smile.

Kamille's expression froze, and she cast a questioning look at Dorian.

"Aye, Lonel's here awaiting his execution, thanks in part to your testimony, Fraulein Kamille."

Wikerus narrowed his eyes. Clearly, Kamille was not here to confront a man who was accused of killing her lover, nor was she here to say farewell to Lonel. She was at the gate to flirt with the soldiers and guards.

"Perhaps you would come up with me to see young Lonel? The boy fancies himself in love with you. I think it would be a comfort for him to see your face one last time. It will also do you good to see and be satisfied that the person who killed Benno will soon pay for his horrific crime."

Kamille wrinkled her nose, but could apparently think of no excuse to refuse, and so she followed the friar and the guards inside the tower. They passed through a dimly lit room, where the gatekeepers were playing at stones, losing money back and forth to each other, and proceeded up the rickety, winding stairs to the small chamber where Lonel sat in darkness. When they walked inside, Lonel scrambled to his feet and shielded his eyes against the glare from the lantern. When his vision adjusted, he fell on his knees in front of Friar Wikerus.

"I didn't do them things they said, Friar! You must believe me!"

Friar Wikerus took a deep breath. He knew that what he was about to do was unkind, but weighing his options, he felt a little intimidation was justified in this matter.

"Well, Lonel, I wish I could believe you, but the costume of a monster was found at your house, and what is more, you were the last person to speak to my young novices before they were killed and their bloodied cloaks discovered in a field outside the city." It wasn't hard for his voice to choke with rage when he mentioned Ulf and Jean-Louis, for he wished their true murderer's soul a merry time burning in hell.

Lonel's eyes grew wider with each accusation. "I didn't kill them! I met those two dummkopfs, yes, and I even spoke to them, but lead them astray and murder them? Absolutely not!"

"Proof, Lonel!" Wikerus leaned his face close to Lonel's until he could feel the warm fog of fear radiating from the boy's body. "Give me proof. If no one but Ulf and Jean-Louis saw you outside the walls, then how can you claim your innocence? Come, boy, you will hang tomorrow! Save yourself!"

Friar Wikerus could see the faintest throb of a blood vessel as it thumped beneath the tender skin of Lonel's forehead. For the briefest moment, the boy's gray eyes flicked from Friar Wikerus to Kamille and back again.

Friar Wikerus lowered his voice to a whisper. "If someone was with you when you spoke to Ulf and Jean-Louis, you must tell me, Lonel, for it could save your life."

"I swear to you on the fingertips of Saint Florentius, I was alone, and although I spoke to your two novices, I did not kill them."

Kamille crept forward, gently placing a hand on Lonel's arm and fluttering her dark lashes. The boy melted into her touch, his face breaking into a smile that could light a room.

And there it is, thought Friar Wikerus. The eyes betray the intentions of the soul. I shall bide my time, for I think I know who is the guilty party here.

Kamille left first, and Friar Wikerus stayed behind, hearing Lonel's confession and asking more questions that could provide clues about the real killer. By the time he walked down the long, winding staircase from Lonel's perch in the tower, the sun blushed the eastern horizon as it brought forth another day. The night guards yawned as they exchanged posts with the day guards. And in the room at the bottom of the tower, Jorges Leporteur was belligerent.

Although he didn't look entirely sober, Jorges' expression was purposeful. Two men restrained him by his tanned, wiry arms. "Take me!" he bellowed for all to hear. "I'll hang. Leave my son, who is in the prime of his life!"

"There ain't enough fat on you to weight the rope and break your neck, Jorges Leporteur," one of the guards said. The big man leaned back on his stool and spat lazily into the filthy straw on the floor, observing Jorges as he struggled in vain against the locked hands of the guards. "Toss 'im out. Better yet, toss him into one of the canals."

"No need," Friar Wikerus broke in quickly. "I'll take Jorges home. Thank you for allowing me to hear the prisoner's confession. I bid you a good morning."

Outside the guard tower, Friar Wikerus supported the weeping Jorges in his arms, dragging him away from the gate and in the direction of Les Tanneurs. The courtyard was empty now, but Friar Wikerus kept thinking about Kamille, who he had seen strutting outside the guard tower like a cat the night before. He suspected she had something to do with the attacks, but what? She was too small to wear the suit of a monster, and not strong enough to kill a shepherd boy. Certainly, she wasn't strong enough to plunge a knife into Benno, who was twice her weight, or to kill two Franciscan novices on her own.

"And what about the tinker and his poor dog? Could she have attacked the tinker outside the walls?" Wikerus asked aloud as he walked. "Impossible!"

"Wassat?" Jorges asked. He sniffed loudly, drawing his sleeve across his nose and leaving a long, wet stain.

"Nothing," Wikerus muttered. "I thought I had a theory, but apparently it's nothing."

A plea falls on deaf ears
In which flimsy evidence is still evidence in some eyes

COLMAR DIDN'T HAVE MANY occasions to hang prisoners. Sometimes it was easier to just send their condemned up north to Strassburg where there stood a splendid gallows, capable of accommodating seven doomed souls at once. But since there were two other prisoners available and waiting in the gate tower, Sheriff Werner's guards and a few local carpenters had already erected a sturdy frame from which to hang them, and it was easy to add one more rope to the crossbeam. All three men condemned to hang that morning looked half-starved and of little combined weight.

"It's too fast," Friar Wikerus said as he paced the floor in Appel's house. "There are too many unanswered questions. Has everyone in this city forgotten there is a second monster running about? Why hang Lonel before we've apprehended the second man – for surely it is a man in another costume, and not a demon at all!"

Nearby, the three alewives and Jorges sat on a bench near the window, shoulders hunched in defeat. Gritta's eyes were red from weeping, and Efi twisted a fistful of wheat straws in her hands until they bled, her face set in an uncharacteristically grim expression.

"We managed to find the killers when others were murdered in Colmar," Appel whispered. "Why can't we find this one? How can this killer be so elusive? Colmar is not a large city. Someone must have seen something and hasn't come forward to tell us what they know!"

"We need more time." Wikerus spun and paced across the room again. "More time to ask questions. More time to find out where the monster disguise came from and how it ended up in a pile of straw behind Gritta's house."

"I know my Lonel didn't put no monster there because he's too clever a liar. If my boy steals and hides, he does it well. A professional, he is!" Jorges said, finishing his declaration with a loud sniff. Tears ran down his weathered cheeks and soaked into his sweat-stained cotte.

"No one who knows our house would have hidden the disguise there," Gritta said. "That out there is a shared pile of straw. We have half the straw for our goat, and Jacques the leather dyer uses the other half for his draft horses." Her eyes widened as she spoke, and she stood.

Friar Wikerus stared at her. "It's shared between you and Jacques Färber? How often is someone out there at the pile of straw?" he asked.

"Once a day at least, and probably more," said Jorges. "That's the bedding for animals plus the straw we strew on the floor o' the house."

"This leaves two scenarios," Friar Wikerus said. His voice was high and excited. "First, if Lonel hid the disguise in the straw pile the night of Benno's murder, it would have been discovered before the sheriff and his men came to search the next afternoon..."

"Or else Jacques Färber murdered the novices, the shepherd, and Benno, then hid the disguise," Gritta finished for him.

"We need to tell the sheriff," Efi said, springing to her feet. "This is important for him to know! It is proof that Lonel didn't hide the disguise!"

"Not so fast," Appel whispered. At first, Efi, Gritta, Jorges, and Friar Wikerus didn't notice her as they all scrambled to find their wraps so they could fetch the sheriff. "I said not so fast!" she said louder. The room fell silent. It was rare for Appel to raise her voice. "Jacques Färber is not to blame," she said.

"But, Frau Appel, how can you be so sure?" Efi asked.

"The day the novices disappeared, Färber was not alone. It wasn't him."

Gritta shook her head and crossed her arms across her skinny bosom. "I should have known. And here I thought sharing a bed with Efi would cure you of all sin!"

Efi looked from Gritta to Appel, her mouth agape. "What's that supposed to mean?"

"Where, Appel? Where have you been meeting him?" Gritta demanded.

Appel looked into her lap. "Mostly outside the walls. That is..." She squirmed. "Until I saw the beast. Then I became too afraid."

"You what?!" Gritta growled. "You saw it? When you had a liaison with Jacques Färber?"

Appel nodded. She couldn't meet their eyes.

"And you never told us?!" Gritta was shouting now.

"Didn't feel it was something you needed to know," Appel said with a shrug.

"Jacques Färber? Why, he stinks of the tanneries, he does!" Jorges said. "Have some standards, Appel!"

"We all stink of the tanneries, and you the most!" Appel snarled.

Friar Wikerus held up a hand, and everyone quieted. "Frau Appel, we can discuss your sins at some other time. For now it is very important to know…did you see the beast in full?"

"No. I saw a bit of his shaggy hide. And I heard his footsteps."

"Could it have been Lonel?"

Appel thought for a moment. She recalled the stillness of the forest, interrupted by the resounding thuds of the beast's footsteps, the tone of its growling voice, and the fear she felt. "No," she said. "Setting aside the fact that it bore not the voice nor the size of Lonel, I know he would never frighten me. He gets into trouble, but he's a good boy in his heart. He wouldn't frighten me." She looked up and met Gritta's eyes. They were shining with tears.

"Thank you," Gritta mouthed.

Appel smiled and nodded. "Always," she whispered back.

When Dorian walked into the gate tower's guard room, he was surprised to find it crowded with agitated people of a peculiar pungency. Pressing a hand against his nose, he called for silence and sized them up. The parents of the murderer and monster impersonator, Lonel Leporteur, were there, along with the Franciscan friar and the two widows who had come to Sheriff Werner's home earlier with wild theories about the murders. The one called Appel was uncommonly attractive, but he was sure that a woman of her maturity would have dedicated herself to a quiet life of piety and abstinence, as a widow should.

"Go home," Dorian said as he settled into a chair behind a large oak table. "It gives me no pleasure, telling you nothing can be done, but the young man cannot find ample evidence to show he's innocent, and four souls departed because of his actions. Moreover, he also terrified the population of Colmar, halting commerce."

"Have you forgotten there are two monsters roaming Colmar, not one?" Efi demanded.

"I have not indeed, and we now believe Lonel was using two disguises to lead the sheriff's attention elsewhere," Dorian replied calmly. This statement was met with roars of outrage from all present, with the boy's mother going so far as to slam her hand on the table and shout, "You are a monster and a foreigner, Dorian of Troyes!" This hurt, for although he was not born in Colmar, he felt he had found a place where he could settle and start a family. The sheriff, seeing Dorian's size and temperament, had immediately asked him to join the militia, which was a relief after spending his entire life working in his father's loomworks with his five brothers.

"Have none of you paused to think about the absurdity of hiding such a damning object so close to his own home? Lonel never would have hidden such a thing where it would be so easily found," Appel said. "And that is a shared pile of straw. Nothing could remain hidden there for long without discovery."

Damn, but she is a fine woman! Dorian thought. "A desperate man will often make rash choices."

"Just you wait until you see what kind of choices a desperate woman will make!" Appel shouted, and she tore the deep-blue wimple from her head, revealing her pewter-colored hair, which was plaited and pinned up so it looked like finely worked silver on a bracelet.

"I understand your dismay. Were my son set to hang this very day, I would also do whatever I could to free him. But harassing me will get you nowhere. I suggest you all go to the church to pray, for your sins, and for the quick passage of Lonel's soul through purgatory."

"You do not understand my dismay," Gritta hissed at him. "And you do not understand the facts. If Lonel was disguised as both monsters, how did Brother Kornelius of the Franciscans see both beasts in the same building at nearly the same time? If Lonel has two disguises, then where is the second one?"

"True, we have not found it yet," Dorian admitted.

"And there is another thing," Appel said quietly. Her face was flushed deep red. "I myself saw the beast with my very own eyes. It spoke to me. But it did not speak with Lonel's voice."

"Where did you see it, Frau Appel?"

"In the forest. Outside the walls a fortnight ago."

Dorian frowned. "What were you doing by yourself in the forest?"

"Never you mind that," Friar Wikerus interrupted. The fact is there are unanswered questions which could prove Lonel's innocence. I beg you to delay this execution, Dorian. Do not allow a man to hang when you still have loose threads!"

Dorian shook his head. "I am sorry, truly. But the jury has decided, along with the sheriff. I do not have the authority to stop an execution."

"Talk to the sheriff then." Friar Wikerus tried to keep his voice as soothing as possible. "Do not let this boy's death cling to your conscience and follow you to your own grave."

There was nothing that terrified Dorian more than the prospect of an eternity in hell, but he shook his head again. "I am sorry. There is nothing I can do. You can speak with the sheriff directly at the execution."

"But by then it will be too late!" Appel cried. "Even now the morning is half over!"

"I'll go to his house right now," Jorges said. "Sheriff Werner don't scare me. Why, I speak with him almost every week on account of him putting me in the stocks when I've had a jolly night out with the lads. We're on amiable terms, we are."

"I doubt that very much," Dorian muttered, but Jorges was already running out of the guard tower in the direction of the sheriff's house, with Gritta and Friar Wikerus close behind him.

Appel bent to pick up her discarded wimple, but Dorian snatched it up first and presented it to her with a small bow of his head. "You're a spirited woman, Frau Appel. It was an excellent display of passion you just showed us." He hesitated. "And I've heard you're full of passion in other ways, too," he heard himself say, and before he had a moment to consider his words, Appel landed a slap on his face that made his vision go dark. By the time he recovered, she was stomping out of the guard tower, her wimple crushed in one hand. Efi marched up to him, and he winced, waiting for a second blow, but instead she only looked at him with narrowed eyes.

"Not only are you rude, but your teeth are yellow, and you smell like a tanning pit!" She swept from the room, following her friend.

"You would know what a tanning pit smells like, wench!" Dorian yelled after her. Women these days, he thought. What is the world coming to?

Eleven Leporteurs and one vital clue

In which Brother Tacitus blunders into brilliance

"Just because I choose to enjoy my widowhood does not make me into the local prostitute!" Appel declared. "I ain't getting paid for my pleasures when I decide to take them!" She was marching, wimple crushed in her hand, toward the sheriff's house, with Efi trotting beside her. "Dorian of Troyes has no right to imply anything about my behavior. Odious man!"

"And besides, if he needs a prostitute, there's always Kamille," Efi snarled. "Why, she has taken the heart of every man in this city who still has enough energy to—"

"Quiet, Efi! I am in no mood for it," Appel snapped.

"But I was only going to say that—"

"Oh, hold your tongue, girl!" Appel stopped at the broad wooden gates of Sheriff Werner's house, which consisted of a great hall, a stable, the kitchens, the buttery, the cellar, and a separate living quarters for the sheriff's immediate family, all enclosed with a high stone wall. They met Gritta, Jorges, and Friar Wikerus, who were being forcefully escorted out by one of the sheriff's guards. Their slumped shoulders and tears were all Appel and Efi needed to see to understand the outcome of their attempts to stop the execution.

"He wouldn't even see us," Gritta whispered. Appel pulled her friend into an embrace, wrapping her arms around Gritta's thin, weathered frame. Gritta began to shake with sobs.

"Sheriff Werner was too busy with his tailor, discussing a new brocade tunic. He refused to meet with us," Friar Wikerus said, his voice grim. He raised a fist and shook it at the great house. "Well, I am sure his fine brocade will be a very uncomfortable fabric to wear in hell!"

"Friar Wikerus!" Efi gasped.

"Frau Efi, I may look like a pious man, but it doesn't mean I can't feel righteous anger sometimes. And what I feel now is nothing short of rage."

"I only meant to remind you, Friar, that dead men descend to hell naked, not clothed in brocade," Efi said.

"Right, of course," Friar Wikerus muttered. Sometimes he wondered if Efi was capable of understanding subtlety. "The prisoners will hang right after the bell tolls for Terce. I will go to Prior Willem and obtain permission to stay with you all during this time if you wish to have me. I assume you will want to be at home and not witness the execution."

"Your presence would be a comfort, Friar Wikerus," Appel said. "Please hurry back. We shall gather at Gritta and Jorges' home to pray for Lonel's quick death and his soul's easy passage."

"Not I," Gritta said. "My boy is frightened, and he needs his mother. I will go to the gallows, I will look into my son's eyes for as long as the light remains in them, and I will stay until the thing is done. You all should stay at the house with the rest of the children."

Jorges slipped his hand over Gritta's, and for a moment they stood, looking at each other. "We were so blessed to have him for this long, our Lonel," he said, tears slipping down his face. "I shall go with you, my dove."

"And I shall go to my prior, for he will deliver the last rites, and I must obtain his permission to miss prayers." Friar Wikerus hurried away toward the church, and Gritta and Jorges walked hand in hand to the gate, for the gallows was set up outside the walls at the crossroads which split the route between Riquewihr and Kaysersberg. Appel and Efi dragged their feet as they slowly made their way into Les Tanneurs. The neighborhood was quiet – as empty as it had been when they all thought a monster was on the loose.

"They've all gone to watch the hanging," Appel said woodenly. "How can they find entertainment in such a thing?"

Inside Gritta and Jorges' house it was crowded. All eleven of the remaining Leporteur children had gathered to comfort each other. Lisette, the eldest, was a pretty girl who lived as a washerwoman in Lord Frider's home. She held little Wina on her lap, and conversed quietly with the wife of Michel, her younger brother. Geld and Noe sat on a bench near the fire discussing Noe's work as a cooper, while Margaret played cat's cradle with

Egilhard, who was nearing his tenth year. She scolded Anstett and Mattheus for some sort of mischief, while Urbe paced the little remaining floor space, clenching and unclenching his fists. Only Rosmunda was missing.

"It's not often to find every one of Gritta's children under a single roof," Appel said, smiling.

"But we're not all of her children, we're all but one," Urbe said, and Appel could see how hard he tried to keep the angry tears from sliding down his cheeks. "I wish I were a knight or a bandit with a sword. I would run the sheriff through until his plentiful guts spilled out."

"Now, young man, anger and violence will not bring you peace," Friar Wikerus said, and everyone turned. He had returned to the house, and with him stood another friar. "I thought you might all be here, and Brother Tacitus, in his wisdom, insisted upon coming along to help."

Brother Tacitus missed the sarcasm in Friar Wikerus's voice. He bowed slightly and folded hand over hook at his waist. "Dear children, I am grieved to hear of your brother's fate. Was Lonel a mischievous young man? Yes. And was he foul-mouthed? Also yes. Did he have any regard for the church? No, he had absolutely none. And yet my heart feels compassion for his soul, which is condemned after this heinous crime."

This preamble was met with silence and icy stares from the Leporteur children, although Brother Tacitus didn't appear to notice.

"Yes, well, thank you for insisting on coming to my aid today, Brother." Friar Wikerus could barely control his irritation. "And now, let us all take a moment to pray for God's peace and comfort to surround Lonel in this time of fear."

"And for the condemned to repent of his sins, as he still has an opportunity to clear his conscience," Brother Tacitus added with another sage bow of his head.

Friar Wikerus ignored his fellow brother and cleared his throat. "Jesu Christi, we beseech you to ease Lonel's journey from this world. Blessed Mother Mary, bring to him your tender comfort so he may not feel terror or agony but only joy for the journey his soul is about to take. In nomine Patris, et Filii, et Spiritus Sancti. Amen."

The room was silent except for a few sobs from Urbe and Appel. Brother Tacitus crossed himself and then raised his eyes toward the heavens in what he hoped was a very holy pose. Then he sighed. "Fate is a cruel mistress," he said, shaking his head. "If only I or Prior Willem had known Lonel was in the wool dyers' quarter when we were there, we could have stopped Benno's murder. He would still be guilty of the sin of contemplating a murder, but having not committed it, perhaps he would not hang today."

Appel looked up and met Friar Wikerus's startled eyes.

"What did you say, Brother Tacitus?" Friar Wikerus asked. "You were in the wool dyers' quarter with Prior Willem when Benno was murdered?"

"Indeed. As you know, Friar Wikerus, I minister to the poor there, now that I am unable to work in the scriptorium." He paused, giving his hook-hand a baleful stare. "Although I admit I am not in the wool dyers' quarter every single day."

Appel leaned forward. "But were you there the day of the murder? Did you see Lonel when you visited the home of Arne and Benno?"

"No, indeed, I didn't go into the neighborhood. Although it was my intention to visit Arne and the homes nearby, as I walked down the lane I saw Prior Willem just ahead of me, walking toward the homes of the most destitute, who live in the hovels against the city wall. Though he is only a Franciscan, Prior Willem is a humble man and often ministers to the poor when he has the time." Brother Tacitus let his eyes dart to Wikerus to see if his insult to the Franciscan order landed. But Friar Wikerus couldn't answer. His mouth hung open in shock, and his eyes were as round as chestnuts.

"Friar Tacitus, I must know if I heard you correctly. The very same day Benno was found dead in his home, you saw Prior Willem near the boy's house?"

Brother Tacitus suddenly felt uneasy. He looked nervously back and forth between Friar Wikerus and Appel. "Why, yes, but it must have been well before the murder happened, which is the tragedy of it all."

"Why do you think the murder had not happened yet?" Efi asked.

"Why, because Prior Willem would have shouted the alarm. After all, he would have visited each home, and... Frau Appel, are you unwell?"

Appel jumped to her feet and paced the room in agitation, wringing her hands and pulling at her wimple.

"Why did you not say anything sooner, Brother Tacitus?" Friar Wikerus demanded. "Why tell us this now?!"

Brother Tacitus was flustered. His face flushed, and a rim of sweat appeared on his upper lip. "I didn't think it was important. After all, the prior didn't kill Benno. No, it was just a sad coincidence."

"Help!" came a cry from behind the house. "Oh, someone help, please!"

Michel and Geld both jumped to their feet. "That's Rosmunda," Geld said. There was a clatter and the thunder of feet as everyone rushed outside and to the back of the house where Rosmunda's shouts came from.

"Clear away!" Friar Wikerus shouted. "Make space, I say!" He pushed to the front, where Rosmunda was on her knees near a stone-lined firepit and a large cauldron of boiling laundry.

"Friar Wikerus. Frau Appel," she said, and held up an object for them to see. "I just found this!"

Efi gasped and covered her mouth. Friar Wikerus once again found himself speechless.

"What's that?" Brother Tacitus asked.

"It's proof of Lonel's innocence," Appel said. "Come!" She grasped Rosmunda's hand and dragged the girl away from the steaming laundry and into the street.

"Where are we going?" Rosmunda panted as she attempted to match Appel's long, loping stride.

"We're going to a hanging. We're going to save your brother."

A fortunate homecoming
In which God calls one resident of Colmar home

IT TOOK SOME TIME for Gritta and Jorges to push their way to the front of the crowd assembled outside the walls to watch the hanging. Gritta recognized the faces of many residents from Les Tanneurs, but this was unsurprising, as an execution always attracted all members of the community. Sitting on a raised dais nearby were Lord Frider and Lady Margueritte, along with some of his lordly friends. The city council and the more prominent merchants also sat in chairs near the front where they could have a good view. But everyone else was on foot, standing shoulder to shoulder with their friends and neighbors.

Gritta had been to an execution or two in her lifetime, but never had she considered the agony of the wives and mothers of the men who died. Jorges was squeezing her hand hard and trying to push away the people who jostled for space. When Sheriff Werner strutted, belly first, onto the platform with Prior Willem and Dorian alongside him, his grip on her hand threatened to crush her bones.

Let my bones break, Gritta thought. It will not hurt as much as the breaking of my heart.

Sheriff Werner held up his hands to silence the crowd and then said some things about the three accused men, none of which Gritta heard. She was watching her son as a guard led him to the gallows, his hands bound behind his back, his head bowed and hair flopping over his eyes. Two other men shuffled in front of him: men in their midlife, with thick gnarled arms like old tree roots. They had been sitting in the tower storerooms under arrest for several weeks after being condemned for robbing and murdering three traveling merchants on the road outside of Colmar. Next to them, Lonel looked like a small and skinny child, despite his seventeen years.

"Why is the prior of the Franciscans here to perform the last rites?" someone behind Gritta mused. "Usually, they send a lesser man of the church for such a task."

Gritta's mind hung on the question. It was unusual for the prior to be there. Was there something more special about having your last rites administered by a higher man of the church? Usually only noblemen had the privilege of a visit from a prior.

When asked if they had any last words, the two condemned thieves shook their heads, but Lonel called out in a wavering voice, "Sorry, Ma! I didn't kill any of those boys, but I would gladly have given Benno a whack on the head, if given the chance!"

This elicited a chuckle from the crowd, which Gritta resented. Then Prior Willem intoned a prayer, and Dorian stepped forward to slip thick hemp ropes around the necks of the accused. Gritta sucked in her breath, and Jorges began to whimper. Her heart was beating so fast and loud she was amazed no one else seemed to hear it. Then the bells of Saint Martin and Saint Matthieu both began to toll, marking the hour of Terce, the late morning. Somewhere deep inside the stone walls of the churches, friars were shuffling quietly from their chambers to pray and sing. In the fields, shepherds escorted their sheep to green pastures, blacksmiths and their apprentices hammered in their smithies, and plowmen urged their oxen in the fields. Life continued as normal for everyone but Gritta and Jorges.

When the last echo of the bells faded over the walls and across the flat landscape, Sheriff Werner held his hands up for silence. "Well then, it's time," he said, nodding to a guard who stood next to a wagon hitched behind a shaggy ox. Lonel and the two criminals stood in the bed of the wagon, but once the ox moved it away, they would be left to dangle, the weight of their bodies slowly strangling them to death.

"Wait!" a voice screamed. "Wait just a little longer! Just wait!"

Gritta and Jorges looked at each other. "Is that Appel who is shouting?" Jorges asked.

"I do believe it is," Gritta said, looking around.

Sheriff Werner narrowed his eyes and nodded again to the guard.

"Hiya!" the guard shouted, and the ox began to walk forward. As the wagon slowly moved under their feet, Lonel and the two prisoners shuffled frantically to keep their weight supported on their legs. Gritta silently commanded her hands to remain at her sides, even though she wanted to cover her ears and close her eyes. Next to her, she could sense Jorges was standing on his toes, as if to will Lonel to do the same, to give him an extra finger's length of relief from the tension of the rope. But Lonel wasn't looking at her or his father. He watched as Appel fought her way through the crowd, waving something over her head like a flag. It was a square of red linen with black silk stitching along the edges.

With surprising strength, Appel shook off the arms of the people who tried to restrain her and launched herself at the ox, yanking back on the harness to stop it from walking forward. Lonel and the two prisoners were barely able to support their weight, with just the tips of their toes still holding them up on the very back edge of the wagon. The ropes cut deep into the skin of their throats, and their faces colored dark red.

"Frau Appel, what is the meaning of this?! You increase the agony of these men by delaying their deaths!" Sheriff Werner shouted. He nodded to the ox driver to continue.

But before the driver could urge the ox forward again, the crowd churned and agitated, and a man swam through the crush of bodies, grabbing people and pushing them behind him as he walked. He wore a voluminous black robe, and his white arming cap was tightly tied under his chin with a neat little bow. Behind him followed a young Dominican friar, also in a black robe.

"What is the meaning of this?" the man bellowed. "Stop this at once!"

One of the oxen shook its head, jostling the cart, and the shortest of the two thieves lost his tenuous toe grip on the edge of the cart and began to swing.

"Back it up," Sheriff Werner barked. The cart slowly backed up, and the thief regained his footing, standing up straight and gasping for air. The black-robed newcomer hoisted himself onto the back of the wagon, and his young servant scrambled up after him.

"With all the respect owed to you, m'lord, this is not an ecclesiastical matter," Sheriff Werner said, but there was an edge of uncertainty to his voice. The onlookers in the back pushed forward to get a better look at the new person on the wagon. The man spoke quietly for a moment with Sheriff Werner and Appel. When Appel grew agitated and began to flourish her scrap of red cloth under the sheriff's chin, the man turned to address the crowd, and the people gasped when they finally beheld his face.

"Prior Konrad," they whispered. "Prior Konrad has returned from Strassburg!"

Prior Konrad nodded sagely. His young servant reached up to fuss with the ties of his cap.

"Oh, do go away, Brother Tielo," Father Konrad snapped. He cleared his throat and said in a loud voice, "It seems there has been a good deal of trouble since I left for Strassburg. The sheriff here tells me he added young Lonel Leporteur to the list of unfortunate men to visit the gallows today because the boy impersonated a demon and killed members of the community.

Well, it is fortunate I felt God calling me back to Colmar when He did."

Some of the onlookers jeered, others raised their fists, but most remained silent. Father Konrad was the head of the largest church in Colmar, and no one felt inclined to be singled out and commanded to do extra penance for rowdiness next Sunday.

Prior Konrad took the piece of red cloth from Appel and looked at it for a moment. After some more hurried conversation between her and the sheriff, he turned to the crowd once more.

"It seems Frau Appel has discovered some evidence that would suggest Lonel Leporteur was not capable of murdering someone unless he could be in two places at one time." He smiled like a benevolent parent. "Now, we all know omnipotence belongs only to God. Let us untie this young man and hear the new information before condemning his soul."

"Oi!" a man from the crowd shouted. "Lonel Leporteur also did murder two novices in the Franciscans' care, and that is an ecclesiastical crime, indeed! He sinned against the church, he did!"

Another onlooker, feeling emboldened, pushed his way forward. "We seek justice for Ulf and Jean-Louis, too!"

For a moment Father Konrad blinked at the two men, and then his face broke into a smile. "Ulf of Hagenau and Jean-Louis of Mulhouse are no more murdered than you or I. They are waiting with my donkeys at this very moment."

The love token

In which only a scrap of fabric stands between life and death

WHEN GRITTA CAME TO, the first things she saw in her hazy vision were the faces of her neighbors from Les Tanneurs leaning over her, whispering anxiously. Jorges swayed in and out of her sight, not because she had just fainted, but because he had consumed a jug of half-spoilt white wine in the space of time between when Lonel was led to the gallows and when he was suddenly acquitted. Where he obtained the cracking goatskin flask of soul brew Gritta neither knew nor cared.

Her boy was alive.

Gritta looked past the worried faces hovering over her and into the blue depths of the late afternoon sky and sighed. Although she hadn't felt the rope about her throat and the stability of the wagon slowly rolling away from her feet, she breathed the air and heard the afternoon chorus of grasshoppers as if she herself had been condemned and then spared.

Her boy would live.

A voice was yelling.

"Get away! Back away, vultures!" Efi's face swam into view, her pale blue wimple askew, with a few burnished gold curls escaping. "Come now, Frau Gritta! Let us follow the sheriff and the jury. There is more evidence in Lonel's favor, which means Sheriff Werner will be caught trying to execute an innocent man. Very humiliating for him, and you wouldn't want to miss his public shame, would you?"

"Never," Gritta mumbled. Her fingertips and lips tingled as she became more aware of her surroundings. The silhouettes of the two remaining condemned thieves swung from the gallows against the horizon, their legs kicking weakly. It seemed that only Lonel received a late pardon.

The crowd had dispersed now as people made their way from the gallows at the crossroads and back through the main gate into the city. Inside the gateyard, the shabby wynstubes and public kitchens were full, and a racket of loud carousing came from within. Gritta, supported by Efi and Jorges, barely heard the sounds. "Where are we going?" she asked weakly.

"To the gatehouse," Efi answered. "After you fainted, Father Konrad said he wanted to resolve the issue as quickly as possible so he could find a tub to bathe and a strong drink."

"Where is Appel?" Gritta moaned.

"She said she will not take her eyes off your boy until he is free. She is also at the gatehouse."

"Oh, Appel, my dear friend." Gritta smiled weakly. "Well, Efi, I could also use a strong drink. But first, let us go to the gatehouse and free my son."

Between the sheriff and his guard, Prior Willem and Prior Konrad, Wikerus, Lonel, the jury, the three alewives, and Jorges, there were too many people to meet inside the room at the gate tower. The wine warehouse for large public gatherings was chilly and damp, so they unanimously decided to retire to Herr Schlock's wynstube, where a large fire burned in his crumbling hearth and few copper coins would buy a fine pitcher of wine.

The low-ceilinged room was dim, as usual, and Herr Schlock bustled about, serving customers who chose to stay inside to warm their bellies rather than watch three men strangle to death on the gallows. When he saw thirteen people troop through his door, his eyes widened and he spilled a pitcher of Rhenish to the floor.

"Out!" the sheriff bellowed to the other patrons in the room. "Begone, all of you! We have business to discuss!" A few people rose and left reluctantly, but most of them settled in, and a few called for more wine. Whatever was about to happen in the wynstube today would be good entertainment.

Dorian stomped around the room, shoving two half-drunk men from a bench and dragging it near the fire for the sheriff to sit. Jorges disappeared and then tottered back a short time later with a clay cup of unwatered wine, which Gritta snatched from him and put to Lonel's lips. "I think the boy needs this more than you, husband," she hissed.

The jurors settled in, shedding their wool cloaks and hoods and accepting clay cups of ale from a serving boy, as more people crowded into the wynstube – many of them with dark spots of rain on their shoulders – who had come from the hanging. Soon the room was so crowded that it wasn't possible to squeeze anyone else in, and so a crowd gathered outside. Appel, Gritta, and Efi were not offered a place to sit, and neither was Lonel. They stood lined up, shoulder to shoulder, with Friar Wikerus nearby. Prior Konrad warmed his hands on one of the hot hearthstones, and Prior Willem took up a place near the back wall to observe.

"Now, Frau Appel," Sheriff Werner asked loudly. "What new information is so important that you would interrupt an execution?" He turned to Lonel. "I want you to understand, boy, there's no guarantee I won't see fit to march you back to the gallows tomorrow morning and watch you dangle."

Lonel tried to flash the sheriff one of his impish grins, but the rope had rubbed an angry red ring around his throat, and all movements, including breathing and swallowing, were painful. Instead, he met the man's eyes and held his gaze for an uncomfortably long time. In the end, it was the sheriff who looked away first. Appel stepped forward and presented the red handkerchief for the jury to see. It was still damp from the laundry, where Rosmunda had found it.

"We found this in Lonel's clothes this morning. This is not the same the handkerchief used to accuse Lonel of being at

Benno's house on the day of his murder, it is a different one, but identical. The handkerchief that was found at Benno's house is no longer valid proof that Lonel was there. Either another of Kamille's lovers also had a handkerchief and dropped it while stabbing Benno to death, or the handkerchief belonged to Benno, himself."

The jurors murmured amongst themselves for a moment. "You could have made your own handkerchief and hidden it in Lonel's clothes for someone to find. How do we know Kamille of Basel gave him this handkerchief?"

"See and feel it, goodmen of the jury," Appel said, holding out the cloth. "This is very fine dyed linen, stitched in silk thread. The Leporteurs could never afford this, but the daughter of a weaver would have access to such materials. Is there anyone in Les Tanneurs wearing and using silk, my lords? Undoubtedly not."

"Are you saying Kamille is responsible for killing Benno the street sweeper? Benno was as strong as a bear, and Kamille only a woman."

Before Appel could answer, Efi stepped forward. "Kamille didn't kill Benno, but I believe one of her lovers did." She stood on her toes, scanning the room. "Stefan the glover, please come here?"

Stefan, who had been standing at the back of the room and watching the unfolding drama with vicious anticipation, froze when all eyes turned on him. "I had nothing to do with this murder," he sputtered. "How dare you! How dare you accuse me, a man of fine reputation in this city!"

"I am not accusing you of murder, Stefan," Efi said coldly. "But I am accusing you of owning a red handkerchief with black silk embroidery."

"You speak lies because you are angry I would not ask for your hand in marriage. You're nothing but a scorned lover, Efi Kleven!"

Efi calmly turned back to the jurors. "Well then, if Stefan doesn't have the handkerchief in his possession, then perhaps he lost it at Benno's house? Perhaps he is the murderer after all."

"Foul temptress. Stinking filthy whore," Stefan snarled. Then he reached into his money purse and drew out a piece of red cloth, which he handed to the sheriff.

"They are exactly the same," Sheriff Werner declared. "Hear ye, all of you!" he called out. "Any man in possession of a red handkerchief like these three must come forward at once and present it. I will send for Kamille to be brought, and when she confesses the names of the men who received a handkerchief from her, we will know if one of you has lost yours."

"Unless she lies," Lonel croaked. "And we all know she will."

Prior Willem stepped forward. "I shall find the girl and bring her. As the leader of her church, she trusts me. If she sees a city guard or a sheriff's man coming for her, she is bound to run."

Sheriff Werner nodded, and Prior Willem squeezed through the press of men and women and out the door. Werner turned to Dorian. "Go to Prior Konrad's wagon and fetch the two novice friars. Let us see what they have to say."

While they waited, more wine was passed and people milled about. Conversation began to hum in the room. A young man withdrew a wooden pipe from his cloak and he played a bright tune. Friar Wikerus felt his nerves jangling at the abrupt change of mood, and he had a distinct sense of unease about how quickly Prior Willem had volunteered to fetch Kamille. Happiness and frivolity were always nice, but Lonel was still under threat of hanging, and there was another monster disguise still unaccounted for. He sipped his wine, and then spat it out in surprise. Pushing their way toward him through the room of revelers were Ulf and Jean-Louis, his two wayward novices whose deaths he had mourned.

"You!" Friar Wikerus and Lonel both shouted the word at the same time. They stopped and looked at each other for a moment, Wikerus with a searching expression, and Lonel with a sheepish shrug. Jean-Louis hung his head, but Ulf's eyes sparkled with mischief.

"Sorry we caused you to worry, Friar Wikerus," Jean-Louis said mournfully. "It was Ulf's idea, you know. I was in favor of staying close to Colmar so we could get back before nightfall, but I let him lead me astray. And once we sold the first batch of shoes, well, there was nothing that could stop Ulf."

Friar Wikerus turned to Prior Konrad. "Where did you find them, Father? I have been sick with worrying about them since they disappeared. I thought they had been killed! I even saw their bloody robes!"

"They were in Strassburg, taking in the sights and smells, and getting into all manner of trouble. I heard them discussing whether to return to Colmar, as this one suggested—" Prior Konrad gestured at Jean-Louis. "Or if they should sneak onto a boat and ride south on the Rhine and disappear, as the other one suggested." He pointed at Ulf.

Now Ulf had the decency to look ashamed. Prior Konrad took a long sip from his cup and sighed. "It is good to be home. The wine in Strassburg does not taste as familiar to me as our Colmar grapes. This is a point I stressed with Ulf and Jean-Louis, too. They owed it to you to return and give explanation for themselves. And to return all the shoes they stole from the Dominicans and the Franciscans."

"What?" Brother Tacitus shouted from where he stood, his normally pallid face flushed with anger. The hemp and rope sandals he wore were in tatters, and his bare toes glowed red from the cold.

Ulf raised his hand. "Ah, meaning no disrespect, Prior Konrad, we didn't specifically steal those shoes."

"Aye, we had a supplier!" Jean-Louis said.

"Silence!" Brother Tacitus screeched. "You have unshod the men of God! You have rendered our feet with blisters! There is no place in the depths of hell deep enough for you!"

"Peace, Tacitus," Prior Konrad muttered as he accepted another cup of wine from Brother Tielo. "The boys won't tell me where they got the shoes, but I do believe they did not steal them."

Jean-Louis set his jaw. "We ain't thieves. The thief is here in this room, though."

Ulf reached over and smacked Jean-Louis on the ear. "Quiet! We said we wouldn't tell!"

Tacitus drew his shoulders back. "Tell me at once, or you imperil your eternal souls."

Ulf sealed his lips tight, but Jean-Louis turned a murderous glare at Lonel. Tacitus followed the boy's gaze and narrowed his eyes. "Ah yes, I should have known," he snarled.

Gritta, who had been talking quietly with Jorges and holding tightly on to Lonel's hand, stomped her foot. "Enough of this nonsense. Where is that vixen, Kamille? How much longer must we wait before I know if my son will live to see the sunset tomorrow?"

Sheriff Werner, who was rather enjoying his second cup of wine, barked an order to Dorian. "Go and find her at her mother's home in the wool dyers' district. Prior Willem must be looking in the wrong place."

Dorian, who always found Kamille's behavior to be far too forward for a woman, gladly left to find her and drag her back before the jury.

"Now then, would Lonel care to enlighten us about the matter of the stolen shoes?" Tacitus asked.

"You have more shoes than you require," Lonel said with a shrug. "I met these two dimwits outside the walls one day, and it was clear they were looking for an adventure. At first I meant to play a trick on them, but when they were so quick to find a ready supply of shoes, we later came up with a business arrangement. I don't see how you can blame me for the whole affair."

Prior Konrad was nodding his head. "Ah yes, this all makes sense to me now. Lonel must have removed the shoes from the storerooms and transferred them to the boys, who sold them in the market in Strassburg."

Lonel nodded at Ulf and Jean-Louis. "They stole them from your storeroom, Father Prior."

"And did they also steal the shoes from the Franciscans, too?" Brother Tacitus asked.

"No!" Jean-Louis shouted. "We would never steal from our own order. And we wouldn't have taken any shoes at all if this conniving snake hadn't tricked us!" He shot another glare in Lonel's direction.

"Who did steal the shoes from the Franciscans, then?" Friar Wikerus asked.

Lonel blushed crimson and looked at his feet. "Well, that I am not proud of."

"So it was you who set the fire in the church orchard?" Sheriff Werner asked, and Lonel flushed even darker.

"Just to make a distraction. I didn't hurt no one." He noticed his mother's enraged expression and continued quickly. "And I decided never to do something so dangerous again. I could have burned the whole church to the ground. I will be straight and true from this day forward."

"I'm impressed by you, lad," Jorges slurred. "That there's a good head for commerce you have. A good head indeed, like your pa!"

Gritta was winding up to rebuke her son and her husband at the same time when Dorian the guard ran through the door of the wynstube, breathless and red-faced.

"They are gone!" he said. "The guards saw Prior Willem riding from the city gates on a horse, and Kamille riding on the saddle with him!"

Suspect suspects
In which a visitor to Colmar provides a vital clue

IT WAS AS IF someone had kicked a beehive from a tree. The people in the wynstube immediately scrambled for the door, some yelling with excitement, others with outrage. They poured into the street, and the men quickly formed into small groups to search. The women retreated to their homes and children, gathering in small clusters in the streets to whisper and theorize about the handsome prior and the beautiful young woman.

Back in the wynstube, the alewives and Friar Wikerus remained, along with Herr Schlock, who stared at the mess of broken cups, overturned stools, and puddles of spilled wine soaking into the straw on the floor. Lonel stood and casually sauntered toward the door, but Friar Wikerus put a hand on his shoulder.

"Stay here, young man. You still remain in my custody until we have located Prior Willem and Kamille." He turned to Ulf and Jean-Louis and gave them a stern look. "And you two miscreants will come with me. Be prepared to shovel every stall in the stable, scour every pot in the cookhouse, and clean every privy pit in the friary until the harvest! Shoes, indeed! You may be more suited to commerce than to prayer, but by Jesu's crooked toes, I'll have your penance from you before you're sent back to your fathers' houses!"

Prior Konrad chuckled. "Strange to see you being so hard on those boys, Brother Wikerus. It was only a few years ago that I was reprimanding you in a similar way."

Wikerus blushed and then rearranged his face into a scowl once again. "Let's go!" he said, pushing Lonel in front of him. "All three of you will go to the friary, where I can keep watch over you."

Appel sat heavily on a bench and sighed. Efi plopped down next to her, and Gritta sank to her seat. "What just happened?" Gritta asked weakly. "I feel as if I've been living in a nightmare. This morning I prepared to bury my son. Now my husband is out with the city guards, hunting for a Franciscan prior nobleman who absconded with a temptress, and I just witnessed Friar Wikerus using strong words of discipline. I hardly know what to think anymore."

A man, his face obscured by a deep-blue cowl, strode into the wynstube, stopped, and looked around.

"Why," he said in a deep voice. "It looks as somber as a clergyman's wake in here."

"We're concluding some legal business, and it ain't no place for strangers. Find your wine elsewhere today, traveler," Herr Gilgen snarled. As a member of the jury, this case had already cost him money and time that he could have spent tending to his granary.

The stranger pulled his cowl back from his face, and Appel drew in her breath so fast that all in the room turned to stare at her. "Heinrik of Strassburg!" she gasped. "What are you doing here?"

"Is a merchant not allowed to travel to this city?"

"Well, the last time I saw you, another murder occurred in Colmar!"

Heinrik was as handsome as ever: tall and dark-haired, with generous streaks of gray at his temples which had grown even more striking since she had met him at a haybarn in Vogelgrun a few months earlier. He smiled at her, and she felt a strong, familiar flutter in her chest.

"Yes," Gritta said, looking at him sidelong. "And he is tall enough to fit into the suit of knives and pass for a monster, too."

"Surely you do not think I have been terrorizing Colmar!" Heinrik laughed. "I only arrived here a few days ago to discuss business with Herr Schlock. Your monster problem began before I even set out on my journey from Strassburg."

"And what is your business, exactly?" Gritta asked. "You've never actually told us."

But Heinrik didn't appear to hear. He was looking at Appel and grinning. Appel smiled shyly back at him. He was younger than her, and undoubtedly of higher social rank. Ever since she had met him in Vogelgrun, though, she found herself tongue-tied in his presence. He carried himself with casual confidence, and his dark brown eyes seemed to look straight through her.

"It took me a while to understand the nature of this crime until Lord Frider gave me the details at his supper table a few days ago," Heinrik said. "Have you caught the beasts?"

"Twice we thought so, but when we sent Prior Willem of the Franciscans to fetch a woman who was witness to the crimes, he fled and the woman with him!" Herr Gilgen said, pounding a fist on his table. "A whole day gone and nothing to show for it!"

"Prior Willem of Stuttgart?" Heinrik asked. All eyes turned on him, and he shrugged. "Well yes, we are acquaintances. I had heard of his transfer to Colmar and planned to visit him at Saint Matthieu's friary before I returned to Strassburg. He is an intelligent man and always good for a lively discussion. And he lays a fine table, too. Nothing but the best food and wine for me when I visit Prior Willem!"

"He has only been Prior of Saint Matthieu's in Colmar since the winter," Herr Schlock sniffed. "Three months at most."

Heinrik frowned and paced the room for a moment. "You speak of monsters..." He trailed off.

"Yes, we speak of monsters," Gritta shouted. "And if you know something, say something! Lives are threatened!"

"While I visited him in his solar in Stuttgart last year, we discussed some of the books he kept there. They were most unusual," Heinrik said with a shrug.

"Books? As in, the holy scriptures?" Gritta asked.

Heinrik nodded. "The scriptures, yes, but there were more. Willem is from a noble family, so he can afford his own books.

One of them caught my eye because I had heard of it but never read it: Naturalis Historia, by Pliny the Elder. He allowed me to look at it, and I saw the drawings therein of the 'cynocephali.' Dog-headed men from the East. We spoke at length about the wonders Pliny described."

"You can read?" Gritta asked.

"Yes. My father isn't a nobleman, but he was a successful merchant, and he could afford to send me and my brother to study at a monastery."

"So Prior Willem knew of the existence of these monsters and believed in them because of his books," Appel said slowly, but Heinrik held up a hand.

"He didn't believe in them. In fact, he considered the stories by Pliny to be nonsense and trickery. To be honest with you, I found it surprising. How could a man of faith and intelligence disbelieve in monsters, especially after all that happened during the Great Pestilence? We had a long debate, the two of us. I argued that he must believe in the supernatural evil with the same vigor as he accepted the supremacy of God. Without evil, how does one understand the divine?"

The remaining inebriated guests in the room were nodding their heads and looking at each other. There could be no good without evil, after all.

"But something happened," Heinrik said, and he chuckled. "The old prior convinced me, too. Why should monsters walk the earth and make themselves known to man in the flesh...when angels do not?"

"The saints!" someone yelled.

"Aye, yes. The saints," Heinrik muttered. "Problematic." He looked around the room and saw the comprehension draining from the onlookers. "Well, I am telling you that old Willem does not believe in monsters, but he knows his congregation feared them – especially as bringers of doom and pestilence. And this makes me think he could have decided to play a trick on his congregation. He could easily have used his knowledge and his powerful status as the head of a church to frighten the people of this fair city. The problem is, I just can't believe that my friend Willem would do something so mean-spirited."

Appel stood up and looked at Heinrik. "He didn't believe in monsters?" she asked.

Heinrik's eyes twinkled. "No, he didn't. And neither do I, Frau Appel."

"And neither do I," Appel whispered. She turned to the crowd, which was leaning forward, collectively attempting to eavesdrop into an intimate moment. "If Prior Willem was, indeed, disguised as a monster, he frightened the citizens of Colmar into staying inside their homes. But why? Why would a man of the church do such a thing?" Appel asked. She was met with silence.

"And why do you keep calling him 'old'? He's young. And he's nice to look at, for a man of God," Efi mused.

Heinrik frowned.

"What about the second monster? The costume discovered in the pile of straw behind my house wasn't of a dog-head, it was a beast with knives and nails," Gritta said.

"Benno made that costume," Appel said.

"What?" Gritta said. "How can you be sure?"

Instead of answering, Appel turned to Brother Kornelius, who had remained in the wynstube and was enjoying a rapidly dwindling cup of sweet white wine. "You were with the sheriff when he inspected the costume, Brother Kornelius, and I heard what you described. Would you mind telling us all?"

Brother Kornelius, very pleased to have been singled out for such an important task, cleared his throat. "Why yes, indeed. It was a rotting hide, poorly tanned and covered with spines, like a hedgehog."

"What were the spines made of? Knives?"

Brother Kornelius shook his head. "A few broken blades, yet. But also splintered bits of wood and bone, bent nails, and a few potsherds."

"All refuse and rubbish!" Appel said. "These are items we rarely see because Arne and Benno sweep them up from the streets. When he was living with me, Arne told us he sells the metal scraps back to the blacksmith for some extra money. He gives the potsherds to the masons, who grind them up and use them in their mortar."

Brother Kornelius paled. "But if Benno made the costume, then how did he come to be stabbed by it?"

Efi gasped and pointed at the door. A group of men were leading a young woman back into the wynstube. She was weeping and clutching her stomach.

"I'll wager Kamille can tell us what happened on the night of Benno's murder."

A confession

In which many words are spoken, and only some of them are true

"Please let me sit down. I am so tired," Kamille begged.

"She ought to be tired," Dorian said. He led Kamille to a seat. "She would have made it halfway to Eguisheim had we not caught her when we did."

Gritta knelt in front of Kamille and took the girl by the shoulders. "Kamille, where is Prior Willem? Was he with you?"

Kamille nodded her head slowly. "He was with me, yes."

"And where is he now? We think he may have done terrible things, and we must ask him questions."

But Kamille buried her face in her hands and began to weep. "He did do terrible things," she gasped between sobs. "So very terrible!"

"Kamille," Appel said gently. "Were you the second monster? Did you kill Helmut and hide the costume behind Gritta's house?"

Kamille took a deep breath and clasped her shaking hands in her lap. "I was not the second monster. But I know who was, and I think he may have killed that shepherd boy, only it was an accident!"

By now, the sheriff and his men were trickling back into the wynstube, and someone sent for Lord Frider. The jurymen settled themselves onto a bench with fresh cups of wine, and soon all eyes were on Kamille. She took a deep breath. "I will tell you everything, only I must first insist that, in exchange for a confession of the facts, the jury and the sheriff will spare my life."

"It depends on the facts, young woman!" Sheriff Werner responded. "You may have sinned so grievously that the only way to truly save you is to repay a life for a life. And if you know who killed Helmut the shepherd and you do not tell us, your soul will be in danger."

"But she says it was an accident, Sheriff," Appel said, laying a hand on the sheriff's arm. "Let us hear what she has to say."

The sheriff grunted and waved at Kamille.

"It is a long story," she replied. "And it doesn't begin in Colmar."

"As some of you may know, I moved to Colmar from Basel with my mother, who is very ill with a tumor in her stomach. Like everyone here, I lost much in the pestilence. My father and two sisters all died in agony. And so did the man I was betrothed to marry. Well, my mother grew ill and witless a few years after the pestilence left, bless her, and I cared for her while we lived off the remaining money from my father's loomworks. My father was an ambitious man. In Basel, where we lived, he made very fine cloth that the nobles would purchase for their cottes and gowns. Despite how well he served the community, no one cared for us after he died, and my mother and I fell deeper and deeper into poverty. I needed to find work, and so I hired on as a laundress at the Franciscan friary in Stuttgart. There, I met Willem, and well, he kept me occupied." She blushed.

"You and Prior Willem were...were..." Appel couldn't find the words to say what they all knew. Prior Kamille and Willem were lovers. Heinrik stood next to Appel, his forehead wrinkled in thought.

"We fell in love. Well, Willem did. But after a while I grew tired of his attentions. He wanted more time with me, and sometimes in those times he would become violent. He seemed to hate me because I didn't always understand what he was talking about. He used to mock me for being unable to read his books and for being a lowly laundress. But he wanted me, so I continued to let him think I was also in love."

"Thanks be to the Virgin that Friar Wikerus isn't here to hear this. It would break his heart," Gritta muttered. Next to her, Brother Kornelius sat with his mouth hanging open in shock.

"Continue the story, young woman," Sheriff Werner growled.

"When my mother found out Prior Willem and I were lovers, she threatened to tell the bishop. I begged her not to, and so instead she agreed to move to Colmar with me. You must believe me, I felt relieved to be away from him. He was arrogant and unkind. Here in Colmar, I met many nice men – like your son, Lonel." She nodded acknowledgement to Gritta.

"You played with Lonel's heart and nearly killed him. You played with Stefan the glover and so many other men in this city. You weren't careful with them, Kamille!" Gritta said, and then she spat on the floor.

Kamille looked at her hands. "I know," she said quietly. "By that time the tumor in my mother's stomach was growing, and she was ill all the time. I found work as a laundress here in Colmar, and some of the esteemed men in this room found me very interesting indeed." She turned a hard stare toward the jury, but none of them met her eyes. "I know my behavior was wrong, but I was so lost. I figured I would never marry, fatherless and penniless as I was, and with my mother to care for. And then one day I met Benno." Her eyes misted for a moment.

More people began to shuffle into the wynstube, and Herr Schlock let out a shout of frustration. "I am finished! There is no more wine to be had! You have drunk every last drop, even the vinegar, you sots!"

Appel took a small boy aside and whispered into his ear, slipping him a copper coin, and he ran out the door. Kamille began to weep quietly, dabbing at her eyes while the jurors shifted uncomfortably in their chairs. Heinrik paced the room again. Then he cleared his throat and leveled Kamille with a hard stare.

"You called Prior Willem a cruel man, and yet you are the only person I've ever met to describe him thus."

Kamille's eyes widened as she stared up at Heinrik. "You've met him?"

Heinrik nodded, and Kamille began to wring her hands. "Well, now I don't feel as if I will have an unbiased audience, since this man here is a friend of the prior. He will surely side with his friend!"

"Oh hush, girl. The jury doesn't know Heinrik of Strassburg any better than they know you. Just be honest with us," Sheriff Werner said.

Two of Gritta's older sons staggered to the door of the wynstube, dragging a two-wheeled cart laden with a massive wooden barrel. "What is that?" Herr Schlock sputtered.

"Strong ale," Appel answered calmly. "Leave it outside, boys, and one of you must keep watch and ensure no one takes more than their portion. Herr Schlock, now you have some drink to serve your patrons, so let us continue with Kamille's story."

Herr Schlock flustered about, ordering a barmaid to fill baskets with cups, and he set up a stool outside next to the barrel. Noe pried the lid off, and Herr Schlock dipped in with a ladle, filling a cup and handing it to a thirsty man. "That will be two hellers," he grumbled, accepting two of the copper coins in payment. Already a line of patrons had formed at the barrel. Appel nodded to Kamille to continue.

"There were several other young men that I knew around Colmar, but Benno was different. He was as large as a bear and as gentle as a lamb." Kamille smiled wistfully. "He needed someone to take care of him, and no one had ever needed me for anything. And he thought I was wonderful. Didn't matter to him that I wasn't educated. Benno was the first man I really loved since my betrothed died in the pestilence."

"So you were not in love with my Lonel?" Gritta asked. "He had a token from you! A handkerchief."

"Yes, those. I had some leftover scraps from my father's loom. I took them with me to Colmar and I sewed those tokens. I thought I could give them to my lovers like the ladies in the minstrel tales. I did give one to Lonel. It was my last one. When I met Benno, the love of my life, I had no more handkerchiefs to give away. I was completely used up, but Benno didn't care." She smiled again and clutched at her abdomen.

"Things were fine until I learned Willem also moved to Colmar and took up a position as the prior of the Franciscans. I was terrified and angry. He began to follow me around, like he did in Stuttgart. I told him if he didn't leave me alone, I would tell everyone about his sin. I would go to the bishop in Strassburg, as my mother had once threatened me. And then, the monster appeared."

"The monster attacked Arne first," Appel said. "But Arne told us he didn't usually take the soil outside the walls because it was usually Benno's job."

Kamille nodded. "Benno was with me that night, but Willem didn't know, so he planned to dress as the cynocephalus to frighten Benno. Instead, he encountered old Arne."

"To maintain the ruse, he must have kept coming out to prowl outside the walls at night," Gritta added.

Brother Kornelius stood slowly. "Prior Willem always insisted on eating his meals alone, in silence, and in the dark of his chamber. I was in charge of serving him. But sometimes when I came to collect his bowl and knife, I would find his tray of food sitting outside his chambers, cold and untouched. I thought he was fasting, but perhaps it was untouched because he had been out prowling for Benno."

"It's possible." Appel nodded. "But then the monster was spotted inside the walls, too."

"Continuing to look for Benno, no doubt. Or perhaps also to simply frighten people," Kamille said. "He thought very little of the people of Colmar, or anyone with less education and money. He seemed to take joy in mocking people's ignorance."

"Nonsense!" Heinrik interrupted.

Kamille clutched harder at her middle. "Oh, I cannot bear to have this man in the room with me! He's in league with Willem, I know it! Please send him away!"

"Heinrik has a right to speak, just as you," Appel said. "Now tell us: what of the second monster? And how did Helmut die?"

"Everyone was frightened, of course, and I suspected Willem was behind the monsters, since he had those books with the terrifying pictures," Kamille said, her voice shaking. Appel turned to look at Heinrik. He had been telling the truth about Prior Willem's books. He met her eyes and smiled. Once again, her insides lurched in a way she hadn't felt for a very long time.

"I finally confessed to Benno what was happening and told him I suspected Prior Willem was the monster, intent on frightening or harming Benno because he was my lover. Well, he wasn't going to stand for that," Kamille continued.

"He made a disguise out of items he found when cleaning the streets, didn't he?" Efi said, and Kamille nodded.

"We made a plan. Benno would sneak into the friary to frighten Prior Willem. Everything was going well until Benno saw Willem wearing his cynocephalus costume and creeping around the novice quarters. I was waiting outside the friary in the dark when I saw Benno, in his disguise, climb over the wall, and then a man with a spear followed him."

"That was Helmut," Sheriff Werner said.

"I was afraid that Benno would be run through with the spear, and so I hid myself in the shadows near the grand canal. When the shepherd ran past, I struck him over the head with a stone. I heard Benno tussle with him for a moment or two in the dark, and then I heard a splash, but I didn't stay to find out what had happened. Then, Benno and I ran back to his house and hid the monster suit beneath it, and the next day I learned the shepherd drowned."

"So, Benno was the second monster and the first killer," Efi mused. "And Brother Tacitus said he noticed Prior Willem near the wool dyers' quarter on the day of Benno's murder."

"I was not in the wool dyer's quarter until after Benno was discovered. If I had come home earlier, I could have given my beloved one last kiss." Kamille broke down into sobs again. "I could have told him that I am carrying his child!" She wrapped a protective arm around her stomach.

"I think I can guess the rest. Willem entered the house, killed Benno in a rage, dropped your token in his haste, and fled without noticing," Gritta said grimly. "But why did he hide the evidence in our straw pile? What grudge does he have against my family?"

"He can tell you himself," a voice announced. Dorian, the captain of Sheriff Werner's guards, walked through the doorway, and behind him stood a bound and bloodied Prior Willem.

Labor pains

In which a trial in the wynstube is cut short

"YOU FAITHLESS HARPY!" WERE the first words Prior Willem spoke when the sheriff's guard shoved him through the door of the wynstube. "Conniving, lying vixen! Every word that crawls from Kamille of Basel's lips is as poisonous as a spider. Untie me at once! Do you hear me, Werner? Untie me, or by the Virgin's pale buttocks I'll ensure you're excommunicated with no hope of return!"

Sheriff Werner shook off any hesitation he had about arresting a man of the church who outranked him in status. He puffed out his chest and turned his mouth down into a deep frown. "I'll hear no more blasphemy from you, Prior Willem! Leave the Virgin and her hindquarters out of this!"

Willem thrashed against the rope tied around his hands. "You mustn't listen to what that woman says. She will tell you whatever she must in order to save herself. She's a skilled liar!"

Gritta stood and regarded Prior Willem for a moment. He was nearly a head taller than her, so she tilted her chin up to get a better look at him. Then she set her hands on her hips. "Why my pile of straw, Willem? Why did you hide your monster disguise where you knew it would hurt my Lonel?"

"I did nothing of the sort, woman! I neither know who your son is, nor do I care."

"As I thought," Gritta said, and she turned to look at the room. "If we can't find evidence that he is guilty of murder, we can certainly prove he makes a poor excuse for a man of God."

"Yes, yes, you're right! Because I'm not a man of God!" Willem shouted. "Now let me go and arrest Kamille. She is the real criminal!"

The alewives, Sheriff Werner, Herr Schlock, and Brother Kornelius all stared at him. They turned as one to look at Heinrik, who stood next to Appel. He blinked a few times, then shook his head.

"No. This is not Prior Willem of Stuttgart. I do not know this man."

Brother Kornelius began to weep.

"He has lost his wits," Sheriff Werner said, shaking his head. "Sin will make a man go mad, but how much worse is it for a man of the church? This is God's punishment for blaspheming the Virgin's bottom."

"He is not a man of God!" Appel and Gritta both shouted in unison.

"I'll ask you again, Prior...er...Willem: why did you attempt to make it look as if Lonel committed this crime? Why terrorize people unnecessarily?" Gritta asked.

Willem opened his mouth to speak, but before he could utter a word, Kamille let out a low groan and fell to the floor, clutching her stomach. "The babe!" she gasped. "My womb is twisting and stabbing! Please, send for help!"

The room erupted into a flurry of activity, with Brother Kornelius scrambling for the door, while Sheriff Werner and Herr Schlock wrung their hands, making excuses for themselves, and Heinrik narrowed a dark stare at Willem. The alewives all looked at each other and reached an unspoken agreement.

"Carry her to my house," Appel commanded. "I have delivered Gritta of five children and many other women in this city, too. I have herbs in my cupboard to ease the girl's pains, and space for her to sleep and cry if her babe dies. This requires the company of women."

The guards quickly lashed Willem to one of the carved wooden posts supporting the ceiling of the wynstube. Leaving Heinrik and a guard to keep watch, Dorian scooped Kamille up in his arms like a wounded calf, and they hurried into the street and toward Trench Lane, but not before Efi marched up to Herr Schlock and snatched his money purse from where it rested in his lap.

"What are you doing, woman?!" Herr Schlock shrieked.

"Compensating myself and my friends for the ale you sold, Herr Schlock," she replied as she calmly counted ten copper coins into her palm. "That's ten hellers to us for selling you the barrel, and you can keep three hellers for your labors."

Herr Schlock reached out to grab the money from her hand, but she closed her fist and crossed her arms over her bosom.

"Stealing from widows seems beneath you, Herr Schlock. You sold the ale we made, therefore we deserve to be paid for it."

"But the barrel is not empty!" Her Schlock sputtered. "I may not sell all the ale before it sours! I will sell the remaining ale back to you, Frau Efi."

"Sorry, no returns," Efi said, and she flounced from the room, smiling to herself as Herr Schlock's chorus of curses followed her across the square and down the road to Trench Lane.

Back at Appel's house, the women set into motion immediately. Gritta ordered Efi to fetch clean water from the stream at Saint Martin's church, and Appel pulled clay jars of roots and herbs from her cupboard, sorting through them and muttering to herself. "Burdock, tansy, rosemary...now did I use all my raspberry leaf on Frau Lena's stillbirth last winter? I must have some more somewhere..."

Kamille lay panting on the wide wooden bench near the window, clutching at her abdomen. "Please, please someone fetch my mother," she gasped. "I must see my mother."

Gritta tutted. "Where is your home, Kamille? I'll find your mother and bring her back."

"Against the walls in the wool dyers' district. Look for a lean-to near the water gate," Kamille said, and Gritta hurried out the door, slinging a wool shawl over her shoulders. For a few moments, there was only Appel, Kamille, and the sound of the crackling fire in the hearth filling the room. Kamille wriggled and shifted, still clutching at her belly. Appel came and sat next to her on the bench.

"How long have you been with child, my dear?"

"It is difficult to know for sure, but my bleed was absent last Sunday, so not very long."

"Well, sometimes the child will decide to leave your womb well before its time. This is the way of things, and you are not to be scorned or blamed for it. Have you been with child before?"

Kamille shook her head and bit her bottom lip to keep it from trembling. "I don't want to lose this baby. It's all I have left of Benno. Please, Frau Appel, you must help me!"

"If only I had raspberry leaves, I could make a tisane for you," Appel said between clenched teeth.

"Frau Berthe may have some. I saw her out a-harvesting in the forest only a few days back. Ask Frau Berthe! Please, this is so very painful, and I am afraid for my baby!"

Appel frowned. "I will wait until Efi or Gritta returns and send one of them. I don't want to leave you alone."

"Nay, please go now, Frau Appel, for these pains are so strong I fear I will die! Please get the herbs from Frau Berthe!"

Appel paused, then picked up her basket and straightened her wimple. "You're sure you will be alright here on your own?"

"Yes, yes, please!" Kamille doubled over, clutching at her stomach even harder and pulling her knees to her chest. Appel hurried out the door, and then, following a growing feeling of suspicion, she walked to the back of her house where another door led into the alleyway. There, she hid herself just around the corner and waited.

The pieces fall into place
In which two stories begin to make sense

"Well, Lonel is locked up and under watch in the larder at the friary, and I have set Ulf and Jean-Louis to work trimming and filing the toenails of all the other novices. That shall keep them occupied long enough to consider the trouble they caused," Friar Wikerus said with a satisfied clasp of his hands. "What happened while I was gone?" He trailed off as he stood in the doorway of Herr Schlock's wynstube, and his mouth opened in shock.

A massive barrel, which he recognized from Appel's house, sat just outside, dribbling a stream of golden ale onto the packed earth. Herr Schlock sat alone at a table in a corner, taking deep swigs from a crudely carved wooden cup. He didn't look up when Wikerus appeared, and his slumped shoulders and slack jaw made it look as if the man had given up his will to live. Nearby sat another man, tall and handsome, with graying temples who Wikerus recognized as the merchant, Heinrik of Strassburg. He also hunched over his cup, looking into its dark depths as if it held the clues to the unanswered mysteries of the world. But most astonishing was the sight of Lord Willem Wilmer von Waldenfroid, the prior of Saint Matthieu's friary, with his hands bound behind his back and tied to a post in the middle of the room. Nearby, a guard dozed against the wall with his spear and helmet askew.

"Prior Willem?" Wikerus asked. He reserved his urge to rush over and untie the man, because the normal expression of bored arrogance on Willem's face had been replaced by something unfamiliar. A feral light flashed in his eyes.

"Wikerus, come here!" Willem whispered loudly, with a nervous glance at the guard and Herr Schlock. "Untie me, so I may return to the church. These brutes are so fearful of monsters and murderers they are willing to detain anyone – even a man of God!"

Friar Wikerus was rooted to where he stood. "You were sent to fetch the woman, Kamille, and you did not return. The men in the square said you ran..." He trailed off. His world had been turned upside-down.

"I ran off in pursuit of her, yes. Perhaps it was unwise, and I must return to Saint Matthieu's so I can make my confession and pray for forgiveness." Willem had abandoned the whisper, and his voice took on more urgency. Still, Wikerus didn't move.

"Where is Fraulein Kamille?"

Now Willem's face reddened. "With those meddlesome women you're so fond of, probably robbing them blind and stabbing them for good measure. Now, untie me and take me to the church. I am your superior, and I order you to do as I say!"

The snoring guard woke with a start, and his spear clattered to the floor. He picked it up and gave Willem a light jab on the thigh. "That's enough out of you! Friar Wikerus knows a bad 'un when he sees one, don't you, Friar?"

But Friar Wikerus was already out the door and running toward Trench Lane.

When he reached Appel's house, Friar Wikerus ran inside without announcing himself. The fire crackled in the hearth and the table was strewn with jars and bowls of dried herbs, but the room was empty. The front and back doors were both wide open, and Wikerus felt his scalp prickle with unease. Appel would never leave her doors open and a fire unattended. As he pondered whether or not to go upstairs and check the second level of the house, he heard a moan from outside.

Appel sat in the dust behind her house, holding her head. Wikerus rushed to her and took her by the shoulders. "Frau Appel, are you alright? What has happened? Where are Gritta and Efi?"

Appel blinked up at him, struggling to focus her gaze. Then she staggered to her feet. "That putrid wench stole my basket!" she shouted.

"What?"

"Kamille was staying here with child pains, but she seemed most anxious for everyone to leave her alone in my house. I hid behind the corner to watch and see if she tried to escape from the back door, but she's crafty. She walked through the front, crept around the garden wall, knocked me over the head, and took my basket," she explained, seeing Friar Wikerus's confusion.

"Why would she hit you over the head, Appel?"

"Because she is no more an innocent person than the so-called prior you hold in such high esteem."

Friar Wikerus felt a deep dread in the pit of his stomach. The shock of seeing his superior bound and undignified in a wynstube had rattled him and aroused some uncomfortable suspicions. He didn't want to ask Appel to explain her disdain for the prior of Saint Matthieu's, but he knew he must. He lowered his gaze.

"Frau Appel, I think Prior Willem may have deceived me and others at the friary."

"Oh, leave your guilt for now, Friar Wikerus! Come, we must catch Kamille before she does something terrible!"

"But didn't you just say she had pains of early childbirth? Surely she would not get very far in her condition?" Wikerus wrinkled his brow. He didn't really understand the mechanics of childlabor, nor did he care to. It seemed a messy, mysterious business – a secret between God and woman.

"She gave birth alright," Appel said. "She birthed lies. Now the question is, where will she go next?"

"When I encountered Willem at the wynstube, he was desperate to get himself to the church," Wikerus mused.

"Because there he will find sanctuary!" Appel finished for him. "Kamille may have the same idea. If she can make it inside Saint Martin's or Saint Matthieu's then she will be protected."

"Not forever," Wikerus added. "But long enough to find a better means of escape."

"Halloooo! Appel? Gritta?" Efi's voice came from within the house, followed by the sound of water cascading from her goatskin flask into the pot hanging over the fire. Appel and Wikerus hurried inside just as Gritta also arrived with a face like thunder.

"Is she gone?" Gritta asked. "Where is that lying pustule of a girl?"

"Yes, gone," Appel responded, massaging the growing lump on her head where Kamille struck her with a piece of firewood.

Gritta growled in her throat. "I searched every lean-to in the wool dyers' quarters and asked around for every bedridden and infirm widow. And guess what I found? Nothing but robust and healthy old widows. Kamille claims she lives with her ailing mother, but has anyone actually seen the old woman? No, they haven't. It seems Kamille has been living alone in her lean-to. When she chooses to sleep there at all, that is."

"What do you mean, Gritta?" Efi asked.

"There's not enough room for so much as a fire pit in that little shack. Kamille spent most of her nights in Arne and Benno's hovel, else she laid her head to rest on the hairy chests of every man in Colmar, and would return satisfied. Do you never wonder why, although she said she was desperately poor, she always seemed plump and healthy?"

"No," Appel said. "I never noticed."

"Well, I did," Efi grumbled. "Seems every man in Colmar did, also."

"She was well fed by her many lovers, and now she's escaped!" Gritta said. "As I was walking back from the wool dyers' quarter, I began to assemble the facts. Prior Willem couldn't have acted alone, and neither could Kamille."

"He's not a prior," Wikerus said, barely above a whisper. "He's nothing worse than a common thief."

"Not common," a voice spoke from the doorway. Heinrik of Strassburg walked inside unsteadily. He shook his head and chuckled to himself. "That strong ale you sold Herr Schlock…it is very strong, indeed, Appel." He sat heavily on the bench near the window and buried his face in his hands for a moment.

"Well?" Gritta snapped. "Did you come here to disagree with us and then take a nap?"

"The man in the wynstube who calls himself Prior Willem is an imposter, to be sure. But I suspect he knew the true old Prior Willem of Stuttgart very well."

The alewives and Friar Wikerus all held their breath, and for a moment it seemed as if Heinrik was about to lay his head on the table and fall asleep.

"Oh, go on then!" Efi cried out. Heinrik jerked his head back up and blinked.

"Ah, right. I'll admit the man looks similar to Prior Willem. A younger version, if you will. If I had to guess, I would say the man tied up in the wynstube is Willem's brother, or a son, heaven forbid it."

"What?" Appel, Gritta, Efi, and Wikerus all said in unison. Heinrik nodded.

"The resemblance is uncanny. The man who has inhabited the friary in Colmar since the winter does look remarkably similar to the real Prior Willem, but it is not him, I assure you."

"He even said so himself. He said, 'I am not a man of God,'" Gritta remarked. "How did he come to be here in the prior's place? And what is his true identity?"

Heinrik scowled. "I don't know much about Prior Willem's family, but I do know there were four sons. One was to inherit his father's lands, one went into the clergy – that was Willem, of course. Another went to serve in the emperor's court, but I know not what happened to the youngest."

Gritta stood and began to pace. "It's brilliant, really. The man we thought was Willem took the real Prior Willem's place somewhere between Stuttgart and Colmar, knowing he resembled his older brother. None of us would be any wiser, and no one from Stuttgart visits our city with any regularity, so it would be possible to keep up such a ruse. But not forever. Eventually, someone would have noticed."

"Did he kill his older brother then?" Efi asked.

"Difficult to say," Friar Wikerus said. "I suppose we could just ask him. But that still leaves only half of this mystery solved.

Who is Kamille? What is her relationship to the man we know as Willem, and why did she flee?"

"And why did she hit me over the head and steal my basket?!" Appel said with a stomp of her foot.

"Well, that one is easy to answer," said Heinrik. "It is a very pretty head. Another woman would hit it if she felt jealous."

Appel blushed, but Gritta narrowed her eyes. "Flattery will get you nowhere, Heinrik of Strassburg, and if I have to lock Appel in her upper rooms to keep her from the likes of you, I will!"

"Is she a young maid and you her mother that you need to defend her so fiercely?" Heinrik asked.

"No. She's a decrepit old woman who has born children and buried a husband. But I'll protect her as if she's my own daughter, and you don't want to see how far I'll go." Gritta shook a skinny fist in Heinrik's face. He laughed and held up his hands in a gesture of surrender.

"You are formidable! I will treat your dear Appel with the respect she deserves! Although I must object to you calling her decrepit. She appears to be in the prime of health."

"Ahem!" Efi cleared her throat loudly, and all eyes turned to her. "So, does this mean Kamille is not with child? I am confused."

"There is someone who can help us clear up the confusion," Friar Wikerus said, his shoulders slumped with resignation. "Prior Willem. Or whoever he really is. Herr Heinrik, please return to the wynstube and bring the man here. Efi, would you be so kind as to fetch Sheriff Werner at my request? This is a twisted tale, and I would like to know once and for all who is responsible for the two murders in Colmar. And who has been in charge of Saint Matthieu's friary these few months."

Heinrik and Efi set off in opposite directions as Gritta helped Appel into a chair and handed her a cup of ale. Soon people began to arrive at her house. First came Sheriff Werner, with a reluctant and irritated Lord Frider in tow. Then Heinrik followed with Willem, still bound and accompanied by Dorian and a bevy of guards. Brother Tacitus slunk in behind the rest and sidled up to Friar Wikerus.

"Do you feel no shame, Wikerus, for always being at the center of the most debaucherous activities in this city? And now you implicate your own prior!"

Wikerus pointed at Willem, who sat miserably on a bench near the window. "That man is not Prior Willem of Stuttgart."

Sheriff Werner cleared his throat. "Well, let us hear what this man has to say now."

Willem pouted for a moment until Gritta gave him a jab in the ribs. "Oh, leave off, you old shrew!" he snapped.

Far from being insulted, Gritta chuckled, which only seemed to annoy the man even further.

"You want the truth? Very well, but you will find I am not the one you seek for murder," he grumbled. "Prior Willem was my brother. Mother's favorite, of course, because he joined the church and quickly rose to power. All my brothers are perfect, but no matter how hard I try, I can't do anything right. I'm not skilled at anything." His eyes misted for a moment, but then he smiled. "Except acting. Truly, I wanted to be a mummer. I love the stage and the lute. I would have been good as an actor, only my father felt it wasn't dignified enough for someone who holds his name."

"Are we supposed to feel sorry for you?" Gritta asked. "You were born with money and influence. We all have things we would rather do than spend our days toiling for pittances. You look as if you never toiled a day in your life."

"Which brother are you?" Heinrik asked. "I know something of your family, but I don't recall your name."

"I am Fritz. The youngest," the disgraced prior said. "And it is no surprise you've not heard my name. No one cares about the youngest in the family."

Heinrik leaned close to Fritz and stared into his eyes. "What did you do with Willem? Did you kill him?"

"No! It's true I didn't love my brother, but I didn't kill him, either. He was already dead when I took his place. He invited me to travel with him from Stuttgart to Colmar because his favorite servant had left his services, but after our second night on the road Willem never woke up. Died in his sleep. Willem and I were similar in size, and before we left Stuttgart he told me he didn't know anyone from Colmar, so I came here in his stead."

"This is true. Prior Willem was sent to Colmar by the diocese. No one living here had ever met him or knew what he looked like until Herr Heinrik arrived here a few days ago," Wikerus said. He turned to Fritz. "The penalty for impersonating a clergyman is severe. You took an incredible risk."

Fritz sighed and buried his head in his hands, which were still bound at the wrist. "It was Kamille who made me do it. She happened upon me while I was trying to decide what to do with my dead brother. She was traveling alone, which should have immediately made me suspicious, but I fell in love with her the moment I saw her face." Fritz sighed. "I cried on her shoulder, and then she kissed me and helped me bury him. The people of Colmar would suffer without a prior in their friary, she told me. And then she said she planned to move there herself and suggested I come along. I was helpless under her spell. I knew I had to follow her. I would have followed her right off a cliff if she asked me."

"She seemed to have that effect on men, although I can't tell why," Gritta said with a snort. "If my Lonel didn't spend so much time locked in the pillory or the gate tower, I'm sure he would have done all manner of foolish things if she asked him."

Sheriff Werner gave Gritta an incredulous look but said nothing. Fritz continued.

"So, I donned Willem's robes and perused his books. My father had us all educated, and I'd spent countless hours in a church listening to Willem drone on and on from a pulpit. It was easy to impersonate him. And while I practiced my grand act, Kamille went ahead to Colmar so we didn't arrive together."

"That's right," Efi said slowly. "She moved into Colmar at almost the same time as you. But if you two were lovers, you certainly hid it well!"

Fritz frowned deeply. "She tricked me as much as anyone else. Yes, she did visit me in my quarters in the friary." He paused and quickly looked up at Friar Wikerus, who was clenching his fists and staring angrily at the floor. "But I heard she was also roaming around town with other men."

"You must have hated to see her behave so brazenly," Appel said. "It must have driven you mad with jealousy."

Fritz nodded. "She flaunted it. Kamille knows how beautiful she is. I tolerated it, but when she took up with that oaf, Benno, I nearly went mad. The other men she seduced had something to give her. I could understand why she threw herself at them. Stefan the glover showered her with gifts and money until his wife discovered their carrying on."

Gritta nodded. "He's right. Stefan's wife put milk thistle into his pottage bowl when she found out about the affair. She bragged the next day in the market that Stefan was spending so much time in the privy with loose guts, that he had no more energy for a young lover."

Efi snorted with laughter, and Fritz gave her a withering stare, then looked back to Gritta.

"And your weasel of a son convinced Kamille he was the heir of a wealthy burgher."

Gritts was rendered temporarily mute. Then she snorted loudly. "How could Lonel possibly convince anyone he's the heir of a burgher? His clothes are more holes than cloth. He's nothing but skin stretched over bones!"

Friar Wikerus cleared his throat quietly. "Although it is not proper for me to discuss what is said during confession, I'll make an exception in this case. Lonel did tell me he acquired a fine velvet chaperon and linen tunic from a wealthy person, although he did not elaborate who the man was or whether the clothes were given willingly."

Fritz was nodding. "It was enough to convince Kamille, although it didn't take long for her to learn the truth. He's a trickster, that one." Fritz nodded at Gritta as he spoke. "But Benno had nothing to offer her at all. He was the lowest of the low, and I hated him."

"So you decided to kill him?" Sheriff Werner asked.

"No, not kill him, just frighten him. As I told you, I had been reading Willem's books. There's not much else to do in a friary. Hellishly dull life you friars live."

Brothers Tacitus and Wikerus both crossed their arms over their chests and glared at Fritz, but he didn't appear to notice.

"The holy books were boring, but Willem also had a translated version of the Naturalis Historia. I read about demons and monsters, and that's when I got the idea to make my own cynocephalus."

"How did you do it?" Efi asked. She was listening with parted lips and blue eyes wide.

"I asked a Vosges huntsman to sell me the carcass of a wolf if he should ever kill one, which he did. Then I sewed it into a cloak. I wore stones strapped to my feet to obscure my footprints." Fritz smiled to himself. "I am rather proud of it, if you must know. Creating costumes is a talent all actors must possess."

"When you frightened Arne instead of his son, why did you continue? Why not stop?"

"Why didn't I stop? The question you should ask is why would I stop? People were so petrified of my monster they trembled with fear when they saw me! I had the entire population of Colmar cowering inside their homes!"

"Wait..." Friar Wikerus held up a hand. "The night when we first realized there were two monsters in Colmar, you were inside the friary dressed as the cynocephalus, weren't you? You were responsible for the bloody robes that I assumed belonged to Ulf and Jean-Louis, and you were the one Brother Kornelius saw in the corridor, but how did you manage all this while also being present as Prior Willem when I discovered the robes? Truly, you must have been in three places at once!"

Fritz grinned. "Did you like that, Wikerus? Don't think you're guiltless in all this. You were still responsible for losing those two dimwits. Since they weren't in the friary, I couldn't have killed them if I wanted to. A few torn cowls dipped in pig's blood made it all the more real. But I'll admit, I was as surprised as the rest of you to learn there was another monster in the friary. If Brother Kornelius hadn't seen me as I was returning from placing the bloody cloaks outside the walls, everything might have turned out differently."

"Kamille told us she and Benno made their own suit in order to terrify you," Appel said.

Fritz snorted. "Oh, she told you that, did she?"

"I believed her," Appel replied. "And I believe she was in love with Benno. She admitted to striking Helmut to save Benno's life the night we were all in the friary."

"Aye, she killed Helmut. She did; not me!" Fritz said. "First, she struck him with a rock. Then she shoved his head into the canal and held him under the water until he drowned. She came to the friary the next night to boast about what she had done." He cast his eyes downward and shuddered. "That is when I saw her for what she really is. Frightening people and playing monster was all a bit of fun. No one was supposed to die, but she didn't appear to care."

"So Benno wasn't a killer either," Efi whispered. "It was all Kamille."

"I did love her," Fritz said softly. "If only she could have restrained herself. I imagined we would flee Colmar one night and make our way to Troyes or some such place so far from here no one would ever recognize us. Why couldn't she just be good?"

"Very touching," Brother Tacitus said coldly, and all eyes turned on him. "And now, tell me why you allowed those two novices of yours to steal shoes from the Dominicans. Have you no shame?"

"I don't care who stole your shoes," Fritz scoffed. "Ours were stolen too, by Gritta Leporteur's foul son, Lonel. And as for the novices, do whatever you like to the lot of them. They are no longer my problem."

"They shall be punished to the fullest extent," Tacitus said, his voice like ice. "My feet and the feet of my brothers require justice."

"Brother Tacitus, perhaps now is not the time to worry about footwear!" Friar Wikerus snapped. "The Franciscans also had their shoes stolen, but none of us are causing a fuss about it."

Fritz turned to Sheriff Werner and Lord Frider, who sat in a corner helping themselves to cups of strong red ale straight from one of the casks. "I didn't kill Helmut the shepherd. And while you waste time questioning me, the real killer is probably on her way to Zurich or Strassburg, or some other large city where she can hide!"

Sheriff Werner wiped his lips and belched. "But you did kill Benno, the street sweeper's son, didn't you?"

"No, another one of Kamille's jealous lovers did that. Or Kamille herself. I don't know."

"You were seen near Benno's house at the time of the murder," Friar Wikerus said.

"Doesn't prove I did it."

But Wikerus persisted. "Her token was found. A red handkerchief with black stitching."

"The handkerchief could have belonged to a dozen men. Kamille gave them out almost as freely as she gave herself. Even Gritta's son has one."

"Very well, if you didn't kill Benno, then what were you doing in the wool dyers' quarter the day of the murder?"

Fritz blushed and then shrugged his shoulders. "Did I want Benno gone? Yes, I did. But I would never kill anyone. All I wanted to do was frighten him a bit. I was getting good at frightening people. I startled that dimwitted tinker so badly he tumbled down a hill and into a particularly nasty patch of thorns."

"Lies," Lord Frider said. "The tinker never mentioned a fall, but he did have a lot to say about monsters."

"He knocked himself senseless. Better for me, too, because he almost got a good whack at me with his walking stick. When I saw how easy it was to scare a man out of his wits, I decided fear would be the perfect treatment for Kamille's lover, too. I hid my cynocephalus disguise under a bridge in the wool dyers' quarter the night before and donned it the next day just to frighten him. But Benno was dead when I entered the house, and so I ran. I put the costume back under the bridge and then came back for it in the night. My only regret is that someone else got to him first."

"How do we know you're telling the truth?" Gritta asked.

"You don't. But I'm not the man who killed him. Call me an imposter, but don't call me a murderer, because it's not true." He dropped his head into his hands. "I destroyed my monster costume when I heard what happened to Benno. It was too dangerous to have it in my possession any longer."

"What did you do with the pieces?" Sheriff Werner asked.

"The wolf skin is on my mattress now. It makes a fine, soft bed to sleep on. The head and cloak I tossed into a canal outside the walls. Both were probably swept into the Rhine."

"Perhaps Kamille murdered Benno," Efi mused. But Appel shook her head.

"Surely not. You heard how she spoke when she was here in my house. She seemed to love him. Why would she do something like that?"

"Kamille is a mercenary of a woman," Fritz said. "She wouldn't put herself at risk unless there was promise of a reward. If you can find a reason why his death would benefit her, then I'm sure you would have your murderer. Or should I say, murderess. One thing I can promise is Kamille didn't love Benno. That woman is incapable of loving anyone."

"And we let her get away," Sheriff Werner said through gritted teeth. "Frau Appel, I wish you had a harder head, that you might have stayed awake long enough to stop her from fleeing."

"And I wish you had more hair on the top of your head, that you might be more pleasing to look at, but we can't all have what we want, can we?" Appel motioned for Efi and Gritta to join her, and the three women gathered in the corner. "This is difficult," she whispered. "It's impossible to know who is telling the truth. Both Kamille and Fritz have given their version of the story, both blaming the other. Each seems plausible."

"Kamille ran, which makes her guilty in my eyes," Efi said.

"And so did Fritz. He would have run again if he weren't trussed up like a sheep," Appel reminded her.

"Perhaps we shouldn't get involved," Gritta said slowly. "Leave it to the sheriff and the jury to decide who should hang and who should go free."

Appel bit her bottom lip. In her mind, she knew the answer was close, but the pieces of the mystery did not fit neatly together. "Fritz talked of being wildly jealous of Benno because he had Kamille's attention. But what else did Benno have?"

"He was very strong," Efi volunteered. "And we know he could craft a half-decent monster costume."

"As the street sweeper, he and his father found things. Strange objects that they would sweep up and dispose of before any of us ever saw them. And because they were out in the earliest hours of the morning, they would be witness to the goings-on that happen when everyone else was asleep," Appel said slowly. "Did Benno see something he shouldn't have? Perhaps he found something of value that Kamille wanted?"

They pondered in silence, which broke when they heard a loud wail echoing across the square. Everyone rushed outside – all except Gritta, who leveled Fritz with an unblinking stare and threatened to thwack him with her mash paddle if he attempted to flee.

They followed the cries to the entrance of the wool dyers' district, where they found old Arne, the street sweeper, on his knees in the dust.

"Gone!" he cried out. "First my son, and now my silver – all of it, gone! What will I do?" He crouched over his knees, his thin shoulders heaving with grief. Friar Wikerus knelt and tenderly put a hand on Arne's shoulder.

"What has happened, Arne?"

Arne pointed to his house on its spindly wooden stilts.

"What is it, Arne? What is under the house?" Wikerus asked.

"What was under the house...my coins. Everything I saved for my son. But look. Look! Someone has dug them up! They are gone!"

Heinrik squatted down and then poked his head beneath the house. "Indeed, there is a hole here. Fresh." He stood and brushed the dirt and cobwebs from his clothes. "If the old man hid his treasure under his house, it is long gone. But how anyone would think to dig here is beyond my comprehension. It's dirty work. You would have to know exactly where to look."

"Kamille," Appel said, her mouth set in a hard line. "If she did kill Benno, I think we now have her motive. Arne, did Benno's lover know about the coins buried under your house?"

"Nay, I don't think so," Arne said, wiping his face with a grubby sleeve. "But Benno did. I told him where to find them in case something should happen to me. I'm not getting younger, you know. Never thought my boy would die before me!"

Appel began to pace. "Here's what we know," she said. "Fritz and the real Prior Willem were traveling from Stuttgart to Colmar when the good prior died in his sleep. Kamille happened along and charmed Fritz, convincing the fool to take his brother's place. Once inside the walls, she claimed to live with an infirm mother and earned her keep around the city by doing a bit of work and extracting gifts from the local idiots, namely Stefan the glover, Lonel, and Benno. Stefan gave her gifts and then his wife put a stop to it, Lonel tricked her into thinking he would give her gifts...but Benno appeared to have nothing to offer."

Sheriff Werner shifted on his stool and cleared his throat. "Well now, there was a night not long ago when Benno was drinking heavily and bragging that he was a rich man for one with such a lowly occupation. He didn't say anything specifically about silver, but he was boasting. Come to think of it, Kamille was in the wynstube that night, too."

Appel nodded grimly. "So she made it her business to get to know him better, and the poor oaf told her he had a cache of coins buried beneath his house. She earned Benno's trust then killed him, dug up the money, and left town."

"No doubt she thought it would be safer to rob and kill a man of lowly status than someone like Stefan the glover, whose death would have caused an uproar," Wikerus said. "Her mistake was not taking into account that the whole city was already in an uproar because of Fritz's monster."

"And if she was angry at Lonel for deceiving her into thinking he was wealthy, she could have placed Benno's monster costume into the pile of straw behind the Leporteur house," Appel said. "So the blame would immediately fall on him."

No one spoke, save for Arne who continued to weep in the dust. "I have nothing left," he sobbed. "Nothing left."

"Poor man," Efi whispered. "He lost so much."

"So did we all, Efi," Appel said, her voice hard. Before the pestilence struck, she would have shown more compassion to a man like Arne. But not now. She no longer had the energy to care, and she felt this absence in herself like a dark pit opening in her heart. There were times when she thought every man, woman, and child on God's earth had become sharp-edged and selfish, too exhausted from managing their own suffering to see to the needs of others. The heaviness of it all smothered her. Her eyes filled with tears – not for Arne, but for all of them: for everyone who survived.

Friar Wikerus knelt and put an arm around Arne's thin shoulders. He raised the man to his feet and supported his weight. "I shall take him to the friary, where he may have a hot meal and a warm bed for a few nights."

"Bless you, Friar Wikerus," Efi said, and Wikerus gave her a sad smile.

"Many years ago, the friars took me in when I needed them most. It is why we are here – to serve the community."

"Well," Sheriff Werner said, hitching his belly up over his braided leather belt. "Let us decide what to do with our imposter of a prior. He may not have taken any lives, but impersonating a member of the clergy comes with its own punishment."

"Punishment that is the responsibility of the church to administer, Sheriff," Friar Wikerus reminded him. Sheriff Werner rolled his eyes and turned back toward Les Tanneurs.

Back in Appel's house, Fritz was belligerent. Gritta stood nearby with her mash paddle pointed at him like a javelin.

"I am not a murderer!" he shrieked. "I demand to speak with a magistrate. I will not have my fate decided by a jury of old codgers and three ill-mannered brewsters!"

"Calm yourself, Fritz, we know you did not murder any of those men, but impersonating a member of the clergy is a serious matter, as is terrorizing an entire city. You may not hang on our gallows any time soon, but you will surely be punished," Sheriff Werner said.

"I will speak with my father about this. Someone send for Lord Wilmer in Stuttgart at once."

The demand was met with amused silence, and the man's expression darkened.

"Oh, for God's sake, someone give me a drink before I die of thirst – ale or water, I care not!" Fritz yelled. Efi stood to pour a small ale from the cask, and Sheriff Werner untied his hands. Fritz leapt to his feet, slapped the cup of ale from Efi's grasp so forcefully that it splashed into the sheriff's eyes. Before anyone had a moment to react, Fritz was on his feet, running out the door, then leaping onto the back of Sheriff Werner's horse. He dug his heels into the animal's flanks, and the horse launched forward, cantering from Les Tanneurs and out of sight.

"He can't go far," Heinrik said, as Sheriff Werner watched the back of his horse disappear out of the square. "He'll never get through the city gates. The line of wagons and travelers is so long at this time of day, he'll not be able to break through the guards who inspect the wares and collect fees."

Sheriff Werner turned to Dorian to issue an order, but his chief of the guard had already jumped into action, ordering two men to pursue on foot and another to warn the gates not to allow the man calling himself Prior Willem through. Sheriff Werner uttered a few choice curses at Fritz of Stuttgart, the alewives, and Les Tanneurs before he turned and trotted after his horse on foot.

All's well that ends

In which things don't end well for all parties involved

Appel, Gritta, and Efi found themselves alone in the house for the first time all day. They looked at each other and laughed. Appel sank into a chair, and Gritta shook her head, setting her mash paddle back on its hook on the wall. "Monsters that aren't monsters, priors who aren't priors, and once again, my family was blamed and found guiltless," she said with a grin.

"Well, that's not exactly true, Gritta," Appel replied. She was leaning her head back against the wall, her eyes closed. "Lonel stole shoes from the Franciscan friary and set their orchard on fire. And you are guilty of sealing a Franciscan friar inside of an ale cask. As soon as the excitement around Kamille and Fritz settles, I think Brother Kornelius is going to remember what you did to him."

But Gritta waved the comment away. "The Franciscans are without a prior, so there is no authority to punish me. And besides, it's not like Kornelius suffered much, for he's a small man and it was a large cask. Really, I ought to charge him two coppers for all the ale he drank."

They heard the merry thumping of Efi's feet as she skipped down the stairs from the second story of the house with a small leather pouch clutched in her fist.

"And just where are you going?" Gritta asked, setting her hands on her hips.

Efi adjusted her shawl and fluffed her blonde curls with her fingers. "To the friary. I cannot replace all the silver Herr Arne lost when Kamille stole it, but I am willing to give him some of the coin I have saved so he is not left entirely destitute."

"But, Efi, that's your dowry money!" Appel said. "And Arne is hardly deserving after the way he treated us when he stayed in our house. You should keep your silver to start your new household!"

"Right you are, Appel. It is my hard-earned dowry money. And I can do with it whatever I wish." Efi stomped out the door before anyone could stop her.

Appel smiled and shook her head. "And just when I was beginning to think there was no kindness and compassion left in this city. What a kind-hearted soul she is."

"Why has she never given me any of her dowry money, is what I wish to know," Gritta grumbled. "I call that very unkind indeed."

But Efi soon rushed back into the house, her face pale. She still clutched her small pouch of silver in her fist. "I've just spoken to Frau Tisserand in the poissonnerie, and she said Fritz escaped through the gates before Dorian could warn the guards. He galloped away on the sheriff's horse and was out of sight before anyone had time to saddle up and go after him," she said, panting.

"Well, I'm not surprised. He did have a good head start, and Sheriff Werner has a fine, fast horse. Fritz would know how to ride well if he was noble born," Appel mused.

"There's more," Efi said. "Kamille has been found. Also outside the walls."

Appel balled her fists. "Good. And I hope my basket is undamaged. It was a gift from my husband, may his soul find peace."

"She's dead. Drowned. The sheriff's men found her body in the canal that runs through the wool dyers' quarter. She must have tried to escape through the water gate."

Appel and Gritta both drew in their breath sharply. It happened sometimes – someone would fall into a canal, and the current would sweep them through one of the tunnels that allowed water to flow out of the city walls. In the spring when the melting snow from the mountains joined forces with the seasonal rain, the water ran fast and it was dangerous to go into the canals. Every man, woman, and child born in Colmar knew this.

"The bag of stolen silver must have pulled her under the water," Gritta said. "Well, God distributed justice, I suppose. Kamille got what was coming to her. Efi, I think you can put your dowry away and hope Arne's silver is retrieved from the canal."

"Gritta, that's heartless," Appel scolded. "It is a sad thing when anyone dies before their hair turns gray. We lost so many people in the pestilence; we shouldn't rejoice when we lose people now."

"What about when we lose murderous people?" Efi countered. "If Kamille had lived, she may have taken more lives."

"If Kamille had lived, Sheriff Werner's men would have caught her and then watched her strangle on the gallows. She would have died either way, Appel," Gritta reminded them.

"I am so tired of death," Appel whispered. "So tired."

There came a gentle tap on the doorpost, and the women turned to see Heinrik of Strassburg standing there, his face serious. "Well, I came to Colmar this week to do business with Herr Schlock, was dragged into a murder trial, and today I helped the sheriff pull a young woman's body from a canal. I feel it is time for me to return to Strassburg," he said. "Frau Appel, do you care to walk with me a while? I would like to turn my mind to happier things before I must pack up and leave."

Appel flushed deep red and felt the heat rising to her face. "I uh..."

"Yes, she will walk with you," Efi said, pushing Heinrik back. "Just wait outside while she puts on her bonnet." She slammed the door, turned to Appel, and grinned.

"Efi, why did you do that?" Appel shouted.

"Just give me a moment," Efi said. She ran to the cupboard and drew out a bowl of freshly picked spring strawberries, crushing one between her thumb and forefinger.

"What in the name of heaven..." Appel started to ask, but Efi shushed her.

"Gritta, find Appel's bonnet, the pale blue one that flatters her eyes. And her blue shawl!"

Gritta sullenly went to the peg on the wall where Appel hung her wraps, while Efi smeared the bright red juice on Appel's lips and then viciously pinched her cheeks.

"Ow! Efi, stop this at once!" Appel snarled.

"There. Now you don't look like you also drowned in the canal," Efi said, satisfied. She tied Appel's bonnet on her head and tucked in a sprig of maiblümchen for a fresh scent, then draped the shawl around her shoulders.

Gritta pulled the door open. "She's ready for you." She looked around to make sure no one watched, then grasped Heinrik by the front of his tunic, pulling his face close to hers. "Take no liberties with my friend, or you'll meet the same fate as Kamille, do you hear me?"

Heinrik laughed and bowed. "I promised once before to treat Appel with respect, and I promise again." He held out his arm, and Appel took it. Her eyes sparkled, the fine web of wrinkles around them crinkling as she looked into his face. They strolled, arm in arm, toward the wynstube with Gritta and Efi watching.

"What will we do if she remarries, Efi?" Gritta whispered. "We shall lose our aleworks!"

"It would be worth it to see her so happy, Gritta," Efi said, and she patted Gritta's hand. "Come. Let's have a drink."

It was nearly sundown when Heinrik returned Appel to her doorstep and then disappeared into the gloaming to prepare for his return journey to Strassburg at first light in the morning. Efi skipped around the table, clapping her hands and demanding the details of their walk.

"Tell me everything," she said. "Every detail!"

"Courting is very different when you're an old woman," Appel said. "We spoke of deep things – of God and kings, the free cities where we both live...and what we want for our futures."

"And?" Efi asked. "Gritta is worried we will lose our aleworks if you remarry."

"Where is the old cow, anyhow?" Appel looked around, hoping Efi would drop the subject of marriage.

"Gone home to tend to the children. Jorges is back in the pillory for urinating on the wall of Saint Martin's church when he was full of drink, and Lonel is serving his time for stealing the shoes of the Franciscans, so he is in the pillory next to his father."

"Ah well, they are both locked up and accounted for, then. Gritta can sleep easy," Appel said with a laugh. She removed her wraps and hung them neatly on their peg.

"But truly, Appel, what is Heinrik's intention? Why did he want to speak with you?"

"He was curious about the work we do," Appel said. "He asked many questions about the ale we brew and was most impressed at how much we have accomplished in Colmar. He seems very interested in the whole ale-brewing business, although I can't imagine why. And now, I would like a little something to eat, and then my bed."

Efi set a bowl of cabbage soup in front of Appel, along with a small cup of ale and a piece of dark brown bread. Then she lit a rushlight and slowly walked up the stairs and undressed for bed. She was fast asleep and snoring when Appel finally followed her up the stairs, and because she was a heavy sleeper, she did not wake up, though Appel tossed and turned all night.

Prior engagements
In which endings bring new beginnings, too

SEVERAL DAYS PASSED BEFORE the alewives saw Friar Wikerus. Even though Prior Willem had turned out to be an imposter, Saint Matthieu's church was in disarray without leadership, and the friars spent their time fretting, praying, and crying, thus very little work was done. The alewives gladly sold the distraught Franciscans several tuns of ale, although Brother Kornelius insisted on bringing another man of the church along with him when he came to pay for the ale, just to be safe. Envoys from Stuttgart and Strassburg were sent for, and the church leaders spent many days in council, eventually deciding it would be best to elevate one of the local brothers to the position of temporary prior while a suitable replacement could be found.

When Friar Wikerus finally did appear at Appel's house, the leafy branch was hanging above the door indicating to passersby that there was ale to sell. Inside, the benches were full of men and a few women taking their ease after a long day of shepherding, blacksmithing, chandlering, tanning, farming, and all manner of occupations that kept the city running smoothly. The doors and windows were all open, and a mild spring breeze gamboled through the room, bringing with it the sweet smell of new grass and the sound of birdsong from outside.

Efi handed Wikerus a generous pour of strong dark ale and ushered him to a three-legged stool in the corner. Appel and Gritta joined, and the four of them huddled with their heads close together.

"Well, what of your errant novices, Friar Wikerus? Have you returned them to their fathers' houses?"

"Hush," Wikerus whispered. "I can only stay for a little while. I have much to do, and the church leadership from Stuttgart and Strassburg are most severe in their enforcement of the rules. Yes, I sent Ulf and Jean-Louis back to their families. Ulf discovered he could earn good money selling the leather shoes in the markets of Strassburg when he ran off, and now he has decided it is his life's calling to be a merchant. And Jean-Louis can't think for himself, so he followed. I'm glad to be rid of them, if I'm honest."

"The other novices in your care are all so timid and well-behaved, you'll get bored without those two around to spice your life," Gritta said with a laugh. "Perhaps I should send my Lonel to you, so your days don't grow too dull in the novitiate!"

Appel and Efi laughed along, but Wikerus stared into his cup. "I won't be working with the novices any longer," he mumbled. The women fell silent. Appel placed a hand on Friar Wikerus's arm.

"I am sorry they took away your responsibilities, Friar. You seemed to like working with the young ones."

Friar Wikerus nodded miserably. "I did," he whispered.

Gritta looked up. "God's bones, what is he doing here? I surely thought we would never have to see Brother Tacitus in Les Tanneurs again!"

Indeed, Brother Tacitus stood in the middle of the room, looking about with a sour expression. When his eyes landed on the alewives and Wikerus sitting in a corner, he sneered. "There you are," he said, pointing a finger at Wikerus.

"What can I get for you, Brother Tacitus?" Gritta asked. "A cup of small ale? A little honey to sweeten your temperament?"

"You try to insult me, but I am impervious to your foul mouth, Gritta Leporteur. Friar Wikerus is wanted, and I was sent, along with others, to search for him. They already punished him by taking away his responsibilities with the novices. I assume there is more bad news in store for you, Wikerus. Best come along quickly." Tacitus looked triumphant as Wikerus took one last sip and then slowly walked from the house, his eyes downcast.

"Our poor friend," Appel said, clasping her hands. "I hope they do not treat him too badly. What if he is sent away to Breisach again?"

They sat quietly for a while, watching the merry patrons drinking their ale and talking at the tables, the din of their voices growing louder with each sip. When the light began to dim, Appel collected the remaining coins owed, while Efi cleared away the thin clay cups and put them in a pot of water to soak.

A few of the men grumbled about having to leave before they were ready.

"When you come to my alehouse bearing candles and an oil lamp, you are welcome to stay past sundown. We do not serve ale in the dark, and we do not have the money to spare on better light," Gritta said as she hustled them out of the house. They had just finished the tidying up when there came a loud knock at the door. The three women all looked at each other with apprehension. It was never a good thing to have an unexpected visitor after dark. Gritta took up the mash paddle, and Efi stood near the lean-to at the back of the room, prepared to run for help if needed.

"Who knocks so late at my house?" Appel called out.

"Wikerus!" came the muffled reply.

Appel glanced back at Gritta, who shrugged. Then she pulled up the bar from the door, and Friar Wikerus stumbled inside, his face pale, his hands shaking.

"Ale, please," he whispered, his voice trembling. "The strongest you have."

"Oh dear, Friar Wikerus! Is your fate at Saint Matthieu's really that terrible?"

Wikerus nodded, eagerly taking the cup Efi handed him. He drank the entire thing in a single gulp.

"Are they sending you back to Breisach? We shall come to visit you and bring along ale and cherry kuchen and many other fine things to remind you of Colmar!" Efi said.

"Worse," Wikerus said. "It's so much worse. I wish I had been sent back to Breisach instead!"

Now Appel, Gritta, and Efi grew concerned. Appel knelt and looked into his eyes. "Friar, do you require help? What has happened?"

But before Friar Wikerus could answer, there came another knock. Friar Wikerus gasped and his eyes grew wide.

"They've found me!" he said and began to wring his hands. The door slammed open, and in walked the person the alewives least expected to see in their house. Prior Konrad of the Dominicans stood there, tall and imperious, with his servant, Brother Tielo, peeking out from behind him. The prior strode into the house, bending slightly so he didn't thump his head on one of the low ceiling beams. "Close the door, Tielo, before someone sees!" he barked at his servant.

The three alewives stepped back and curtseyed, but Wikerus remained seated, staring into his cup and looking perfectly miserable.

Prior Konrad's expression softened. "Come now, Wikerus. It won't be as terrible as you assume. And it will not last forever. You must return with me before you are found here."

"But why me, Father? Of all the brothers in Colmar, why me?"

Father Konrad sat on the bench at Appel's large trestle table and looked up at Gritta. "A cup of small ale, if you do not mind, Goodwife Gritta."

Gritta hurried to get his drink, and Prior Konrad looked at his hands, deep in thought. "An example must be set for the others," he said finally. "It was not a recommendation I took lightly, and the envoys from Strassburg and Stuttgart have no other options. Believe me when I tell you there are some men inside my very own church who would have gladly taken your place."

Wikerus nodded and set his cup down. "I like my life, Father. I am content—"

"And this is why you must do what we ask of you, Wikerus. You are too comfortable."

Gritta stepped forward and nervously curtseyed again. "Begging your pardon, Prior, but this ain't fair nor right. Friar Wikerus didn't lose those two novice boys – they deceived him and ran away. I've raised eight sons, and there's Lonel who causes twice as much trouble as the others combined. If a boy is determined to do something he oughtn't, he will find a way."

"You are good to defend your friend, Frau Gritta, but Prior Wikerus is not being punished. He needs to accept the responsibilities given to him."

Gritta's eyes widened, and behind her they heard a clatter as Efi dropped a clay cup, shattering it on the ground.

"Prior Wikerus?" Gritta asked.

Prior Konrad smiled, and Wikerus turned bright red with embarrassment. "Indeed. Prior Wikerus. Without any leadership at Saint Matthieu's, and with no available alternatives for now, I advised the church envoys from Strassburg and Stuttgart to elevate Wikerus to prior until a suitable man can be found for the job. And since they are not familiar with the brethren in Colmar, they made their decision based on my endorsement of our friend here." He turned to Wikerus. "It is your duty, Wikerus. While your hesitation is understandable, you must rise up to this new challenge. What Saint Matthieu's needs, after the betrayal by Fritz of Stuttgart, is a man of humility."

"It is truly temporary?" Wikerus asked. "Do you believe a replacement prior can be found soon?"

Prior Konrad rose to his feet, and Brother Tielo rushed forward to straighten his robes.

"Stop that at once!" Prior Konrad swatted his servant's hands away. "I cannot tell you how soon they will find a replacement, but I can assure you if you do not accept this position, then a far worse man will take your place. What Saint Matthieu's needs right now is stability, Prior Wikerus."

Wikerus looked around the room, and finally at the alewives, who were standing in a tight huddle, their eyes wide. He grinned sheepishly. "A prior of the church cannot frequent an alehouse," he said. "Dear alewives, it may be some time before I will sit at your welcoming hearth again."

"Indeed, a leader of the church must be seen to be without blemish," Prior Konrad said. "And I must go, for the same applies to me. Were I to be discovered here—" He stopped speaking abruptly and looked toward the door. Lamplight flickered uneasily through the knotholes in the wood, and the sound of several pairs of sandal-clad feet shuffled outside.

"Open up!" called the voice of Brother Tacitus. "This is church business, and you will open this door at once!"

Wikerus and Brother Tielo jumped to their feet, their expressions terrified, but Prior Konrad merely looked annoyed. "God grant me patience with that hook-handed vigilante," he grumbled.

At once, the alewives sprang into action. "He could probably fit into an ale cask," Gritta said, pointing at Brother Tielo as she sized him up, "but not the rest of you."

"Shut up, Gritta!" Appel hissed. "Efi, show them out through the lean-to in the back of the house. I'll get the door."

As the three men slipped quietly through the back door, where only a few days before, Appel had been clobbered unconscious by Kamille, Wikerus hesitated. "Farewell, my friends," he whispered. "God's blessings upon you!"

"You need blessings more than us," Gritta said, and Wikerus grinned again before he disappeared into the darkness. Appel was fumbling with the bar at the door, and she wrenched it up as soon as Prior Konrad, Wikerus, and Brother Tielo were gone.

"Why, Brother Tacitus, what an unexpected surprise at this time of night," she said, keeping her most serene smile on her face. Tacitus stomped inside, his dark robes floating like the wings of a bat.

"I heard voices. Men's voices! Where is he?"

"Where is who, Brother?" Appel asked.

"Friar Wikerus. I've heard the most alarming rumor about him, and now Prior Konrad is missing, too. I am sure they are together."

"The prior of a church would not be caught dead or alive inside an alehouse, Brother Tacitus," Gritta said.

Three more friars – two Franciscans and one Dominican – filed into the house carrying oil lamps. Brother Kornelius looked balefully at the cellar door and pointed at it. "Best to check the ale casks, just in case that old witch nailed Prior Wikerus inside," he said.

Tacitus turned on him, his normally pallid face flushed with rage. "Friar Wikerus!" he snapped. "Until it is official, he shall be known as Friar, not Prior!"

Efi fluttered her eyelashes, opened her blue eyes wide, and asked in her most innocent voice, "Why, did something happen, Brother Tacitus? You seem agitated."

Tacitus ignored her. "They're not here," he said, turning to go. "Let us continue our search at the wynstube."

The four men hurried outside with a few glowering backwards glances at the alewives, and Appel slammed the door behind them and shoved the bar firmly into place. "There! The next man who hammers on my door will receive a cold pitcher of canal water over his head!"

"Friar Wikerus is now the prior of Saint Matthieu's church," Gritta said slowly. "I never thought I would be close friends with someone so elevated!"

"He doesn't seem well pleased about it," Appel said. "And I doubt it will help us in any way. But I am glad to see Father Konrad recognizes the value in Friar Wikerus."

"Prior Wikerus," Efi corrected her.

"Indeed. Come now, Efi, let's off to bed. I expect there will be an uproar tomorrow when Brother Tacitus wakes and discovers his worst fear has come true."

Efi gave her a questioning look, and Appel chuckled. "I can only assume he wishes for something to incapacitate Father Konrad so he can become prior, himself. Ah, the very thought of his irritation will give me happy dreams tonight."

A few days passed, and the envoy from Strassburg bestowed the mantle of leadership on Wikerus, elevating him to prior of the church of Saint Matthieu. With no more threat of monsters and murderers in the city, the citizens of Colmar ventured cautiously from homes, and soon the streets and squares were bustling with movement, color, and noise. Locked in the pillory again, this time for drunkenly proposing marriage to a mule, Jorges enjoyed watching the people as they walked past him, a few stopping to chat or to toss a piece of stale bread at him. Lonel was free to roam, and quickly found himself in love once more, this time with a laundress who worked in Lord Frider's city house.

In Herr Schlock's wynstube, the large cask of ale that had been rolled there during the trial of Fritz of Stuttgart was empty, and he had it converted to a table for his patrons, since it was no good for storing wine. Sheriff Werner swaggered inside on a sunny afternoon and sat on a groaning three-legged stool. "Bring me something sweet and fresh, Schlock!" he called out.

"I would, but all the maidens of Colmar are spoken for," Herr Schlock called back, and the rest of the men in the room roared with laughter. He produced a cup of petal-pink wine and pulled up a stool of his own to join the sheriff.

"So, has there been any word of the whereabouts of Fritz Willmer of Stuttgart? He may not have killed anyone, but he certainly caused chaos in Colmar."

Sheriff Werner wiped his lips with his sleeve. "He fled back to his home, and his father made a generous donation to the bishopric in Strassburg to smooth things over."

Herr Schlock scowled. "So that is it? No punishment?"

"No indeed. All is forgotten!" Sheriff Werner laughed heartily, and Herr Schlock got a good look at the money purse hanging from the man's belt. It was filled to bursting with coins. He wondered how much of Lord Willmer's "donation" to the bishopric of Strassburg ended up in the sheriff's purse. He looked slyly at the inebriated man before him.

"More wine?"

"Yes indeed, Schlock!" Sheriff Werner shouted. "Schlocky schlock schlock!" He slurred his words slightly and laughed at himself.

Herr Schlock smiled and bowed. He would earn his portion from the bribe paid to the sheriff – not through negotiation, but through libation. And besides, his meetings with Heinrik of Strassburg had been fruitful. Soon he would have control not only of the wine sales in Colmar, but ale as well.

He looked out the door of his wynstube and saw Appel, Gritta, and Efi walking arm in arm across the square, talking and laughing uproariously.

"Foolish women," he muttered to himself. "Don't know what they have to be so happy about." He thumped another cup of ale in front of the giggling sheriff and held out his hand for a coin.

As the three alewives strolled past the wynstube, Appel took a moment to look back at it and bit her lip with apprehension. What was Heinrik of Strassburg's business there, anyhow? He always managed to evade the question when she asked him. Underneath her growing affection for the man was a vague sense of unease that battled with the fluttering in her heart whenever he wandered into her thoughts. *It's nothing,* she thought to herself. *It has been so long since I've felt love that I no longer trust myself, nor the man I fancy.*

"Well, girls, what do you suppose I heard this morning in the market?" Gritta asked, and waited for Appel and Efi to grow sufficiently impatient. "Prior Wikerus has convinced the city council to accept a new member. Can you guess who?"

Of course they could not guess. Efi suggested Peter the stonemason, who she had once considered a potential husband. Appel suggested Herr Fisker, the head of the fisherman's guild, and Gritta was so pleased with her secret that she practically burst with the news.

"Arne, the street sweeper. He's in charge of all matters pertaining to the cleanliness of the streets and privies. Instead of sweeping, he now has two young sweeps working for him."

Appel and Efi were dumbstruck. "But how is this possible? He's of lowly status, to be sure," Appel said.

"Can you imagine one of those other pompous council members being concerned with the common privies? They were happy to accept Arne. I'm sure he'll be treated very poorly by them, but he no longer has to toil with his broom and his cart."

"Well!" Appel said. "This is a wonder, indeed! What a world we live in, my friends, where women can rule their own destinies, where paupers become leaders, and timid friars are elevated to church prior. What a world, indeed."

Author's Note

In which the author muses to herself about monsters and men

I'LL ADMIT, I HAD the idea for this book because I've always been intrigued by the premise of the M. Knight Shyamalan movie *The Village*. Whether or not it's a very good movie is debatable, but I appreciated the exploration of how an idea, a fear, or some cleverly embedded dogma can cause panic and be used to manipulate or trap a whole community. And if there was one thing that defined the Middle Ages, it was dogma and control. So now, let's discuss medieval monsters, shall we?

My first challenge was the word "monster". It seemed to be such a modern term. I searched and searched for something that sounded less anachronistic, but I discovered that the word "monster" goes back hundreds of years. For a historical fiction author, this creates something called "the Tiffany Problem," a term coined by the fabulous historical fiction author Nicola Cornick. The Tiffany Problem arises when an author needs to write about something that is commonly thought to be a very recent name/place/term/phenomenon but it's actually quite old. For example: the name "Tiffany" didn't burst forth from the ether in the 1970s. It's actually been around since the 1600s. Surprise!

Back to the topic of monsters.

My fantastic editor, Craig Hillsley, pointed out that it could be challenging to convince a modern audience that the threat of monsters and other supernatural beings was very real in the Middle Ages. To our post-enlightenment minds, monsters are fairy tale creatures, but what would a medieval person think? After all, several of the great travel writers of the Middle Ages and early modern period mentioned monsters in their manuscripts, from mermaids and unicorns (these aren't Disney creatures, they're menacing!) to the cynocephali (dog-headed monsters). There were the headless blemmyae, with their faces embedded in their torsos, and the skiapodes, who would lay on their backs, dangling their single, giant foot above themselves as a sunshade. We may laugh at them now, and think it absurd that anyone would truly believe in such creatures, but when information was difficult to come by and the world was full of very real but unexplainable dangers (such as plagues and earthquakes) there was no reason to think a monster could not also be incredibly factual.

Even more disturbing in my mind is the *concept* of the 'monstrous' as something very human but not fitting into a narrow band of acceptability. Our modern minds think that monsters are creatures less than human, and we imagine talons, misshapen limbs, towering strength, and slavering fangs. But the monstrous in medieval times could be more mundane – and far more offensive. Monstrous were women's bodies, which were defined as "deformed men's bodies". Monstrous were Jews,

Muslims, people from the African continent, the disabled, and anyone else who didn't fit a Western European ideal. And then, of course, there are people who are monstrous because of their actions. In researching this book, I had opened a can of worms, indeed.

When the only lifeline in times of terror was religion and what one could see with one's own eyes, how could a medieval person comprehend phenomena that deeply affected them but had no explanation in the natural world? During the Black Death (aka the pestilence, aka the great mortality), priests, nuns, and monks died at rates even greater than the general population because they were often selflessly visiting the dying and delivering last rites. So it was clear that being pious or holy didn't protect from the horrors of the disease. Scapegoating Jews was always easy, but even though many Jews were mercilessly sacrificed in the name of public safety (look up the Colmar Treasure for more information about the horrors that the Semitic population suffered during this time), the pestilence carried on. Blaming monsters or the devil was convenient because there was no way to disprove their existence, therefore also no way to disprove that monsters, demons, and the devil caused pain and suffering on earth.

There are so many misconceptions about life in the Middle Ages. No, people didn't wallow in filth. Yes, they adored their children and grieved when their loved ones died. But there is a truth about this time that, with some empathy from our modern sensibilities, makes sense; there was a LOT that they didn't know. And in the absence of a logical and provable explanation, people filled in the gaps then as they do now. This is how something like the specter of monsters, which seems silly to us, could take a strong grip on a population.

These people, seven hundred years our ancestors, don't deserve scorn, they deserve compassion. Life was full of terrors and wonders, and who among us wouldn't blame the unexplainable on sin or the supernatural? Some among us still do.

Acknowledgements

In which the author confesses that she needs a lot of help

THE THING I STRUGGLED with the most while writing this book was focus. So many things happened to derail my focus that I consider it a miracle I finished this manuscript at all. There is no way I could have done this without the support of many people who have helped me through the most difficult time of my life – and yes, I said that in Acknowledgements of *Sleight of Hand*, blithely unaware that things were about to get harder for me.

Thanks are owed to the team of geniuses, whiz kids, and miracle workers who have contributed to this book. Olly from More Visual created another amazing cover for me, and John Wyatt Greenlee of Surprised Eel Maps Ltd. drew the map inside the front cover (can you spot the eels?!). Craig Hillsley, my developmental editor sent the manuscript back to me, politely describing it as "relentless", and offered suggestions for how to make the whole mess come together. Editor, Sarah Dronfield, put her magnifying glass on every sentence, identifying each inconsistency and misplaced semicolon, which is why it's now in a readable state. My beta readers took unpaid time from their lives to read something that wasn't finished and offer me essential guidance to the plot, especially the unmatched MJ Porter, who informed me that there were over a billion instances of the word "that" in the manuscript, and if I managed to remove even half of them she would be 'a very happy bunny'. I also must thank a very special advance reader, Gabriele Sauerland, who spotted several typos mere weeks before the book launched and alerted me to them, for which I am very grateful!

I received support from the usual lineup of patient, supportive, detail-oriented super star authors who I don't think I can live without: MJ Porter, Kelly Evans, Jan Foster, Christine Herbert, and Jim Keen. Thanks, always, to James Whittaker and the writing group at Side Hustle Taproom in Kirkland, WA, who have been staunch supporters and early readers. And so much gratitude is owed to my friends, family, and neighbors who helped me this last year. Rachel Kelley and the whole Kelley family have enthusiastically welcomed me and my very high-maintenance husky, Riva, into their open arms. The hundreds of times that they let Riva stay at their house so I could write, undisturbed, made this book possible. My brother, Christian, sister-in-law Emily, and adorable niece brought so much joy into my days when I needed to take time away from the keyboard. And my brilliant, handsome son, Soren, kept me laughing, encouraged me, and reassured me that it's ok to pursue a dream, even when it's not lucrative.

And then there is my dad, Louis W. (the third), who this book is dedicated to. He claims that he was gifted his sense of humor by his grandmother. Well, her legacy lives on. Thank you for showing me how to take joy in the absurd, how to always search for the very best adverb, and for teaching me how to check my car's oil. That saved me more than once.

About Elizabeth R. Andersen

In which the author introduces herself

Photo by Mallory MacDonald

Elizabeth R. Andersen is an independent historical fiction author living in the beautiful Pacific Northwest of the United States. She is passionate about reviving (and eating) historical recipes, reading and supporting other indie authors, and exploring the stunning Cascade mountains with her teenage son and Riva, her energetic Siberian husky. Elizabeth is a member of the Historical Novel Society, the Crime Writer's Association, and is also represented by History Through Fiction.

Join Elizabeth's monthly newsletter and receive *Nasira*, the free prequel novella to *The Two Daggers* series for free. Sign up at https://www.elizabethrandersen.com or follow her on your favorite social media sites.

Also by Elizabeth R. Andersen

In which we discover that the author also writes other books

The Alewives of Colmar series
The Alewives
Sleight of Hand

The Two Daggers series
The Scribe
The Land of God
The Amir
The Marquis of Maron
The Two Daggers (coming 2026)

Printed in Dunstable, United Kingdom